BEHIND THE SALUTE

A Cadet's Journey
INSPIRED BY TRUE EVENTS

MAURICIO LUCHO

Published by Mauricio Lucho
1942 W Gray Street #1323
Houston, TX 77019

This novel is a work of fiction, written in the form of a memoir, and
inspired by real experiences. While certain themes, settings, and
emotional truths reflect lived events, all characters, dialogue,
institutions, timelines, and incidents have been fictionalized,
combined, or re-imagined for narrative purposes.

Any resemblance to actual persons, living or dead, or to real
organizations or events is coincidental or used fictitiously and is not
intended as a factual portrayal.

Cover art by Damonza Studio
Damonza.com

The Amazon Endure typeface was designed by 2K/DENMARK in
2025.
Template id: ST-414D415A-25-A01
Printed in The United States.
1st Printing

ISBN: 979-8-9941672-1-2
Ebook ISBN: 979-8-9941672-0-5

For my partner, whose encouragement never wavered throughout this journey.
For my family, whose love and support have always been unconditional.
For Brett, Jay, and Kevin, who shared their talents and time and helped me grow as a writer and storyteller.
For the true friends who stood beside me and helped guide the way.
For David, who loved to hear my stories.

CONTENTS

PREFACE

Some stories demand to be told, not because they promise neat or happy endings, but because they reveal something true—about culture, shame, honor, duty, fear, love, and the relentless pull between who we are and who the world expects us to be. This is one of those stories.

For almost thirty years, I rarely spoke about what had happened during my freshman year of college. I locked that chapter away, burying it beneath layers of shame, culture, and expectations. Then, while packing for a move, I opened an old box I had nearly forgotten about. Inside were journals, insignias, photos, and fragments of a past that had once defined me. Holding them in my hands transported me back to those two semesters—two semesters that changed everything.

I grew up in a Catholic family that worked hard and valued education. My brother, Apolo, enlisted in the Marine Corps, and I saw the pride it brought to our parents— immigrants from Mexico who had given everything in pursuit of the American Dream. I wanted to follow in his footsteps, to serve my country, to uphold my family's honor. But there was one truth between us, a difference I worked tirelessly to suppress, fearing it would unravel everything I had built.

Joining the Corps of Cadets at Texas Farming & Engineering University, a nationally recognized ROTC program, had been my dream—the path to becoming a Marine Corps officer. But along the way, something happened that I never felt prepared for: a friendship that quickly deepened into my first love. Justin, a fellow freshman, was unlike anyone I had ever known. Loving him, while respecting that he was straight, became both beautiful and devastating in ways I didn't yet understand.

But **Behind the Salute** is not only about friendship and courage. It's also a story about power—how easily it can be twisted and how devastating its grip can become. During that year, my squad leader, Ari Strait, turned his authority into a weapon. His mental and physical abuse targeted our entire freshman class, but once he discovered that I was closeted, I became a particular focus of his cruelty.

This novel—written in the form of a memoir drawn from my journal—is about that journey: my freshman year as an

ROTC cadet and how I survived it. It traces the moments that shaped me, the friendships that saved me, the trials I faced, and the tremendous loss I endured—both in the open and deep within me. At its complicated core, it's about striving to become the best version of myself, even when I wasn't sure who that was.

It is written for those who have battled to belong and felt torn between duty and identity. The cost of that struggle is rarely small.

This book also honors my Mexican heritage—the culture of my ancestors that shaped me, the sacrifices of my family, and the wisdom passed down through generations. My mother's voice, firm and unwavering, has echoed in my mind for as long as I can remember. Her dichos—timeless expressions filled with wisdom, values, and resilience—guided me when nothing else could. Those lessons are as central to this journey as the path itself.

If I've learned anything, it's that the hardest fights aren't always waged in uniform. More often, they rage within us. And yet, through every struggle, family and true friends—those who love us fully—can be our greatest sources of strength. They stood by me when I needed them most. I hope this story reminds others that they're never alone in that struggle, even when hope feels distant.

1 MY CALL TO DUTY

October 1994. At seventeen, nothing mattered more to me than our Naval Junior Reserve Officers Training Corps (NJROTC) unit at Houston Aviation Academy. Looking back, NJROTC gave me purpose, structure, and a sense of belonging I'd longed for my entire life. Our unit had earned a reputation as one of the best in Houston, Texas—a distinction we wore with pride.

I still remember my freshman year, standing in line as they handed me my first set of uniforms. The moment I put one on, something clicked. Purpose took root. Discipline, drill competitions, community service projects—NJROTC became my world.

By senior year, I had earned the title of executive officer—XO—the second-highest-ranked cadet in our 200-member unit, responsible for helping lead the entire company.

My life blended both American and Mexican cultures. My parents had immigrated from Mexico in the early '70s, carrying with them a heritage that shaped me. Papi worked tirelessly as a painter, moving between interior walls and scorching exterior jobs in the Texas heat or the rare, biting cold. One blistering summer, after a single week working beside him, I admitted I didn't want to labor like that for the rest of my life. He laughed, wiped the sweat from his face, and told me to study hard, or I'd end up in a blue-collar job like his. "Don't waste the opportunities I never had," he said in Spanish.

Papi also filled our home with stories from Mexico—legends, memories, and mischief—that sparked my love of storytelling. Mami's faith and her dichos grounded me in morals and tradition. Their love was undeniable.

But even in that warmth, I carried a private conflict I could not share. I was already learning that silence could be its own kind of armor—and sometimes its own kind of prison.

Machismo, Catholicism, and the newly implemented "Don't Ask, Don't Tell" policy made revealing my truth unthinkable. I hid behind girlfriends, medals, and discipline, terrified of being exposed.

My older brother, Apolo, was twenty at the time, and he was more than anything my mentor and role model. After high school, he enlisted in the Marine Corps, a decision that shaped my own dream of becoming a Marine. Without scholarships for college, he chose to enlist and serve four years so a veteran's program would cover his college education afterward. But he wanted something different for me. He pushed me to become a Marine Corps officer—urging me to apply for scholarships and college ROTC programs. He saw how committed I was to NJROTC and believed in me.

My two best friends and fellow NJROTC cadets, Marisol and Antoine, were determined that all three of us would go to college. We were inseparable throughout high school—bound by our commitment to NJROTC and by the trust that comes from years of showing up for one another. We spent countless hours practicing for drill meets and helping manage the unit. Weekends often meant traveling to competitions or being at one another's homes, eating dinner with each other's families, training and studying together, or daydreaming about growing old side by side. Our classmates—and even a few teachers—called us the three amigos affectionately. And once Antoine got his first car, there was no telling where we'd end up around Houston or down in Galveston.

It took months of mental preparation before I could bring myself to come out to my two best friends. Even with all the love and trust between us, shame and discomfort around my truth held me silent far longer than I ever intended.

One evening, during one of our usual drives to Galveston Island to look up at the stars, something in me finally shifted. Antoine parked along the seawall, and the three of us sat on the wall with our legs dangling over the edge, listening to the waves. Under the glow of the moon and stars, I felt both safe and deeply vulnerable.

I took a long breath—one I'd been holding for years—and said, "I've got something to tell you. I'm embarrassed to reveal this part of me, but I hope you'll understand. Even though I had a long-term girlfriend for several years until recently... I'm actually gay."

As soon as the words left my mouth, my whole body tightened and my heart rate spiked. Years of hiding—of watching my words, my gestures, my thoughts—crashed over me at once. Then the tears came.

Marisol put her arm around me. "Mauri, you're our brother. We love you no matter what."

Antoine rested his hand on my shoulder and grinned. "Yeah, I don't care. Proud of you, XO. I'll always have your back—even if you get an ROTC scholarship and end up at my university's archrival."

For the first time, the weight lifted. I felt—for a brief, fragile moment—free. Their immediate reactions of love and support put me at ease, and I let them ask me questions.

"Mauri... how long have you known?" Marisol asked. "And have you told anyone else, or are we the first?"

I nodded. "Since I was a kid, and yes—y'all are the first."

Her expression softened even more. "You carried this alone all these years? That must've been so heavy," she said. There was a pause before the next question. "Are you scared about 'Don't Ask, Don't Tell' if you go military?"

"Terrified," I admitted.

Antoine leaned toward me, studying me with that familiar mix of concern and humor. "But seriously… do you feel relieved at all? Like you can finally breathe?"

Marisol squeezed my shoulder. "What do you need from us? We're right here."

"Yeah," Antoine added. "And if you want to tell anyone else, or if you don't, we'll back you either way."

They believed in me and encouraged me to apply for ROTC scholarships. But when the applications asked whether I'd ever experienced "homosexual tendencies," I lied. "Don't Ask, Don't Tell" was new then, and if I wanted any chance of serving, hiding the truth was the only option—a charade I'd been performing since junior high.

Texas Farming & Engineering University—better known as Texas F&E—and its Corps of Cadets were my dream. The Corps promised tradition, discipline, and camaraderie, everything I craved. A recruiting poster outside Captain's office became my window into that world. I would stop and stare at it, picturing cadets marching in formation and the echo of commands bouncing off the dorm walls. In those daydreams, I was already there.

Stories from Houston Aviation Academy alumni fed those dreams: the Corps produced exceptional officers, demanded everything, and gave back purpose. Freshmen earned their place through sacrifice and dedication— official bans or not, everyone knew hazing persisted. I mailed my application for a campus and Corps of Cadets visit early senior year and listed P-Company Pirates as my preference. Mac Walsh—a Houston Aviation Academy grad two years ahead of me—was there. He'd been larger-than-life at our school: a natural athlete with a sailor's son swagger who made P-Company sound like a crucible and a family.

Antoine and Marisol wouldn't be joining me; their hearts were set on Capital College in Austin—Texas F&E's fiercest rival. If everything went as planned, the three amigos would soon trade friendship for rivalry, at least on paper.

Three weeks later, my acceptance for the late-October campus visit arrived. Captain suggested I take the train. "University Station, grew up around the tracks," he said, and I loved the idea.

As the train pulled into the station, Mami slid a sandwich into my bag "just in case." Papi's hand on my shoulder tightened as he said, "Ten cuidado, mijo. Call your mother when you arrive." He slipped me a twenty and, in a rare show of softness, pulled me into a hug that landed somewhere deep. At the platform, Mami cried and whispered the refrain I'd heard my whole life: "No confíes en nadie. Ten mucho cuidado. Y Dios te ayude." Don't trust anyone. Be very careful. And may God help you. Her words became the armor I carried aboard.

University Station wasn't grand, just a modest pavilion and a gravel lot. A rattling station wagon taxi took me straight to the ROTC Museum. Inside, glass cases held over a century of uniforms, flags, and letters; a room of folded American flags, each with a name and class year, stilled me. Service wasn't just history—people had made the ultimate sacrifice. I wanted to be worthy of that legacy.

The P-Company recruiting sergeant walked me to the living and training area of the Corps—referred to as "the mile"—where the dorms were arranged around a large, paved drill deck, decorated with ornate shields. The recruiting sergeant explained that each shield represented a company. "You'll learn the rest by living it," the sergeant said, slipping me an agenda. At McKibbin Hall, he suggested I grab dinner with another visitor who had just arrived—if I could wait, we could go together.

A minute later he returned with the other visitor. "Justin Fischer," he said, and a tall cadet with hazel eyes stepped forward. He carried himself with a deliberate steadiness, every movement precise, like someone who understood the weight of first impressions—his clothing was pressed to match. The handshake was firm and confident. Something about him felt familiar, though I couldn't place it.

We were both starving, so we headed to a burger joint west of campus. By the time we crossed the mile, our conversation already felt natural—family stories, drill meets we'd both attended without realizing it, and why the Corps called to us. He told me about his family's four generations of Texas F&E alumni, his plans for mechanical engineering, and his Marine Corps scholarship. I admitted what I rarely said aloud—that I wasn't sure if I would be admitted or receive a scholarship.

On the walk back from dinner, we talked nonstop until we stopped at a war memorial in front of the columns at the mile's entrance. I ran my fingers over the names of former cadets who'd served and died in various wars. The stone was cold, but the weight behind those names hit me hard. In an instant, I was back at the Vietnam Memorial in Washington, D.C., standing in front of that endless wall of names, feeling swallowed by a grief I didn't yet have words for. The same heaviness washed over me—part sorrow, part gratitude, part fear for whatever future I was walking toward.

Justin didn't rush me. He just stood beside me, supportive and quiet, like he could sense my emotions.

Back at the dorm, a cadet named Kent welcomed us, ran through the agenda, and suggested we shower before lights out. He explained the "head" protocol—in military language, a "head" simply means the bathroom. The heads in the dorm included toilets, urinals, sinks, and showers. Freshmen got the first stall, then sophomores, and so on. He added that in the Corps, hallways were called passageways and doors were referred to as hatches.

When we stepped inside the head, the freshman shower stall was occupied and there were no curtains. I told Justin to use the sophomore shower, and I'd wait.

The freshman turned as the water cut off, lean and muscular, built like someone who lived in the gym. My eyes lingered a second too long as he reached for his towel. He caught me looking, and a bolt of heat rushed through my body as I snapped my gaze to the wall in front of me. While he dried off, I felt him staring—unblinking, assessing. I stayed completely still.

When he finished, he stepped close, not raising his voice, just near enough for his breath to brush my ear. "What's your name?"

"Mauricio Lucho."

"I won't forget it. If you come back next year, you'll address me as Mr. Strait. How will you address me?"

"Mr. Strait, sir," I said.

He didn't need to shout. His future seniority alone demanded deference—an automatic respect given to those above us in the hierarchy. He'd be a sophomore the following year with authority over me, and he wanted me to feel that power, to understand exactly where I would stand beneath him.

He smirked, stepping just close enough to make the moment unsettling. His voice slipped out low, almost gentle. "That's right. I'll be here… waiting for you."

When Justin finished, he waited for me so we could walk back together. He asked what the encounter was about, and I brushed it off, saying that the freshman had just wanted to introduce himself. We returned to the room, made up our bunks, killed the lights, and lay there in the quiet.

"Why the Corps?" Justin asked out of the blue.

I told him the truth I could share—that my brother's enlistment had lit a fire in me, that my parents' pride and sacrifice mattered, and that I wanted to be the kind of man the uniform demanded: good, loyal, honorable, disciplined.

He listened, then said softly, "Mauricio… I've always had a read on people. It's just something I can't turn off. And

7

everything in me tells me you're a good man. You're exactly the kind of person the Corps needs." His words brought me back to one of Mami's dichos: "Dime con quién andas y te diré quién eres"—tell me with whom you go about, and I'll tell you who you are. To her, the company you keep revealed your character. Lying there in the dark, with Justin's confident voice above me, I felt like I was keeping the right company.

The next morning came with the thunder of feet pounding the passageway and a bell so loud it felt like it could wake the dead. Visitors weren't allowed to participate in physical training, so we followed Kent to chow instead—2,000 cadets moving in a perfectly chaotic harmony. Freshmen sat silent and ate their meals with precision, bald heads level, eyes forward. Upperclassmen watched, speaking freely. Control governed everything, and I knew any misstep would be noticed.

We watched the drill platoon after breakfast—the crack of rifles, the surgeon's precision of each toss—and sped through a campus tour that felt less like sightseeing and more like glimpsing a life I wanted. Lunch brought a surprise: Mac Walsh, grinning through a hangover, promising I'd do fine at F&E and with P-Company. "You'll fit right in," he said to both me and Justin.

When it was time to go, Justin and I shook hands longer than I expected. "See you next year," he said, like he had the power to manifest it. Something in that moment felt like the start of a friendship that might last a lifetime. His confidence and ease were magnetic—and yes, he was easy on the eyes—though I tried not to let myself see him that way.

On the train home, I replayed the visit—the museum's flags, the energy of the mile, the way Justin stood quietly beside me at the columns. Hope rode with me—so did a shadow.

Mr. Strait's smirk and his words stirred a fear in me that

he'd seen more than I meant to show.

Still, despite that warning, I held onto one belief: that the Corps of Cadets—with all its trials—might shape me into the kind of man I wanted to be.

A good man.

An honorable man.

An officer of Marines.

2 FRESHMAN HELL WEEK

The letter from Texas F&E arrived in February, thin enough to feel like rejection. My hands trembled as I tore it open. Across the table, Mami gripped her rosary so tightly the beads dug into her skin. Then the words leapt off the page—I'd been accepted.

"I got in!" I shouted, my voice cracking with relief and joy.

Mami burst into tears and ran around the table to wrap her arms around me. "Thank the Lord! I knew it, son. You'll be the first Lucho to go to college!" she cried out in Spanish. Making her and Papi proud was its own reward, worth every late night, every drill, every sacrifice.

When we told Apolo, his joy came rushing through the phone, filling the house with excitement. For a moment, the whole family was bound together by pride, hope, and the dream that had finally become real.

Six months later, on Sunday, August 20, 1995, Papi and Mami drove me to University Station for the start of Freshman Hell Week—better known as FHW. The boot camp-style program indoctrinated incoming freshmen, teaching Corps customs a week before the start of classes. The sweltering ride in our old Ram Charger, with no air conditioning, left me stewing in doubt.

I'd had doubts before, but these last-minute ones hit harder as my freshman year loomed. I wondered if I was truly ready for the Corps and if I could convincingly pass as straight in an all-male unit where every move was watched and there was no room for modesty. One slip—a glance too long, a word too soft—could ruin me.

Then came the rank reset. In high school, I'd been XO of my NJROTC unit—the second-highest-ranked cadet—won more than thirty awards, and earned Marine Corps, Air Force, and Army ROTC scholarships, something that had never happened in the history of my unit. But in the Corps, none of that mattered. Everything I'd accomplished was stripped away. While the reset was disorienting, it also lit a fire in me. I'd proved myself once; I could do it again. I was ready to start from square one as a freshman—freshman Lucho—no rank, no ribbons, no accolades, earning every bit of it back the hard way.

Not knowing who my bunkmate would be set my nerves on edge. What if he snored loudly? What if he was a slob? Sharing a room wasn't the issue—I'd done that with Apolo—but doing it with a total stranger was different, and the thought unsettled me.

Academics didn't worry me much, but the hazing did: the brutal workouts, the sleep deprivation, the nonstop yelling. I'd survived a few weeks of it in high school, but two full semesters felt like a different beast. For the first time in months, a flicker of self-doubt crept in, and those small jitters made me question whether I was as ready as I'd convinced myself I was.

Still, my North Star was clear: to become a Marine officer. Leaving home carried excitement too—new friends, student clubs, even parties—my first taste of independence.

At McKibbin Hall, Papi and I hauled my footlocker up to the fourth deck while Mami followed close behind. I'd just gotten my room assignment, and as we made our way down the hall, a mix of excitement and concern buzzed through me—the moment had finally come. I was about to meet my bunkmate. When I pushed open the hatch, he turned toward us with a genuine smile. "Hey, I'm Richard Donnelly—your bunkmate," he said, offering his hand. His grip was firm without trying to prove anything. A native of the Dallas area, majoring in mechanical engineering and a high-school soccer player, he seemed put together in a way that immediately put me at ease.

Our small talk paused when a couple of seniors dropped by to welcome us. One of them spoke Spanish with my parents, and I could tell it both surprised and comforted them. They rarely felt confident speaking the little English they knew, so hearing their native language—even just a few friendly phrases—put them at ease in a place that, I imagined, felt overwhelmingly foreign.

As departure neared, my forced smile masked the anxiety gnawing inside. Mami broke first, clinging to me before turning to the window to privately wipe tears from her face. Papi's hug lingered, his grip reluctant to let go. Years of sacrifice had led to this moment, and I thanked them, promising I'd be okay.

When the last parents left McKibbin Hall, FHW officially began. Richard and I were assigned to Mr. Strait's squad—a detail I suspected was no accident. It wasn't until I saw his face that it clicked: he was the freshman I'd seen in the shower stall during my campus visit the year before—the one who caught me staring at his naked body. I hadn't forgotten the way he'd leaned in, the warning that he'd be waiting for me, the shame that had hit me all at once in that moment. And there I was, assigned directly under him.

Our class gathered in the fourth-deck ready room—a classmate's room near the center of the deck where we assembled to receive instructions, prepare for the day, and wait for whatever came next. I stuck close to Richard and Justin—familiar faces in the crowd. The sophomores drilled us relentlessly under the watchful eyes of our Company Commander and Master Sergeant, with a few upperclassmen, including my old friend Mac, assisting.

Monday began with our first campus run. The pace wasn't brutal, but Company Commander promised it would build.

Apolo's gift—a pair of running shoes—carried me through, though the heat left me drenched.

We finished in time to fall in with the Corps for morning chow. Every unit marched in perfect unison, the beat of shoes striking the drill deck. Inside the dining hall, squad leaders barked the rules in rapid fire: "Grab a tray. Pick up your chow. Four water pitchers per table. When your table's full, ask to sit. Eyes front. Eat with speed and intention—don't taste, just swallow."

The chaos of hundreds of freshmen proved efficient enough; in under twenty minutes, we were done.

Back at the dorm, Master Sergeant shouted, "Get to your rooms and strip down. Grab a towel, toiletries, shower shoes—move it!" Richard and I grabbed towels, claimed opposite corners of the room, turned our backs, and wrapped ourselves up.

After my classmates and I assembled in the passageway, Master Sergeant made it clear there was no room for modesty. Unexpectedly, he ordered us to remove our towels and hang them on our left shoulders. Everyone complied.

There was the Class of '99—four of us per section, nine bulkheads, thirty-six naked bodies. I'd never felt so exposed. I stared directly at the chest in front of me and fought not to look anywhere else.

Our side of the passageway marched to the southern head and was packed so tightly that the kid behind me lost his balance and pressed into my ass. I leaned back to avoid the classmate in front of me, which made the intrusion from behind worse. He mouthed an apology; there wasn't much he could do. It happened two more times as we advanced, and he apologized each time.

In the head, the sophomores explained "buddy showers"—first cadet steps in, rinses, steps out to lather; second cadet does the same; first cadet steps back in, rinses off, done. Everything rushed. Everything watched. The usual "don't drop your soap" jokes flew; there was nowhere to hide.

I dried off and raced back to the room, trying to avoid upperclassmen. I pushed the hatch open and froze. Richard stood at his desk, face pale; Mr. Strait was chewing him out.

"Stand at attention," Mr. Strait snapped, then unloaded. "You two numbskulls took too damn long in the head. You're in my squad—you move faster than everyone else." He ordered twenty-five pushups in towels and shower shoes, then twenty-five more when he decided we were still too slow. Fifty pushups weren't a problem for me, but if he'd demanded one more set, I wasn't sure I had anything left to give.

Determined not to give him another reason to punish us, I snapped to attention, and my towel slipped to the deck. For a split second, fear spiked through me. Apolo had warned me there was no room for modesty in the military, and I was comfortable being naked around others. Instinct made me reach for the towel, but I caught myself just in time.

"Lock it up, freshman Lucho—you didn't request permission to move," Mr. Strait shouted as he cut across the room. He circled me with a stare that felt violating. I'd never felt so exposed under someone's gaze. My jaw clenched as I stood there, forcing myself not to flinch.

He leaned in so close his breath warmed my ear. "Now you know what it's like to be on display, buck naked. Feels different when the eyes are on you, doesn't it?" His voice dropped, menacing. "You two belong to me now. My word is law. Understand?"

We answered together, loud and automatic: "Sir, yes, sir."

He stormed out, leaving the room buzzing. My hands trembled as I got dressed, and I could still smell his breath on my skin—an unwelcome reminder of how close he'd been.

The day rolled on with dorm, mile, and campus protocols, plus hazing in the passageway—yelling, spit in the face, endless calisthenics. We were issued uniforms, physical training gear, bed linens, a blanket, and the Polaris, a booklet of Corps facts, traditions, and rules that needed to be memorized.

That afternoon we marched to the student center for the FHW "four-inch white walls" buzz cut. Most classmates arrived with thick hair that left their pale scalps glaring under the lights after. I had a buzz cut since ninth-grade JROTC but still sat for the ritual.

By Wednesday morning, before swim qualifications, Mac slipped into my room, worry etched on his face. Richard was in the head, so it was just us. "A couple of your classmates already quit the Corps," he said, lowering his voice. "And your name's at the top of the list of who might be next."

His words made my stomach tighten as if I'd been sucker punched. I'd been pushing through, doing everything I could to survive the days—but hearing that they saw me as a quitter made everything feel suddenly, painfully real. I was confused, too.

Was I there to be weeded out, or were they actually trying to set me up for success in the Corps and beyond?

Mac promised to have my back however he could but was also transparent: "The sophomores will threaten you, break you down any way possible—spread rumors, even say you're gay. Don't let them win. It's all a test. You've got to be resilient."

FHW didn't just test my endurance—it began teaching me who I would have to become to survive.

He also shared what I already sensed: Mr. Strait carried a heavy chip on his shoulder. His class had lost most of its members, and he seemed hell-bent on passing the pain down to us.

I told Mac quitting wasn't an option. Outwardly I sounded confident, but his mention of gay rumors sent a cold jolt through me. The thought left me feeling exposed, unsteady, and suddenly unsure of who I could trust.

Later that morning, I passed all three swim qualifications. Those who failed would retest the next day.

Afterward came a new term—freshman boil. None of us knew what it meant, only that it sounded like punishment in a cauldron.

Whatever it was, I knew it wasn't meant to be survived comfortably. We didn't ask any questions.

At lunch, Master Sergeant dropped the bombshell: our first personnel inspection was the following day. It would cover rooms, uniforms, personal appearance, and knowledge of Corps history from the Polaris. If even one cadet failed, the entire class failed—and the price would be our first freshman boil.

Unity wasn't optional. It was survival.

Richard and I spent the night cleaning, studying, and getting everything ready for the inspection. I'd been through inspections like this countless times in high school and at camps, so I walked him through every detail, even though it cost us precious sleep. By dawn on Thursday, we felt ready for inspection—hoping the rest of the class had put in the same level of work.

After dinner, Company Commander marched us back to the dorm, his face grim. "You failed inspection," he announced. My stomach sank—failure meant the dreaded freshman boil. He ordered us to our rooms to change into physical training gear and wait.

Richard and I rushed upstairs. Inside, our room was wrecked—sheets, mattresses, and trunks overturned, shaving cream and toothpaste smeared across the vanity, toiletries gone. I said to my bunkmate, "Forget the mess for now. At least they didn't touch our uniforms. Let's get ready."

We changed clothes quickly, then stood in silence by the sink, waiting. The call to fall out ripped through the passageway. Master Sergeant commanded, "Fall out, class of '99. Find a bulkhead. One to a bulkhead." Richard and I exchanged a reassuring glance—the kind that said we're in this together—before running out into the passageway.

Sophomores in camouflage uniforms—with matching brown-and-green painted faces and Smokey Bear hats—lined the passageway, playing drill instructor with a level of intensity I hadn't seen before. I stayed close behind Richard until a sudden, brutal shove from Mr. Strait sent me crashing into a bulkhead hard enough to rattle my teeth. He picked my bulkhead for me and said, "Lock it up at attention."

We spread out, thirty-six bodies pressed along both sides of the passageway, one to a bulkhead. The air reeked of tension and fear.

Then the barrage of calisthenics hit—pushups, flutter kicks, burpees, mountain climbers, monkey fuckers—each one shouted before I'd even finished the last. The pace was relentless. I forced myself to keep up, but within minutes my lungs were on fire. Sweat poured down my face and back, soaking my shirt, stinging my eyes. My arms shook, my core burned, and every muscle felt one command away from giving out.

The worst came with duck walking—squatting low and waddling down a stairwell, across the third deck, and back up to the fourth—two times. By the time we stopped, my legs were vibrating so violently from the physical strain that I wasn't sure they'd hold me up. Gasping for air, my thighs knotted with cramps, and for a moment I couldn't rise. That's when I thought about my dad. If my father could work twelve-hour days in Houston's brutal heat to keep food on our table, I had no excuse.

When Master Sergeant called us to attention, I heard the command, but my body wouldn't move. Muscles locked, I struggled to rise, every nerve screaming.

Mr. Strait saw me struggling and rushed in, his voice

cutting like a blade. "What the fuck are you doing? Attention means on your damn feet, freshman Lucho."

I forced myself upright, legs wobbling, and met his glare. "A little slower next time. Hell, take all day if you want," he sneered.

Then Master Sergeant told us to return to our rooms and grab our uniforms. We bolted for our rooms, the halls thick with sweat and noise. When I arrived, Richard was already at the hatch, uniforms in hand, his face flushed. I grabbed mine, steadied my breath, and followed him back.

At the bulkheads, we were ordered to raise our uniforms straight out, elbows held fully extended. It was manageable at first, but the weight intensified quickly, and my arms started to shake with strain. Then Mr. Strait appeared again, pressing down on my load until my muscles quivered. "Ready to quit, Lucho? Keep 'em high, or I'll make it worse."

Then came the ambush. His voice filled the passageway, dripping venom. "Rumor is you've got extra sugar in that tank? Whose biscuit you looking to butter?"

Chuckles from a few classmates hurt worse than the ache in my arms. He demanded I admit it. I shouted back, insisting the rumors were lies. Because if he—or anyone—learned the truth, I knew exactly what would follow: a board of inquiry, an investigation, and losing everything—the Corps, my scholarship, any chance of becoming an officer, my family's pride.

He finally turned away, but the damage lingered. His words stung harder than the punishment.

My body reached the breaking point, and my vision began to blur. I fought to stay upright. I would not pass out. I refused to give them that satisfaction.

At last, Master Sergeant barked for us to stash the uniforms. I sprinted to my room and back under a countdown, running on the last fumes in my tank. The drills went on a little longer—leg lifts, low crawls across the floor, skin scraped raw.

The air grew thick with sweat and vomit. Some freshmen lost their dinners, and the stench filled the passageway, turning my stomach as much as the exercises had.

Nearly two hours in, we were herded into the ready room, the smell following us like a curse. Then the hatch slammed open. Mr. Strait stormed in, eyes blazing.

"Looks like you pussies have had enough," he said. "You got off easy. Next time you fuck up—and you will—I promise you'll boil twice as long."

Relief and dread crashed together. The torture was over, but Mr. Strait's threat hung heavier than the stench in the room.

Mr. Strait ordered us to shower in our physical training gear to rinse off the sweat and vomit. Then we had to clean the third- and fourth-floor passageways. Rest would have to wait.

After rinsing off with Richard, we wrung out our soaked gear in the sink and checked each other's scrapes under the harsh fluorescent light. The bruises ached, but nothing was serious. Together with our classmates, we cleaned well into the night.

Before bed, Richard gave me a warm smile. "Congrats on surviving your first boil. Don't let Mr. Strait's words matter." His calm certainty steadied me. I managed a smile, though I fought tears. His kindness meant more than I could admit.

We stowed our gear and crawled into our sleeping bags. I whispered, "Five will quit by morning." Richard chuckled, "Three. And don't be one of them—you're too good at shining shoes." We laughed, and I finally passed out.

At morning physical training, the pace quickened. The jodies helped—those call-and-response cadence songs meant to keep us moving in unison—but my legs screamed in agony. A sharp, stabbing pain shot through my shins—unfamiliar and unwelcome. Still, I refused to quit, dragging myself across campus with the stragglers.

Mr. Strait saw me struggling and mocked me as a future

"sloth platoon" member. I didn't know what the sloth platoon was, but the way he said it sounded degrading. Even with that uncertainty hanging over me, finishing the run felt like its own victory—proof that whatever he thought of me, I could still push through.

At breakfast, Company Commander's tone shifted as he made the announcement: President Clinton had declared war in the Middle East. Classmates with family members already serving were promised a phone call home. He added that reservists could be next.

The words paralyzed me. My mind jumped straight to Apolo—my big brother, an enlisted Marine. If anything happened, he'd be among the first sent. Then came the concern for Mami and Papi. I could picture them hearing the news, imagining worst-case scenarios, crying, praying.

The weight of it pressed heavy on my heart—fear, uncertainty, and a sudden understanding of how close war really was.

Back in the dorm, each step up the stairs stabbed like knives. I confessed to Richard that my shins were killing me. He thought it might be shin splints, told me to ice them, but warned me I'd likely have to stomach the pain for some time.

Later in the head, relief evaporated when a classmate shifted away from me in line. My stomach dropped—I knew that he wanted to avoid showering with me. He either heard Mr. Strait, or rumors had reached him.

Richard and I were nearby when the classmate leaned toward Justin, whispering something I couldn't catch. Justin's puzzled look prompted him to repeat it louder. "Freshman Lucho may be queer."

I stood frozen, breath shallow. I didn't dare look at Richard—I wasn't sure what I'd see in his eyes: judgment, confusion, or something worse. Justin cut the classmate off. "Watch what you say. It's none of your business."

For the first time that week, I knew I wasn't completely

alone. Justin's defense made me feel seen—someone worth defending. In that moment, I knew I had an ally.

Buddy showers were already awkward, maneuvering the small shower stall with a naked classmate as others watched. The homophobic remarks made by Mr. Strait and then my classmate made things more uncomfortable. They were a stark reminder: gays weren't welcome.

Friday evening, Company Commander announced that the Middle East campaign was escalating and Texas F&E was on high alert. "Why would we be a target?" I wondered. Nothing was clear since I was cut off from the outside world. The order was to sleep in full gear.

Just as I closed my eyes, the hatch slammed open. Heavy metal music blared in the passageway, and Mr. Strait stormed through the doorway, yelling that we were under attack. Richard and I scrambled out of our racks, low crawling toward the ready room as red lights flashed in the passageway.

Inside the ready room, Mr. Strait ordered our entire class to lock arms in a tight circle. "If we get one of you, you all suffer," he warned. We knew exactly what that meant. In the Corps, being separated was the quickest way to get singled out and punished, so locking arms wasn't just obedience—it was survival. A solid mass was harder to pick apart.

When the upperclassmen charged in, hands grabbing for anyone on the edge, we clung to one another with everything we had, moving as a single unit. The moment the command came, we stumbled together out into the night, refusing to let anyone be dragged away. Across the mile, other freshman units were doing the same—tight clusters of bodies fighting to stay whole as they staggered toward the columns.

Master Sergeant revealed the truth when we reached the columns. The "war in the Middle East" was a hoax—we were really there for a pep rally, the first of many before football games. Relief flooded me, but beneath it simmered something else—anger at how easily they'd weaponized our families. I thanked God that Apolo wasn't being sent into combat and that Mami and Papi weren't at home imagining the worst. The panic, the sprint across the mile, the chaos—it had all been engineered to test us.

He congratulated us for not losing anyone. "The sophomores will leave you alone during the pep rally," he said. Only then did we finally exhale.

The university band's music hit me harder than I expected. It reached places I'd been trying to seal off—feelings I'd buried all week so I wouldn't be vulnerable in front of the upperclassmen. For a moment, it was as if the sound lifted a weight I'd been carrying throughout FHW.

Then the cheerleaders stormed the stage, pulling us into a series of chants and songs. Even without the full band, the school songs struck something deep—pride rising in my chest until tears blurred my vision. The upperclassmen could punish my body, humiliate me, test every inch of my resolve, but they hadn't broken my spirit.

When I looked around—Richard laughing, Justin shouting the songs, the rest of our class pressed shoulder to shoulder—I felt it. The stomping of our feet sent vibrations up through my legs and a hum through my chest. For the first time, the belonging wasn't imagined or hoped for. It was real. I was part of a brotherhood, and in that moment, despite the chaos and fear of FHW, I knew I'd made the right choice to join.

Afterward we huddled again, bracing for the walk back. The sophomores taunted, but adrenaline carried us. At McKibbin Hall, Company Commander congratulated us for not losing a single classmate. FHW was officially over, and weekend liberty started the next morning.

Back in the racks, Richard and I whispered jokes in the dark. For the first time in days, I prayed for my family and fell into a peaceful sleep.

Sleeping in a couple of extra hours on Saturday gave my body a much-needed reset. The day was lighter—laundry off campus, games, food, even a movie with Justin, Richard, and a few classmates. We also started a gory dorm banner for the next weekend's football game against the Baton Rouge Bobcats. Justin took the lead, sketching the design while the rest of us added ideas and color.

That evening our entire class crammed into a few cars for our first liberty dinner. The restaurant near campus was packed with non-Corps students, so we waited nearly an hour before the staff squeezed us into tables near the bar. Once seated, conversation and laughter spilled out easily. We talked about home, family, and girlfriends. As a cover, I told everyone that Marisol was my long-term girlfriend and that they'd all love her. The lie appeared to land smooth, but it sat heavy in my chest—another reminder of how much of myself I still had to hide.

Justin stood out—charming, quick with a joke, magnetic in a way that pulled people in. I mostly listened, content to take in the banter and feel the growing bond among us.

We also talked about the twelve classmates we'd already lost—FHW had broken all of them. By the end of dinner, we'd made a pact: if anyone ever felt like quitting, we'd talk to each other first. We were in it together. Despite the bruises, hazing, and the sting of homophobic jabs throughout FHW, I felt optimistic about the year ahead because of my classmates. And sitting there among them, I made a quiet promise to myself: I wouldn't quit.

The ride back to McKibbin Hall was quiet, everyone heavy with food and fatigue.

By Sunday night, Richard and I had polished every piece of brass, squared away our room, and shined our shoes. Climbing into my rack and sleeping bag, I paused to reflect. Twelve classmates were gone, but I was still there—carrying my family's hopes and pride with me. I hadn't expected FHW to weed out so many freshmen. It felt less like training and more like survival.

Still, thirty weeks remained, and I swore I would endure them all. My parents hadn't raised a quitter. The boy who tore open that acceptance letter was still in me somewhere—bruised, exhausted, but unbroken.

Outside, the campus finally fell quiet. In the stillness, I let myself breathe and closed my eyes, ready for the first day of classes.

3 THE WEIGHT OF SILENCE

Author's Note

This and subsequent chapters contain depictions of sexual abuse, coercion, and homophobic language within a military training context. These scenes are included to portray the realities of power, silence, and survival during the era depicted.

The first football game of the season was a victory against the Baton Rouge Bobcats—and the energy ignited at the pep rally. The stadium was filled wall-to-wall, bodies pressed shoulder to shoulder. The student body and alumni roared with a force that rolled across the field like thunder. When the team ran out of the tunnel, the place erupted. Even the concrete seemed to vibrate beneath my shoes.

But the week leading up to that game had already gone sideways. Our dorm banner—meant to rally support for the showdown with the Bobcats—had barely been hung before it drew the fury of the higher-ups, known among cadets as "Top Brass." The mix of officers and enlisted service members overseeing the Corps ordered us to take it down immediately after breakfast on Monday. We had wanted to live up to our reputation, and our upperclassmen were pleased with the uproar. But apparently, our depiction of a decapitated bobcat squirting blood and a pirate holding its heart in one hand and a dripping sword in the other went too far. We were warned to tone down the violence for the next game against Tornado State.

From the first day of classes, my biggest challenge was simply staying awake. Other cadets fought the same battle—heads nodding forward in lectures, snapping back up during evening study hours. One day, I even fell asleep on the toilet—clear proof of how far my exhaustion had sunk. Cadets were supposed to be sharp, alert, unbreakable. I felt none of those things.

That same morning, I discovered what Mr. Strait meant by "sloth platoon" during FHW. After morning chow, Master Sergeant announced—loud enough for the whole company to hear—that four classmates and I who had lagged during the FHW runs now faced extra physical training as sloth platoon members. The shame struck fast, and every muscle in me tightened.

Mr. Strait stormed down the passageway and closed in on me. He said nothing, but his glare looked like he wanted to kill me.

I didn't look out of shape. At 5'9" and 190 pounds, most described me as beefy and muscular. But late-night tacos and burgers with Antoine and Marisol in high school, followed by Mami's full dinners, had added extra pounds. Sloth platoon wasn't just extra physical training—it was a mark, a target. Another reason for Mr. Strait to hound me harder.

Surprisingly, Mac, my friend and the iron man of P-Company, volunteered to lead us. He committed to training us with care and discipline, pushing endurance while teaching us about nutrition. For the first time, I saw a real path forward—a version of myself that could run long distances, built up by Mac while Mr. Strait worked just as hard to break me down.

Richard pitched in too, offering to jog with me on weekends, repeating his soccer coach's mantra, "Breathing right is the key, bunkmate."

Justin also offered to help me build my endurance. Before the Bobcats game, we jogged to the obstacle course. I kept pace better than either of us expected.

Despite my shin splints, I surprised him with my speed on the course. When I reached the rope climb and rappelling wall, I soared up to the twenty-foot knot with ease.

"Holy shit, Mauricio!" he said. "You might be in the sloth platoon, but you move like a beast on this course."

I warned him not to spread it around—the last thing I needed was more attention. The obstacle course was short enough for me to sprint; long-distance endurance was where I struggled.

He grinned and sealed his lips. "This stays between us, Speedy Gonzales."

Justin encouraged me in his own way. "Mauricio, I think I already know the answer, but how do you feel about being in sloth platoon? And those shin splints—you ever think about the campus clinic?"

Being in the sloth platoon embarrassed me, I admitted, but I was determined. A doctor would only tell me to rest, which I couldn't afford. Justin didn't push. Instead, he promised to help train me. "You've got sprint speed, I've seen it. And hey, did you know sloths can swim three times faster than they move on land? Maybe that's your secret weapon at the aquatic center."

He laughed at his own joke, and I couldn't help laughing with him.

As we circled the rappelling tower, Justin spotted a rappelling rope on the ground. His eyes lit up. "Have you ever tied a Swiss seat before?"

The question took me back. A Swiss seat—a makeshift harness you tie around your waist and legs for rappelling— was something I hadn't practiced in over a year. "A while back at summer camp," I said. "But I'm rusty."

He picked up the rope with a confident smile. "Watch this. I can tie one in fifteen seconds."

I raised an eyebrow and told him to prove it. After he asked me to count, his hands blurred—looping, weaving, cinching the rope around his body with practiced ease. Eighteen seconds later, he stood there with a perfect Swiss seat.

My jaw dropped. "Where the hell did you learn that?"

He laughed, untying the rope. "An Army Ranger drilled it into me, and I practiced for months until I could do it in the dark. I got addicted to beating my own time."

On our way to chow, he promised to train me too. "We'll get your Swiss seat time to fifteen seconds. No excuses. And I'll get back to fifteen seconds, as well."

I agreed immediately—partly to sharpen my skills, but mostly because I wanted every excuse to spend more time with him. Justin made me feel safe in a way I couldn't quite explain—lighter, almost—like the grind of Corps life loosened its grip when he was around. He made me laugh without trying, and there was an ease between us, a quiet intimacy, that I didn't feel with anyone else.

Back in the dorm, Richard caught me grinning. When he asked why, I answered honestly. "Bunkmate, you, Justin, and Mac really care about me, and I care about you. Truthfully, it's pushing me to reach my goal. It's going to be a long road, but I'm grateful for all of you." I let myself savor it, unaware of how badly I would need that feeling in the days ahead.

Two weeks into the semester, amidst the relentless grind of Corps duties, I faced my first quiz. Determined to do well, I hurried down the passageway during Sunday study hours to request an "exemption pass" from Master Sergeant. The small black card, slipped into the nameplate on my hatch, signaled to upperclassmen that I'd be missing morning physical training. It was a golden ticket: one morning without physical training, one night of uninterrupted sleep.

Prepared for the quiz, I slid the pass into place on the hatch with a sense of satisfaction.

After I brushed my teeth, Richard, perched atop his rack, greeted me with a sarcastic remark, telling me to wipe the grin off my face. Undeterred, I replied, "I feel prepared for the quiz!"

"I'm glad to hear it, bunkmate," Richard responded with a reassuring nod. "You've put in the work, so I have no doubt you'll destroy that quiz tomorrow."

Assured of my preparedness, I told Richard that I felt better than I did a few days prior. It was after lights out, so I undressed and stowed away my books in the dark, looking forward to a restful night's sleep.

At 0545 hours, Richard's alarm clock shattered the silence, and he intentionally made extra noise as he got dressed for morning PT. He relished giving me a hard time, but when he returned from physical training, he let me sleep.

It was a sleep that, as Mami would say, aimed to compensate for the accumulated sueño viejo, or "old sleep."

At 0800 hours, my alarm blared, jolting me awake. I moved quickly to shut it off, listening for any sign of movement in the passageway before I headed to the showers.

Hesitation crept in; it was the first time showering alone, without classmates running interference. A second pause followed before I opened the hatch—ear pressed to the cold surface, straining for any telltale sign of movement.

A faint shuffle of footsteps echoed in the passageway, accompanied by the distinct sound of a head's hatch closing—a sure indication that upperclassmen were around. I guessed it came from the far end.

Praying whoever it was had already vanished, I swiftly exited the room and locked the hatch behind me. Something in my gut told me to wait. I should've listened. Just one more minute.

As I began to execute a left face, a flicker of movement

caught my attention, tightening every muscle in my body. Midway through my turn, I froze, staring down the passageway.

To my dismay, Mr. Strait stepped out of his hatch—naked, aroused, a towel slung carelessly over his shoulder. My eyes betrayed me before I could stop them, flicking where they shouldn't. And worst of all, my body jolted—an involuntary, unwelcome spark of attraction I wanted no part of. Heat rushed up my face, not just from embarrassment but from the desperate need to numb out and silence every trace of my gayness before it exposed me.

The moment I realized he'd caught me staring, I snapped to attention, desperate to recover, but the damage was done. Seeing him naked in the showers was challenging enough. Seeing him erect was something I never expected. Oh God. He knows I looked—again.

I threw myself against the bulkhead and stood at attention. "Good morning, Mr. Strait, sir."

He stopped directly in front of me and chuckled, low and menacing. "Well, well. Freshman Lucho. You keep denying you're a cock-sucking faggot, but here you are, checking me out again. Do you like what you saw? We both know the truth. Just admit it."

I felt trapped—pinned down by his words and intimidation. I shouted at the top of my lungs, "Sir, no, sir."

True to form, he intensified the situation, likely to fuel his ego and hunger for power. Mr. Strait looked down both ends of the passageway to confirm that no one was around. Then he leaned in even closer to me, toward my right ear. His voice dropped to a whisper. "Is that what you want, freshman Lucho. On your knees, mouth open, just aching for it. Because from the way you've been eyeing my cock, I think I know the answer."

A cold grip of dread tightened around me. This wasn't hazing. This was something else—something darker. I yelled, "Sir, no, sir!" Praying that someone—anyone—

would walk out into the passageway and put an end to the situation.

Worse, his tone wasn't just intimidating—it was practiced, manipulative, almost seductive. I felt helpless and exposed. It was the first time he'd cornered me completely alone, with no witnesses and no escape. The passageway suddenly felt too narrow. My hands trembled at my sides as he pressed himself into my leg. Panic shot through me. Please, God—don't let me get aroused. Not now. Not here. Not in front of him.

Despite my attempts to thwart his unwelcome interrogation, he persisted, "I can feel you shivering, freshman Lucho. Wonder what your classmates would think if they knew how rattled you got after being caught staring at my cock. Tell me, does it feel good? Or maybe, just maybe, you want more."

"Sir, no, sir," I shouted.

But Mr. Strait escalated his abuse of power further to test and antagonize me. He pressed himself against my leg while he tickled my ear with his nose and exhaled from his mouth onto my cheek. My trembling continued to quench his thirst for control, and it took every ounce of my willpower not to have the physical reaction he was hoping to provoke. After several seconds that felt like minutes, he reached down and squeezed my package over my towel.

Failing to cause the reaction he wanted, he groaned, "Not even a twitch, freshman Lucho? Still, I caught you staring, again, and I believe you're a faggot. You can deny it all you want, but I see right through you. Keep your eyes where they belong, or next time, you'll regret it."

He stared at me as he slowly backed away. Just before he entered the head, he glanced back at me and muttered, "Guess it's time to deal with this morning wood."

I remained motionless against the bulkhead. Then I remembered hearing that his girlfriend, Brittany, was out of town over the weekend. For a moment, my mind tried to file it under "sexual frustration," to make it make sense. I hated myself for even trying to rationalize his behavior.

He left me paralyzed against the bulkhead. After he disappeared into the head, I glanced both ways down the passageway before reaching inside my towel to confirm what I suspected.

I hadn't gotten hard, but there was still precum—proof my body had reacted in ways I wanted no part of. The violation and humiliation hit hard, and all I wanted was to hide in my room until he and any other upperclassmen were finished in the showers. But with a tight schedule, I still had to shower, shave, and get dressed.

I ran into the head, turned the corner to face the shower stalls, and immediately saw two other sophomores showering in the freshman and sophomore stalls. They were speaking to each other and turned around to look my way when I greeted them. Mr. Strait was not in my line of sight because he was in the third shower stall, for juniors.

One of the sophomores must have seen the exemption pass on my hatch because he gave me permission to use the coveted senior stall, the farthest from the entrance and the most private.

"Just don't let a senior catch you, freshman Lucho."

I nodded and made my way toward the stall, walking past the two sophomores.

The moment I stepped in front of the junior stall, Mr. Strait's voice cut through the steam.

"Stop. Face me."

I stopped and turned toward him. He stopped masturbating and stepped forward—lathered in soap and fully erect. I fixed my eyes on his chest.

He leaned in closely, his voice low and deliberate. "You're gonna stand right here and be my curtain until I'm finished. Don't move a muscle, freshman Lucho."

His hand pressed down on my head, forcing me to look down and watch. I stood rigid, my breathing rapid and uncontrollable, as he continued to rub himself.

The two sophomores continued talking only a few feet away, oblivious. If one of them walked over, would they have stopped him? Laughed? Reported me instead?

His breathing quickened as the stroking intensified. He watched me the whole time, eyes narrowing with a cruel kind of satisfaction, feeding on my fear, my inability to move. I wanted to disappear.

Then, with a sudden tug, he yanked my towel away.

I stood exposed, mortified, and—against my will—fully aroused.

My body betrayed me in the worst possible way. His quiet chuckle told me he felt triumphant.

Our eyes locked, and I knew he had what he wanted—proof.

He stepped closer and placed his free hand on my shoulder, and what followed happened fast. When he finished, he wiped his hand across my stomach as if I were nothing more than a rag.

I stayed rooted in place, my sense of safety drained down the shower floor. Whatever this was, it wasn't a fantasy. Whatever thin line I once imagined between hazing and real harm had been erased.

Mr. Strait signaled for me to go away, so I bent down to reach for my towel and toiletries. The coast was clear, and I backed out and staggered to the senior shower stall.

I turned the shower handle as far toward hot as it would go, and within seconds the scalding water hit my skin. It didn't bring pain—just tears. I scrubbed and rinsed over and over, as if I could scour away the morning, the humiliation, the shame lodged beneath my skin.

Once the upperclassmen finally cleared out of the head, I dried off and rushed back to my room. Even though it was forbidden, I locked the hatch behind me the moment I stepped inside. Then I slid down to the deck, pulled my knees close, and bawled as quietly as I could, desperate not to draw any attention.

The tears eventually stopped. I forced myself to get dressed and head to class. During the quiz, I was physically present, but my mind replayed the shower scene over and over. Every question blurred, and I had to read each one twice.

If I told anyone, they'd turn it on me. Top Brass had made it clear: the hazer and the hazed both faced expulsion. And if Mr. Strait exposed my truth under "Don't Ask, Don't Tell," I'd lose everything—my scholarship, my degree, my chance to be an officer.

The thought of involving Justin, Richard, or Mac twisted my stomach. I couldn't burden them with this, couldn't risk dragging them into the fallout.

The memory of their laughter and support—Justin's rope tricks, Richard's jokes, Mac's encouraging push—felt a world away. I couldn't risk losing them, so I shut them out.

With so much on the line, I decided that keeping my mouth shut was my only option. I would bury the truth about what Mr. Strait had done and sacrifice justice. After all, he was my squad leader—a dark cloud I couldn't escape.

Silence became my shield, but it also became the heaviest burden I carried.

And one question gnawed at me: what would happen the next time he had me cornered?

4 RAMPANT DISCRIMINATION

In just over a month, my eyes were opened to pervasive acts of discrimination toward women and minority cadets. There was also constant mockery and ridicule aimed at gays and those perceived as gay, including me.

As a young man raised to live by the golden rule, I valued respect and fairness. Most of my formative years were spent with people from various countries and backgrounds in Houston, so I learned early on to appreciate different cultures.

The scale weighed heavily toward overt racism from the start of the year. For example, word quickly circulated that Mr. Strait's paternal grandfather, a former cadet, had been a grand wizard in the Ku Klux Klan (KKK). Mr. Strait was revered by several cadets in the Corps because of this family association.

I unfortunately didn't realize that many of our university's early senior administrators were officers in the Confederate States Army and members of the KKK. A handful of statues and memorials on campus had the inscription C.S.A.—a subtle attempt to obscure its meaning. We also paid homage to these heroes as part of Corps tradition.

There were also references to the Civil War and Confederacy both on and near campus, such as the Confederate flag displayed at local businesses. A prominent example was the most popular bar in town just west of campus. Its branding and artwork were unmistakably modeled after the Confederate flag.

While seemingly harmless, the weekly viewing parties orchestrated by Mr. Strait, featuring reruns of "The Dukes of Hazzard," a TV show that originated in the late 1970s, held a deeper, more unsettling significance. During our first viewing, I realized the show's nod to the Confederacy. The iconic car, practically a character in itself, bore the name of a Confederate general and prominently displayed the Confederate battle flag on its roof. The car's horn also played the song "Dixie," the unofficial anthem of the Confederate states.

There was one Black male in our dorm, and my daily count of Black cadets I saw on the mile never required more than one hand. This experience was a stark contrast to my high school years at Houston Aviation Academy, a predominantly Black school.

Homophobic treatment didn't come as a surprise because I had endured every slur and insult since sixth grade. Years of experience helped me form a thick skin. Although there were rumors and banter, there was no evidence to confirm my sexual orientation. Fortunately, most believed that Marisol was my girlfriend. Regardless, some of the upperclassmen continued to make gay jokes about me. "Better watch yourselves in the showers, boys— you wouldn't want to drop the soap around freshman Lucho," and "Don't bother asking if freshman Lucho is a fag, because he can't tell you."

One unexpected realization for me was how limited the opportunities were for women in the Corps. Most companies—including mine—didn't admit women at all. Our dorm had just one woman, and only a handful of companies admitted any. It was a stark contrast to Houston Aviation Academy, where nearly half our company was female—and where they excelled. Marisol, especially, had been one of our strongest cadets.

Unfortunately, the misogynistic culture within the Corps Drill Platoon came to a head that week—and Justin became one of its casualties. It wasn't something they put in the recruiting brochures: no woman had ever been allowed in the platoon. Past instructors had ensured that, and the current ones were just as determined—clinging to their version of tradition even if it meant crossing lines and hurting the very cadets they were supposed to train.

When the call for Corps Drill Platoon volunteers was issued at the start of the semester, a handful of my classmates valiantly answered, including Justin. Admittedly, a mix of excitement and slight envy coursed through me; being in the Corps Drill Platoon would elevate their status in our pecking order—good for them, not so good for me. However, I was honest with myself—any additional commitment requiring a significant amount of time would be detrimental.

Justin updated me frequently and said that Corps Drill Platoon tryouts were consistently intensifying. However, the drill field was empty most evenings. Instead of teaching the drill routines, the instructors were more focused on physically challenging and hazing the cadets. Our classmates returned drenched in sweat after every practice. They were being physically pushed to the limits and forbidden from talking about their training at all.

Finally, I called Justin one evening after hearing the group return to the dorm much later than usual. Practice had gone way past the standard time. "Justin, what the heck is going on? What are they doing to you guys? Why are they putting y'all through the wringer like this?"

Initially, there was silence followed by Justin taking a deep breath. He wanted to tell me, but fear was clearly holding him back. Reassuring him helped break the silence. "You know you can trust me with anything, Justin." It was important for him to know that his words would be safe with me.

Justin slowly exhaled, his voice low and serious. "Mauricio, this stays between us. Not a word to anyone—

not even your bunkmate. Do you understand? Swear to me you won't repeat what I'm about to say."

Keeping a secret wasn't an issue for me. "I swear, Justin. Whatever you say stays between us."

"The drill instructors... they're putting us through absolute hell, all to weed out the last two female cadets who refuse to quit." Justin's voice wavered, heavy with frustration and concern.

I didn't hesitate to press for more details. "How much longer is this punishment going to last? And where's Top Brass in all of this? They go on about bringing more diversity into the Corps, yet this bullshit is still happening. It's unbelievable. These trials aren't just grueling, they're reckless. They're putting your life on the line."

Justin lowered his voice to explain the disturbing truth. "Mauricio, this isn't going to stop until every last woman cadet is gone. Our Top Brass advisor? He's right there during training—a former Corps Drill Platoon member. The drill instructors are dead set on keeping tradition alive—no woman will ever make it into the Corps Drill Platoon. To them, having a woman cadet in the ranks is a bigger disgrace than losing a national championship. They're going to turn up the heat until the women break and walk away on their own."

Justin continued and told me that a "hell day" was planned for Saturday. It was devised to break the remaining two women at any cost. Worry consumed me for my friend and other classmates. Moreover, a sense of shame washed over me knowing I was associated with the discrimination at play.

Saturday morning came around and the Corps Drill Platoon began its "hell day" while everyone else enjoyed liberty and sleep, including myself. By midday, there was no sign of the Corps Drill Platoon. Richard and I joined a few classmates for lunch in the dining hall and then went to the laundromat to knock out one of our weekend chores.

Upon returning to the dorm, my concern increased because our Corps Drill Platoon classmates were nowhere in sight. I presumed that the two women cadets were giving the instructors a run for their money. Dinner time approached, and we discussed evening plans—some of the gang was heading to the movies and others were going to the new dance club on the west side of campus. Richard and I chose to wait around for our classmates.

Richard and I were in our room and listening to music when we heard Mr. Strait yell through the passageway, "Class of 99, get your asses downstairs—now! Your worthless classmates need your help."

My classmates and I flung open our hatches, and we bolted down the stairwells and found Justin and the others hunched over on the benches in front of the dorm. They were covered in mud and sweat, appeared delirious, and gasped for air. Helping Justin was my top priority. "What the hell happened? Are you okay? And what are you covered in because it smells like crap?"

Justin took a long, shaky breath before slowly admitting, "I can't take another step, Mauricio." His whole body trembled with fatigue. "My fingers are so weak I can barely hold onto my rifle… and this crap all over me? It's burning every open wound I've got."

My instincts kicked in—our classmates needed help. Raising my voice with a sense of urgency, I took command. "Alright, classmates, listen up! They need to get upstairs to shower and rest but can't walk. Pair up, grab an arm, and get them on their feet. Let's move!"

We swiftly divided and one of our classmates collected the rifles. Richard and I helped Justin stand up and got him into the dorm. When we arrived at the stairwell it was clear that the three of us wouldn't fit.

Every nerve in my body lit up at once. I hoisted Justin onto my shoulders in a fireman's carry and began the trek up to the fourth deck. My legs were on fire by the third deck, but

I refused to quit.

When we reached the fourth deck, the stench quickly flooded the passageway. The familiar smells of sweat and vomit mixed with manure and God knows what else were pungent. I asked Richard to help Justin to our head while I retrieved soap, a washcloth, shampoo, and towels.

I entered the head, and Justin was sitting on the floor in the freshman stall with water spraying down on him. Richard looked relieved to see me. After joining him in the stall, I knelt down beside my friend, keeping my voice steady and calm. "Hey there, look up. Look into my eyes, buddy. Come on, right here." He looked into my eyes, and I gave him a small grin. "You look and smell like absolute shit, so let's get you cleaned up before you scare my bunkmate off."

Richard volunteered to retrieve snacks for the guys because it seemed they had been fed little to nothing throughout the day. After Richard left the head, attention turned to the task at hand—the arduous process of bathing Justin.

Starting with his head, his short, fuzzy hair was thoroughly shampooed and scrubbed to wash away the dirt and sweat. A washcloth was used to gently cleanse his face, ears, and neck. Then I unfastened his camouflage blouse, removed his t-shirt, and scrubbed his torso, back, and arms. The trembling continued, and Justin told me that his vision was still blurry but improving.

Remaining calm seemed crucial, even as frustration and fear simmered inside me. "Close your eyes and relax. Take deep breaths. Let the cold water cool you down. Just focus on your breathing."

As I worked the soap through his hair, Justin let out a low sigh. For a moment, he looked completely worn down—eyes half-closed, shoulders heavy. Then, out of nowhere, that familiar spark of humor flickered back to life.

"Hey," he said, tilting his head slightly toward me, "mind

scrubbing my scalp a little more, Mauricio? I'm starting to think this is what a fancy spa feels like."

Despite everything—his pain, the exhaustion—I couldn't help but laugh. Leave it to Justin to find a way to make even this feel lighter.

"Real funny, mister. Now focus on your breathing."

After getting him to his feet, the boots, socks, and trousers came off, revealing his legs coated in sludge that lined the inside of his trousers. His white briefs were black and drooped like a soiled diaper. I hesitated to remove his filthy underwear at first, but then a glance into his eyes was met with a nod to proceed. Despite the discomfort, he laughed, calling out the sludge's presence in his ass crack as well.

We both chuckled, and I looked into his eyes with a sense of determination. Placing a reassuring hand on his shoulder, I said, "Don't worry, my friend. In a few minutes, you'll be clean. Just relax and let it all wash away."

With a tired but genuine smile, Justin whispered, "Thanks, Mauricio. I mean it. You always have my back."

I scrubbed his body with care to avoid further discomfort. Before long, the shower room floor began to flood as the sludge clogged the drains. Justin sat on the shower stall bench while I worked on clearing the drains.

After the water began to flow, getting him on his feet was necessary to clean his lower body. I handled the cleaning of his genitals with extra care because of potential chafing or cuts. He noticed that I was getting drenched, but this was no inconvenience. After helping Justin turn around, I washed his backside, hamstrings, calves, and feet. Fortunately, he was chafed but not bleeding.

Once he was clean, I shut off the water and dried his body. I wrapped the towel around his waist and sat him down on the shower stall bench. Then I continued to dry his torso and head with a second towel.

Richard returned with Justin's shower shoes, a protein

bar, and beef jerky. Justin was starving and ate the snacks while we watched. Richard reported that the others were being cared for and that Master Sergeant said we should lay them down in their racks to rest and bring them dinner. They can clean their rifles later.

Justin stood up, stepped into his shower shoes, and declared that he could walk to his room. Despite his confidence, Richard accompanied him while I stayed behind to take a shower.

After finishing up, I reunited with them in Justin's room, my mind set on getting some food in his belly. "This man needs some Mexican caldo de pollo—good old chicken soup. Too bad there's no way we're finding caldo on campus. Any ideas where I can find a decent bowl of chicken soup?"

Justin remembered that the student center made a delicious chicken and dumplings soup, and I offered to pick up a bowl for him. Meanwhile, Richard said that he was going to shower and meet up with some of our classmates.

While Justin rested, I walked to the student center and returned with two bowls of chicken and dumplings. After pulling up a chair beside his rack, my offer to spoon-feed him was obviously unexpected. Justin let out a surprised laugh. "Wait—you're really offering to spoon-feed me? I can't even remember the last time that happened."

I grinned and shrugged. "Well, I've never spoon-fed anyone before, so I guess we're both in uncharted territory."

I blew on the spoon to cool the soup before holding it up. "Alright, open up. Justin, it was horrifying to see you guys like that—completely beat up and weak. You were on the brink of heat exhaustion, red face and all. I don't get it, why didn't they call for medical help? Hell, they didn't even make sure you all safely returned to the dorm. The whole thing seems reckless—irresponsible as hell."

It was obvious that my words caught him off guard. Then

he stopped me from shoveling another spoonful in his mouth and said that what I did was the most caring act anyone had ever demonstrated toward him.

Justin let out a tired chuckle. "I can't believe you hauled me all the way up to the fourth deck, Mauricio. You're a beast. I owe you one. Seriously, thank you for taking care of me, my friend." His gratitude also radiated through his sincere smile and hazel eyes.

I shook my head and looked directly into those eyes. "You don't owe me anything, Justin. Just tell me this ordeal you've been living is finally over. Did the last two women cadets quit the Corps Drill Platoon?"

Justin confirmed, "Mission accomplished. The last two women cadets tapped out—along with a few guys. Damn good cadets, but honestly, I don't blame them for quitting." He paused for a moment, his eyes lost in thought. When he spoke again, his voice was quieter. "Mauricio, you wouldn't believe the hell they put us through..."

Although I was relieved to hear that the hellish indoctrination period was over for Justin and the others, I felt disheartened for the women who simply wanted to be a part of the Corps Drill Platoon.

When Justin finished telling me about the unbelievable hazing he experienced, I told him a story about an event that left a meaningful impression on me while I continued to feed him. It happened at mini-bootcamp in Pensacola during the summer of 1992. Ironically, Justin and I missed each other by one week that summer.

It was chaos after I landed in Pensacola. There were drill instructors yelling and loading us and our bags on buses. I was frightened, sat at attention, and looked ahead as instructed. As I entered my first military base, I glanced at the sign and learned that the Naval Air Station was home of the Aviation Officer Candidate School. Later, it became clear that we were sharing the same base facilities with that summer's class of aviation officer candidates.

On one side of our living quarters, a dormitory-like building, there was a huge sandbox bordered with logs the size of light poles. For the first few days, I wondered about the purpose of the sandbox.

Around the halfway point of mini-bootcamp, in the middle of a hot and humid Florida afternoon, the purpose of the sandbox revealed itself. As my platoon practiced close order drill in the street facing the sandbox and our living quarters, I observed the officer candidates undergoing training. A closer look revealed one woman in the group.

Training that day had the officer candidates low crawling across the sandbox, starting on the side of the sandbox near the street and us. Two Marine Corps drill instructors positioned themselves on the corners of the sandbox farthest from the street, wielding high-pressure water hoses aimed at the officer candidates.

One drill instructor focused his hose on their faces, blinding and forcing them to gasp for air. The other pounded their arms and legs as they tried to move forward. The water hit with brutal force, and the candidates fought to advance. Soaked utilities—camouflage uniforms, known as utes or cammies—and heavy combat boots turned every forward motion into a fight.

Despite the blinding and stinging water, the candidates slowly advanced one movement at a time. Each time they crossed the sandbox, they circled back to the entrance, dropped to the low crawling position, and repeated the arduous routine. I watched them every time they started over, and they appeared exhausted but never quit.

By the tenth round, the woman officer candidate stopped advancing because she was completely depleted. Instead of aiming the hoses at the other candidates, the instructors focused both hoses on her, clearly increasing the difficulty of the challenge. Unexpectedly, one of the drill instructors shouted, "We never leave anyone behind." At that moment, it became clear they were teaching the officer candidates a lesson.

After hearing this, four of the other candidates instinctively low-crawled over to her. One grasped her left forearm, another her right, while the remaining two secured her ankles. In a synchronized motion, as if rehearsed, the four men low-crawled while aiding her, moving across the sandbox one final time.

My hopes that they were done for the day were quickly shattered. Once they cleared the sandbox, the drill instructors ordered them to lift one of the logs onto their shoulders, and they ran down the street and away from us.

The motto, "leave no man—or woman in this case— behind," became real for me in that moment. Regardless of gender, race, or national origin, Marines were taught to have each other's backs. What I observed that day was a powerful lesson.

The way they forced the women out of the Corps Drill Platoon, hazed everyone until they quit, went against my values. It was the complete opposite of what I saw that day in Pensacola.

I looked at Justin, knowing how much this meant to him, knowing his family legacy left him with no real choice. "I get it, Justin. Walking away isn't an option for you, and I respect that."

Justin said that he understood and that he would remember to help others when they were down. He promised to never leave anyone behind.

He finished his bowl of soup, and I gave him a nod. "Alright, my friend, now that you've got some food in your belly, it's time to sleep and recharge." I glanced at my own bowl, realizing the soup was probably cold, but I didn't mind. "I'll hang out here and finish mine while you drift off to sleep. Just rest, and if you need anything, call me."

Before I pulled my hand away, he reached for it and thanked me one more time. If there was any silver lining from the terrible "hell day" experience, it was that I got to nurture my injured friend back to health. We had a strong connection, with a shared commitment to supporting each other.

It struck me afterward that I had never bathed another person, not even a family member. The experience wasn't sexual in any way, but it was deeply intimate—closer than I had ever been to anyone outside my family. Something inside me stirred, something I tried to silence the moment I felt it. I cared about Justin, maybe more than I should have, and tending to him that way revealed feelings I wasn't prepared to confront. I wanted to stop them, to push them down, to stay in the safety of friendship. But even then, I knew it wasn't that simple.

The two female cadets were on my mind as I sat at the desk eating my soup. They and the others before them simply wanted to be a member of the Corps Drill Platoon. Imagining their untapped potential triggered empathy and a sense of injustice.

They were likely future military officers, and yet, despite their passion, the Corps Drill Platoon didn't extend them a welcome. It was a stark reminder of other barriers, like the U.S. military's rejection of openly gay members. Those in power went to great lengths to eradicate or marginalize others.

It had become painfully clear that bigotry and discrimination ran rampant within the Corps. Witnessing injustice forced me to confront a question I had never dared ask: What does it cost to belong here? In a place with whose values were so fundamentally at odds with my own, that question began to torment me.

5 TORCH THE TOWER

Despite the soreness, blisters, and sunburn, my mind stayed fixed on something far more painful: my relationship with Justin. All weekend, I circled back to one of Mami's dichos: "Árbol que crece torcido, jamás su tronco endereza."—a tree that grows crooked can never straighten its trunk. She meant it as a warning about character, about how hard it is to change who we are at the core. The metaphor haunted me, making me wonder if I was the crooked tree.

The world felt complicated because I'd grown up surrounded by messages that something about me was wrong—crooked, even. I had spent years hiding the truth of my gay identity, the part of me society had taught me to see as flawed. That shame lived just under my skin, shaping how I moved.

On Friday, September 29, just before weekend liberty, the sophomores ordered us into the passageway to hear our next assignment. Master Sergeant stepped forward and told us it was time to begin working toward the long-standing tradition: Torch the Tower. For weeks, cadets would haul lumber and pour in countless volunteer hours to build the centerpiece of the event—a full wooden replica of Capital College's iconic clock tower. Each year, on the eve of the big football game, crowds of students and alumni gathered for the largest pep rally of the season to watch the structure go up in flames, celebrating our archrival's symbolic downfall.

Master Sergeant explained how it got started. According to folklore, we lost a game to our archrival in the early 1900s. This angered an unknown cadet to the point that he drove to Austin and lit the university's clock tower on fire. Charges were never filed because his identity remains unknown to this day. Fortunately, no one was injured, and the damage wasn't extensive, but the act shaped a tradition that has lasted almost a century.

Every year, the tons of lumber required to build the tower were manually chopped down by students, mostly cadets. Safety gear and tools were required. Once again, we assembled a core team to make a shopping run to the military surplus store and purchase helmets, gloves, machetes, spray paint, tape, and axes. Everyone chipped in.

To distinguish ourselves from the other companies, we also needed to tap into our creativity and design unique helmets. Before dismissal, Master Sergeant informed us that the first tree chopping would start the next Saturday, rain or shine, because that day's game against Lubbock University was an away evening game.

In the ready room, my classmates and I discussed our new project before breaking for weekend liberty. Everyone was on board with Justin creating the design for our helmets because of his creative talents, and we quickly organized ourselves. We agreed on who would make the supply run and formed two working groups for the first and second shifts to incorporate Justin's design onto the helmets over the weekend. We committed to nightly work shifts during the week to finish the project.

Before we parted ways, Justin unexpectedly leaned over and whispered that if I was free that evening, he could use some help with our helmet design.

"Just us two?" I babbled, trying not to blush or grin too hard.

With a slight grin and puzzled look, Justin nodded, "Yeah, just us two."

The invitation delighted me, and we agreed on a pizzeria for dinner. After suggesting two pizzas for us and his bunkmate, he mentioned that he would be alone for the weekend. His bunkmate was driving home to see his folks.

When I got to my room, I called Justin to see if he was okay with me crashing in his room for the night. Without hesitation, he chuckled, "A slumber party sounds fun, Mauricio. Just promise to keep the snoring to a minimum."

Beyond my personal excitement to spend more time with Justin, this situation turned out to be beneficial for Richard as well. Visitors were allowed to spend the night in the dorm, so Richard's girlfriend was driving to University Station for the weekend. My absence provided them with some much-needed privacy.

After a quick shower, I returned to my room to get dressed. Richard was sitting at his desk anticipating a phone call from his girlfriend. He was grateful and relieved by my plans for the weekend. Up until then, he was nervous about asking me to have the room to himself. I looked at Richard and said, "This is what bunkmates do for each other, and don't ever be afraid to ask me for anything." Seeing him that happy made my day even better.

Richard excitedly rushed to shower, and I dug around my desk for the pizzeria flier. After packing my sleeping bag and toiletries, I called Justin before heading over, and he picked up right away. "Hey, come to my room when you're ready," he said casually, "I'm about to take a shower, but I'll be back in a few minutes. My hatch will be unlocked, so just come in and make yourself at home."

"Justin wants to be your friend. Respect that. Don't cross any lines. Don't push the boundaries." These thoughts echoed in my mind as I grabbed my things and headed out the door. Admittedly, it was obvious to me and others that Justin and I shared a special friendship, and the feelings toward him that were forming deep within me were unprecedented. Regardless, he wasn't gay, and I needed to demonstrate willpower.

When Justin returned to his room after showering, I was seated in his bunkmate's chair with my head resting on the desk. He stepped inside, turned the lock on the hatch, and walked over to his chest of drawers. We weren't allowed to lock our hatches, and the small click caught me off guard.

I didn't ask why he did it, but a quiet question flickered through my mind—was he simply seeking privacy, or was he creating a subtle, unspoken kind of intimacy?

Unknowingly, I swiveled around in the chair, and there he was facing me—completely naked, casually toweling off. After what sounded like a satisfied sigh, he grinned, "Man, that was one of the best showers I've had since we got here. The water pressure felt like a massage, and I had the head all to myself—no interruptions, no rush. Pure bliss." Justin appeared anything but bashful and standing naked in front of me seemed natural to him. On the other hand, I found myself trying to avoid blushing because I sat at eye level with his package. My eyes remained mostly fixed on the floor, with occasional upward glances to sneak a peek.

With a playful smirk, he caught me off guard. "Is it just me, or is it hot in here? Or wait...are you blushing, Mauricio?"

I quickly glanced at the window and blurted out the first thing that popped into my head. "Yeah, it's definitely hot in here. Um, let's turn down the temperature so I can actually get some sleep tonight."

Justin turned around and gave me a full view of his firm glutes and muscular back while he continued to slowly towel off. Richard and I never took that long to dry off, and we also didn't face each other naked. As I shamelessly gawked, he casually spread his feet apart and bent down to dry his calves and feet. Despite being completely dry, he continued to towel off at a snail's pace. It occurred to me that he was allowing me to savor the moment.

Finally, after several minutes of watching Justin dry off

and being secretly aroused, relief came over me when he casually tossed on boxer shorts and a t-shirt. Before putting on a Pearl Jam CD, he unlocked the hatch. He never explained why he'd locked it—and I didn't ask.

He grabbed his notebook and a pencil, and I joined him on the floor in the middle of the room to talk and watch him sketch some initial designs.

Before long, our growling stomachs indicated that it was time to order pizza. In less than thirty minutes, the delivery man dialed Justin's room, and I ran downstairs to pay and retrieve our dinner. We placed the pizza box on the floor between us and devoured our halves. Fortunately, Justin wasn't a fan of garlic, so I enjoyed the melted garlic butter with my pizza crust, and he ate the banana peppers.

After we ate and changed the CD, discussing our siblings made for some funny stories, but our perspectives and experiences were quite different. He was the oldest, the big and responsible brother, and I was at the opposite end, frequently referred to as the spoiled baby who was lucky to get away with more than my older brothers. Despite this difference, we both loved our siblings very much.

We gloated about our mothers, and he said that his mom was the strongest and most loving person he knew. I told him about the close bond I had with Mami and that she was constantly praying for her sons. She consistently shared her wisdom and repeated dichos to help shape our perspectives. I explained how dichos are Mexican expressions ingrained into our values and behaviors.

I lost him for a moment, but the blank stare in his eyes was telling—he was struggling and carefully crafting what he intended to say next. Then he continued and explained that his mother was raising him and his siblings alone because she became a widow when Justin started high school. His tragic loss rendered me speechless because none of my friends had lost their father. Divorced parents, yes, but not deceased.

I paused feeling the weight of his pain. "I...I'm at a loss for words, Justin," I started, struggling to find the right ones. "I can't even begin to imagine the depth of your pain, and I'm so sorry for your devastating loss. Losing Papi...it's difficult to even wrap my head around."

Justin's words seemed carefully measured. "Death... it's not a comfortable subject, so most people steer clear of it. I appreciate your words, Mauricio. Even though it's been years, I still grieve. Let's change the subject for now— talking about my dad still brings up a lot of pain."

We switched over to the topic that most young men greatly enjoy discussing—sex—losing our virginity, our favorite positions, our more adventurous sexual acts, and the Hollywood celebrities we fantasize about. I had to embellish that last part and couldn't tell him about my physical encounters with men. He described intercourse with his girlfriend as making love, and my perspective was a bit more transactional, less emotional and more physical. Masturbation came up, and we laughed about how open the upperclassmen and some of our classmates were on the topic.

After putting the final touches on the class of '99 helmet rendering, we called it a night. We brushed our teeth and crashed out.

Bright and early Saturday morning, our classmates made the rounds to collect money for the supplies. Without knocking, one of our classmates stormed into Justin's room and found us sleeping. He woke us up and said that he was surprised to see me. My excuse was that it got late, and Richard invited his girlfriend to spend the night in our room. "My bunkmate needed some alone time with his girl."

Justin hopped down from his rack to retrieve his wallet. When he turned around to hand our classmate the money, his morning wood was poking out of his boxer shorts. Our classmate awkwardly coughed and muttered, "Brother, you need to adjust yourself." I remained silent and watched him struggle to remedy the situation.

Seeing Justin's morning wood instantly aroused me, so I inconspicuously reached down into my sleeping bag to adjust myself before hopping out of the rack to retrieve money. Justin also distracted our classmate by sharing the helmet design.

We joined a few other classmates for breakfast after the group left for the supply run. Then the first group met behind the dormitory and worked on the helmets throughout the morning.

When the second group began to arrive, Justin asked if I wanted to spend the rest of the day with him. He wanted to have lunch, spend the afternoon in the recreation center, and then head to the movie theatre for dinner and a show. He also invited me to spend the night in his room again. The invitations were music to my ears, and I agreed.

The recreation center was a fun and much-needed escape. In the diving pool, we leaped off multiple platforms and diving boards. The hot tub was relaxing, and we had it all to ourselves. When our fingers looked more like prunes than skin, we made our way to the locker room to rinse off and get dressed.

As Justin and I entered the communal shower room, I opted to use a shower at the opposite end, giving us both some space. Justin's playful nature surprised me when he slipped out of the room while I lathered up with soap on my face. He returned with ice cubes in hand and threw them at me.

Taken by surprise, I burst into uncontrollable laughter. I quickly rinsed the soap from my face, ready to retaliate. This nude horseplay lasted for several minutes, and it felt completely natural.

For a split second during our horseplay, I felt like I was being watched. Justin didn't appear to notice, but my gut was right. I caught a glimpse of someone lurking in a shower stall and watching us through an opening in the curtain.

When we settled down, we stood across from each other in the shower room and let the rushing water massage our heads and backs. Justin caught me looking down at his package a few times, but he didn't appear fazed. I also caught him looking at me. From my experiences, it seemed natural for men to look at each other for comparison reasons.

A guy approached us as we were getting dressed in the locker room. He glanced over his shoulder to ensure no one else was around. He shocked the hell out of us when he said, "It's great to see an open couple, especially in a place that's so homophobic."

Justin looked at the guy and his head slightly tilted, clearly caught off guard. "Whoa, hold up. You've got us mistaken. We are not a couple."

The guy's face turned red as he apologized for his bold insinuation, then swiftly made an about face and raced off. I told Justin I had a suspicion that the guy had been watching us in the shower room. He shivered and muttered, "That's seriously messed up and creepy. Are you okay?"

"Yeah, I'm okay. Thanks for asking," I replied, trying to brush off the unsettling encounter. Then, with a forced grin, I added, "Forget about that guy. It's time for dinner and a movie."

We went to the town cinema and enjoyed hot dogs, popcorn, and the gory movie, Mortal Kombat, based on the arcade game that we both loved playing during high school. The theatre was obviously full of cadets because the audience cheered every time someone lost an appendage.

After returning to the dorm and getting comfortable in our underwear and t-shirts, Justin reached into a drawer and retrieved a small bottle of vodka. Once again, we sat on the floor in the center of the room and talked as we sipped vodka.

Justin paused after the third swig and looked directly into my eyes before he began to talk about his dad. I could see the emotion welling up in his eyes.

The dad he described sounded identical to Justin—hard working, extremely intelligent and creative, quick-witted, handsome, and everyone loved him. Unfortunately, he was diagnosed with Parkinson's disease, and he wasn't the same halfway through his battle. Justin's voice cracked as he described the pain he felt watching the strongest man he knew deteriorate before their eyes. He questioned his faith in God and didn't understand why such a good person would be put through this trial. He repeatedly asked his dad to not answer the call from God. From Justin's point of view, his father was too young to answer the call and had a family to raise and love.

Tears streamed down his cheeks as Justin talked about begging God to end the suffering. Justin knew that the end was near and didn't want his dad to suffer another minute. He also saw the toll on his mother and wished for the pain to end.

What felt like an eternity finally came to an end. They were all by his father's side when he took his final breath.

Despite the lengthy preparation leading up to his father's funeral, the day of the service still overwhelmed Justin with grief. Months of emotional preparation couldn't shield him from the shock and sorrow that engulfed him as he faced the reality of his loss.

In lieu of flowers, his mother asked guests to donate to a worthy cause. Still, more than a dozen arrangements were delivered. Among them were lilies, their scent settling into Justin's memory. His voice grew heavy as he recounted it: "Every time I smell lilies, I'm right back in that moment—standing there, thinking about my dad.

Justin described the unexpected weather that day. The forecast was sunny and dry, and there wasn't a cloud in the sky on the way to the funeral service. However, the weather suddenly shifted after the service. A torrential downpour started immediately after the funeral home side doors were opened to load the casket in the carriage. Justin was shocked because rain wasn't in the forecast—he had checked.

The minister stepped to the microphone and solemnly said, "These are not just raindrops. They are tears from the heavens, a reminder that God is welcoming His son home. Have faith, for he is now in the Lord's embrace." Hearing this interpretation of the rain brought Justin a sense of comfort.

Justin continued, speaking in the awestruck tone of someone still trying to make sense of what he experienced. "Everyone stood in silence and just watched. It took less than five minutes before the downpour stopped, and suddenly, the sky was topaz blue, not a cloud in sight."

He went on and described how family and friends improvised at the graveside service because the sand in the bucket was soaked. Instead of sand, each guest removed a flower from the arrangements and tossed it into the grave and onto the casket. Justin stood and watched in silence.

When Justin stopped talking, I realized tears were pouring down my cheeks. There we were, two eighteen-year-old young men sitting on a dorm room floor, crying and looking into each other's eyes. In that moment, I couldn't help but imagine a younger Justin grappling with the emotional trauma of his father's illness and passing, and it felt like a dagger to my soul.

An urge to comfort him arose, and instinctively, what needed to be done became clear. Rising to my feet, I gently encouraged Justin to do the same, then opened my arms wide.

The floodgates opened then, and Justin, this tall and strong young man, completely melted into my arms. His tears flowed, and I could feel his pain in every sob. "I miss my father so much," Justin cried out, his voice shaking with raw emotion. "I think about him every single day. I just don't understand why the Lord took him from us so young.

I know He has a plan for us, but my prayers to understand it all—they continue to go unanswered."

I gently rubbed his back, offering whatever comfort was possible. "I truly believe your father is with you every day, Justin. He's a guardian angel now, watching over you and your family. And I can promise you this—your father and your whole family are so proud of you. You are so loved, by them and by all of us. You're a special person, Justin."

It suddenly became clear that a tremendous internal conflict was unfolding within me. On one hand, I desperately wanted his pain to stop, to ease the sadness he carried. But on the other hand, a selfish part of me didn't want the moment to end, to let go of the connection we shared in that raw, vulnerable space.

As Justin bared his soul and revealed his deepest vulnerabilities, desire and sexual tension reared their ugly heads within me. It was an intensely intimate moment, unlike any I had ever shared with another man before.

My instinctive reaction was to keep holding him, offering him all the comfort I could. "Please, let it out, Justin. Say whatever you need to say. Don't hold anything back. Let it all out. You're not alone, and everything is going to be okay."

His voice cracked when he began to speak, expressing his appreciation for me staying over because he didn't want to be alone. I looked directly into his eyes as if I was looking into his soul and said, "I wouldn't want to be anywhere else or with anyone else right now. You're not alone in this, Justin."

When I reached for his cheek to wipe away some tears, my gesture initially startled him. Yet, after a moment's hesitation, he allowed me to brush away the tears.

A few minutes after we were in the racks and Justin turned off his desk lamp, he knocked on the headboard and whispered, "Are you still awake, Mauricio?"

I was staring up at the bottom of his mattress. "Yeah, I'm

still awake, Justin."

He confided in me, "Thank you for listening and being there for me. That was the first time I sobbed and talked about my dad with anyone. I've always had to be strong for my family, especially my younger siblings."

I smiled softly, wanting him to feel the sincerity in my words. "Don't mention it, Justin. I want you to come to me whenever you feel alone, hurt, sad, or lost. Even though our friendship is just starting out, I have a feeling that you're going to be very important throughout the rest of my life."

Justin softly whispered, "I hope so, Mauricio. And I'm going to pray for it. Good night."

By the time the next Saturday rolled around, my classmates and I were ready for the first tree chopping of 1995. We had finished the helmets during the week, and everyone—including the upperclassmen—was pleased with the result. They were spray-painted black, with P-CO on the front, a skull and crossbones with dripping blood on one side, and 99 on the other.

The first tree chopping was quite a spectacle with hundreds of volunteers converging at the site. Among them were alumni, current students, community members, men, and women, all coming together to be a part of this longstanding tradition.

Master Sergeant appeared to be hungover when he delivered the safety guidance and told us which trees we were allowed to cut down.

The morning and lunch break flew by, and the temperature steadily climbed. Hours of direct sunlight were wearing on me, but I was consistently hydrating to avoid heat exhaustion. I was physically present and going through the motions in the hot sun, clearing brush and undergrowth with my machete, but my mind and heart were stuck on the prior weekend. Justin overwhelmingly occupied my thoughts. The moments and emotions we experienced, even the uncomfortable one when the stranger assumed we were a gay couple, were special, but each triggered my internal struggle.

Living up to our P-Company reputation, our upperclassmen selected the largest tree in our area. Boys will be boys, and size matters, no matter what people say. We checked with the other units, and everyone agreed that it was the largest and could be a contender for the center log of the tower. The tree was enormous and easily over one hundred years old.

The tree wore out every member of our unit. Master Sergeant took the final swings and just as the sun fell below the tree line, it cracked like thunder as it began its descent. Several cadets shouted, "Timber," while others cheered. The ground vibrated when it struck the ground, then there was a silent pause followed by roaring cheers. I locked eyes with Justin, and his smile filled me with joy.

Our final task for the day was to carve P-Company in huge letters into the bark. Master Sergeant wanted everyone to know who was responsible for the mammoth tree.

My classmates and I were both exhausted and hungry after the day's work. It marked the beginning of weeks dedicated to constructing the tower. Upon returning to the dorm, several of us made plans to reconvene for dinner and the game after showers, eager to celebrate the completion of our first tree chopping.

At dinner, Justin and I predictably sat next to each other at one end of the table. I mostly listened, which is unusual. Justin's voice was low and concerned as he leaned closer, his breath warm against my ear, "You okay, Mauricio? You seem distracted." I quickly tried to play it off with a smile. "Yeah, just trying to take in all the Torch the Tower excitement," I responded, though the truth, my thoughts were consumed by him.

For a moment, I clearly heard my mother's warning about the crooked tree. Unlike the perfectly straight trunk we'd chopped down and added to the tower, I felt more like the bent, twisted one she always described. And if she was right, then I was fighting a futile battle with my own identity, destined for an outcome I could never fully escape.

6 ABSOLUTE POWER CORRUPTS ABSOLUTELY

One Friday in early October before the start of weekend liberty, my classmates and I anxiously stood at attention along the passageway to receive our assignment for the upcoming game against the Texas Methodist Stallions. Out of the corner of my eye, Master Sergeant was slowly approaching. He looked stiff, as if he had just dismounted a horse.

He stopped in front of Justin with his back to me, and Master Sergeant's bare ass was exposed as he was wearing cowboy boots, a jock strap, chaps, a vest, a red handkerchief tied around his neck, and a cowboy hat. Master Sergeant asked Justin, "What am I wearing, freshman Fischer?"

Justin responded, "Sir, you're wearing the freshman stallion riding uniform, sir!"

Master Sergeant confirmed, "Correct, freshman Fischer. And can you tell us what I'm holding in my hand?"

"Sir, you're holding a lasso, sir," Justin shouted.

Master Sergeant praised him and explained that wearing the stallion riding uniform was a rite of passage for the freshman class. It was a tradition dating back over a century. Corps freshmen annually wore the stallion riding uniform the week leading up to the game against the Stallions to show support for the football team.

We were instructed to shop at the Seventh Star Surplus store for the stallion riding uniform. "P-Company" and his class year were embroidered on the back of the vest. Our vests needed to match, and the store offered embroidery services. One benefit was that we were allowed to wear jeans throughout the school week.

Early Saturday morning, a few of my classmates and I volunteered to drive to the Seventh Star Surplus to place the orders. We were intent on arriving before droves of other Corps freshmen. In the meantime, a handful of our classmates claimed our usual space along the sidewalk behind McKibbin Hall and began working on the dorm banner for the Stallions.

The store gathered the getups and completed our vests just before they closed on Saturday. The dorm banner was also completed, and we repeated our theme of decapitating the opponent's mascot and defecating on its bloody head.

The weekend turned out to be a fun bonding time because our entire class stuck around to contribute to the projects. We hopped between several rooms in the dorm Saturday evening, shared embarrassing stories and laughs, ordered my favorite pizza, told jokes, and even listened to one of our classmates play his acoustic guitar and sing. Beyond his good looks, he was quite talented.

There was an awkward situation as well. A few of my classmates were sitting on the couch and floor in a junior's room watching porn. After I walked in on the group, I envisioned a circle jerk. The arousal and discomfort compelled me to leave before the climax.

Wearing the stallion riding uniform throughout the week was embarrassing at first, but the majority of students across campus looked forward to the annual tradition and cheered when we entered a classroom or general area. As a final show of support, we wore our stallion riding uniforms at both our dorm pre-party and the pep rally on Friday evening.

Missing the second march-in of the season because of excessive drinking and a brutal hangover weighed heavily on my mind, so I was intentional about pacing myself with alcohol consumption before the Friday night pep rally. I was determined to avoid Everclear at all costs. Otherwise, I would most likely repeat vomiting on the football field, one of the most sacred campus landmarks. I also didn't want to let my classmates down by missing another march-in.

My limit was two beers during the dorm pre-party, and I declined several offers to take shots with classmates. The idea of taking shots didn't appeal to me and made my stomach churn.

During the pre-party, I also spotted Mr. Strait accompanied by his alluring girlfriend and noticed him pointing me out to her. To avoid making eye contact, I instantly looked away when I saw them glancing in my direction. I suspected that he would call me over to haze me and demonstrate his power.

The trek from the dorm to the pep rally was a lively one because most of the group was feeling the buzz. My classmates and I secured several rows of bleachers when we arrived at the football stadium. Everyone from P-Company gathered in a circle along with our guests, and Justin stuck close by my side the whole time.

Our upperclassmen hovered around us throughout the evening. At first, Mr. Strait and his girlfriend were near the front rows, and Justin and I stood toward the rear of the group.

As the night continued, they stealthily crept their way to the back of our group, like a pair of hyenas plotting an attack. Just as I was lost in the camaraderie, a tap on my shoulder jolted me back to reality. I spun around, only to find Mr. Strait, of all people, standing there with an unexpected grin on his face. I immediately snapped to attention.

In a surprising departure from his usual demeanor, Mr. Strait walked toward me with a smile on his face, accompanied by a very attractive woman. "Freshman

Lucho, this is my girlfriend, Brittany. I've been telling her about you, and she wants to see how you announce when it's time to go."

A racist caricature performance that had been ordered by a senior a few weeks prior amidst the monotony of formation before evening chow had become the talk of the upperclassmen. It was humiliating, to say the least. Despite my discomfort, the upperclassmen continuously requested it, leaving me with no choice but to comply.

With everyone around us looking, I got into character and performed like a court jester, "Arriba, arriba, ándale, ándale, señor!" Instantly, laughter erupted from all around.

Sadly, I heard laughter from some of my classmates. They seemed oblivious to the insensitivity and racism underlying the performance. Justin, on the other hand, appeared perturbed.

Alas, in the world of comedy, one man's dignity was another man's punchline. My role was the jester, feeding Mr. Strait's appetite for amusement and power, and I repeated the performance when he asked me to do it again.

Mr. Strait and Brittany couldn't stop laughing, likely fueled by the alcohol. When they simmered down, Brittany unexpectedly leaned down from the bleacher above me and whispered into my ear, "As silly as your performance is, you still look adorable. Ari mentioned you're a good-looking Mexican, and he's not wrong."

Taken aback, I stood still as she carefully examined my face. She offered compliments while her fingernail traced a line from the side of my face down to my neck. "Why, your skin is as flawless as porcelain, and those almond-shaped eyes and long lashes are positively mesmerizing. And those lips—heavens. What I wouldn't give for full, luscious lips like yours. It's such a pleasure to finally meet you, freshman Lucho. Ari has spoken volumes about you, about how you're… not like the others. Isn't that right, Ari? Every single detail?"

The thought crossed my mind that he might have told her about me being gay, but the extent of what he had shared with her was shocking.

Mr. Strait sounded annoyed. "Drop it, Brittany. Let's move on."

Mr. Strait and other upperclassmen consistently made digs at us because Justin and I were inseparable. They attempted to degrade us with insults, but Justin and I took the ridicule with a grain of salt. Brittany's facial expression suddenly changed when she heard the name Fischer.

Brittany appeared surprised when it clicked that she knew Justin. "My, what a small world! Well, if it isn't Justin Fischer from Bedford, Texas? Why, it's been years, hasn't it? I didn't recognize you with a shaved head. What a delightful and unexpected surprise to see you, Justin. I do hope your family is doing fine. Please be sure to send my regards to your precious mama and let her know I said hello."

Justin thanked her and said that it was nice to see her as well. He asked Brittany to pass along greetings and well wishes to her family.

After their brief conversation, she turned her attention back to me. Sensing Justin's discomfort, I made a mental note to inquire about it later.

Brittany, clearly fueled by alcohol and seeking more amusement, loudly insisted, "Ari... Ari, order him to do it one more time before we leave."

Mr. Strait snapped at Brittany, "Stop yelling in my ear. You give the order this time. Because of me, he has no choice but to obey. Isn't that right, freshman Lucho?" Up to that point, I hadn't been asked that question, nor had I faced a similar situation. Upperclassman privilege and power apparently transfer to girlfriends in Mr. Strait's book. I followed his lead to make him feel powerful.

When I acknowledged that he was correct, her disposition immediately changed. One look into her squinting eyes and malicious smirk was enough to reveal her enjoyment in this transfer of power. The unconscious facial reaction was familiar to me. "Well, do you mean to tell me that he has to do absolutely anything I command?"

Mr. Strait confirmed, "That's right, anything."

Emboldened by her newly recognized power, Brittany looked directly into my eyes and said, "Oh my stars, this kind of power in the wrong hands could be downright dangerous—or dare I say, irresistibly tempting." She then asked if I was returning to the dorm after the pep rally, and I confirmed, "Ma'am, yes, ma'am." She raised an index finger to her cherry red lips and appeared to be contemplating something sinister.

Brittany shouted, "Well, you two love birds... I'm just teasing, boys. Y'all enjoy the rest of the pep rally, and we'll see you back at the dorm later." Then she pressed her finger against my lips. "I certainly do envy those full lips."

Onlookers, including Mr. Strait, appeared as confused as I was. When she finished, it looked like he tightly gripped her hand and led her down the bleachers to the front of our group. I overheard Mr. Strait ask Brittany about Justin, referring to him as freshman Lucho's boyfriend.

Justin waited for Brittany and Mr. Strait to be out of earshot before asking what that was all about. I didn't have an explanation as it was completely out of left field for me as well. "Fill me in on the backstory with Brittany later," I whispered to Justin. He nodded, replying, "Sure thing. It's a long story. I've known her since I was a kid."

Brittany's behavior seemed oddly flirtatious to me. Though I suspected Mr. Strait might have mentioned my sexual orientation to her, I doubted he disclosed details about our encounter in the shower room. Or maybe he did. Eventually, the cheering and festivities diverted my attention from thoughts of Mr. Strait, and I allowed myself to enjoy the moment.

Among my many talents, I lacked the ability to sing well.

Regardless, I belted out our cheers throughout the night at the top of my lungs and could barely speak when the pep rally concluded. Fortunately, none of our classmates vomited on the football field or had to be hauled off.

During the walk back to the dorm, I couldn't shake the image of Brittany's reaction when she realized I would obey her every command. Without a doubt, the surge of control went straight to her head. I was keenly aware of the transformative nature of power, having experienced its effects firsthand. Brittany's response resembled my own initial reaction to authority, prompting me to recall a memory from high school.

Promotion to cadet chief petty officer came early in my sophomore year, and it felt like a major milestone. My rapid rise surprised a lot of my peers—and, if I'm honest, it went straight to my head. Within days, I let the new rank get the better of me. I yelled at an underclassman so aggressively that he burst into tears and reported me.

The fallout was swift. Captain reprimanded me for what he called "an unacceptable failure of leadership." He chewed me out publicly, demoted me on the spot, and then pulled me aside when the room cleared. His tone shifted from fury to something quieter and far more serious.

"Absolute power corrupts absolutely," he said, repeating a lesson he'd learned early in the Navy.

He warned me that power—even the small amount I had—could twist a person if they weren't vigilant. My mistake wasn't catastrophic, but he wanted the lesson to stick, to leave a mark I wouldn't forget. And it did. Standing there in my downgraded uniform, shame burning through me, I made a private promise—to never use rank or authority to diminish someone else again.

The festivities continued when we returned to the dorm. There was a keg left in one of the heads, so Justin and I filled up some cups and retreated to his room to get away from the ruckus.

It came as a surprise to learn that Brittany and Justin had grown up as close neighbors, with their parents being good friends. They played together as children and were schoolmates in elementary school and junior high, but life took them in different directions during high school. While Justin became an exemplary JROTC cadet, Brittany turned into a glamorous debutante. They rarely saw each other during high school and eventually lost touch.

Justin told me that he and Brittany attended summer camps together for years, but there was one terrifying summer when he missed seeing Brittany by a week because she went on a trip with her mother.

He recounted the near-death experience seared into his memory, triggered by a severe allergic reaction to nuts. Compounding the danger, the camp staff were unaware of his allergy, as the intake form detailing his dietary restrictions had mysteriously vanished.

Brittany's father volunteered to be the camp doctor and came to Justin's rescue one day. Justin struggled to breathe during lunch in the cafeteria because his throat was swelling up. Fortunately, Brittany's father acted fast, retrieved a nearby EpiPen, and stopped the allergic reaction.

Justin's voice sounded sincere as he reflected, "If not for Brittany's father, I wouldn't be standing here today. That man saved my life." He paused, then added, "It was a wake-up call. I never eat without carrying an EpiPen now. That's a lesson I'll never forget."

A sudden banging on the hatch startled us. Exchanging worried glances, we watched as the hatch suddenly flew open, revealing Mr. Strait with bloodshot eyes. We snapped to attention, and the overwhelming stench of cheap alcohol hit me as he stumbled into the room. Brittany stood silently in the doorway, taking a sip of her drink as she watched.

Mr. Strait looked back and forth at me and Justin as if he was confused. Then he began to babble, his voice laced with mockery. "Seeing you two together is exactly what I expected. You see Brittany, it's just like I told you earlier. These two are inseparable, and it's only a matter of time before they get caught buttering each other's biscuits."

Brittany approached me with an air of mischief, her eyes glinting with intent. She traced her finger down my nose and lips, and the scent of tequila was heavy on her breath.

"Aren't you just the most handsome Mexican thing, freshman Lucho," she purred, her voice dripping with charm. "I reckon those lips of yours could work some real magic."

Mr. Strait interrupted her with a cruel chuckle. "I bet freshman Fischer can tell us what those lips are capable of doing."

Justin and I remained silent, hoping they would leave us alone. Finally, after a few more minutes of harassment, Mr. Strait and Brittany left the room.

We listened for Mr. Strait to close his hatch before walking to my room. Richard was still out, so I had the room to myself. I stripped down to my underwear, brushed my teeth, and hopped into the rack.

Just as I began to drift away, the telephone rang and startled me. I fumbled around in the dark and answered the call. At first there was silence. I figured it was one of my classmates playing a prank, but then there was a voice. It was Brittany.

She commanded me to meet them in Mr. Strait's room. Her debutante's accent faded into a direct tone as she delivered the instructions. "Walk into the room with your eyes closed, lock the door behind you, and stand in front of the vanity. I will give you further instructions when you get here. Come now."

Obedience was the only option. I hung up the phone, jumped out of bed in my underwear, and ran down the passageway barefooted. My mind raced with uncertainties about what could be waiting for me in Mr. Strait's room.

After taking a deep breath outside the hatch to calm my nerves, I slowly turned the knob and pushed the hatch open to reveal the dark interior.

As instructed, I shut my eyes before taking a step into the dark room. Then I closed and bolted the hatch. Music was playing in the background. I cautiously took four small steps into the darkness and stopped in front of the vanity. Then I sensed someone standing directly in front of me and recognized the tequila breath.

"I have a little proposition for you, freshman Lucho—one that I believe will be beneficial for all three of us." Brittany informed me that Mr. Strait wanted a blowjob, and she refused to comply. Putting her lips on a man's genitals was an impropriety that she wasn't willing to commit because she thought it wasn't ladylike. She also said that she was a virgin but gave him hand jobs and let him perform oral sex on her.

These two twisted individuals were either testing me or playing a practical joke to see my reaction. But then she continued. She said that she had a favor to ask, or rather, it was an order, and Mr. Strait was on board.

"How about you put those luscious lips to work while he puts his mouth to work? This way, we all benefit and get something that we want, if you know what I mean, freshman Lucho."

I was utterly speechless, feeling as if my head might explode. It dawned on me that they were serious, leaving me completely shocked.

She reached for my hand and reminded me to keep my eyes closed. She guided me over to the rack where Mr. Strait was lying down with his legs spread apart and hanging over the side. She instructed me to get on my knees and inch forward. Then she put my hand on his inner thigh and guided my other hand to his crotch. His cock was limp at first touch, but it began to swell when I gently squeezed the base of his shaft.

Brittany wanted to be in control and asserted her dominance. She cupped the back of my head and instructed me to open my mouth. With gentle pressure, she pushed my head forward. The warmth of my mouth triggered a rush of blood, and the stimulated Mr. Strait instructed Brittany to sit on his face.

Brittany climbed onto the bed, and I opened my eyes to see what was happening. My eyes needed a few seconds to adjust to the faint moonlight seeping through the open window. Then I watched as she smothered his face.

Adrenaline rushed through me. To be honest, the erotic situation was stimulating. Mr. Strait and Brittany were also trembling. Their heavy breathing increased as the pressure mounted. They moaned with pleasure, but his moans were muffled because she was practically suffocating him. Several minutes passed and Brittany orgasmed multiple times before Mr. Strait was ready to burst.

When he was close, he tightly gripped the back of my head to pull me lower down his shaft. He struck my gag reflex when he thrust his cock deep down my throat. Tears instantly began to flow from my eyes. He lifted Brittany off his face and said between panting that he wanted to watch me swallow his load.

Mr. Strait then confirmed that I heard. "Did you hear me, freshman Lucho? Every last drop."

Unable to speak, a few nods signaled that I understood.

Brittany watched as he gripped my head again with his large hands and rapidly steered my mouth up and down his cock. His body suddenly began to convulse and without warning, he repeatedly unloaded in my mouth and down my throat.

After the throbbing ceased, he released my head, and I pulled away. He leaned back, drawing slow, measured breaths to steady himself. I stayed on my knees and waited for their next order. "Well, I'll be, freshman Lucho. I'll be danged if that wasn't the best blowjob I've ever received.

That level of sucking is what I'd expect from a gay boy. Now you listen to me gay boy. You're not to repeat a word to anyone about this—not even your boyfriend, freshman Fischer. Do you understand me?"

When I nodded to show I understood, Mr. Strait leaned forward. "Get the hell out of my sight, gay boy."

I jumped to my feet in an instant and exited the room despite being fully erect and in my underwear. Back in my room, I closed the hatch softly behind me and scanned the darkness for any sign of Richard's return. Finding none, I leaned against the hatch and lowered myself to the floor, whispering to myself, "Did that really just happen?"

In that moment of disbelief, the words returned to me with brutal clarity: "Absolute power corrupts absolutely." I had never felt their truth more sharply. Brittany's newfound taste for power—stoked and sanctioned by Mr. Strait—had warped her. Together, they weren't just aligned; they were feeding each other's worst instincts.

A few minutes later, I was taken aback when I felt the hatch pressing against my back, assuming it was Richard returning from his night out. To my surprise, it was Mr. Strait. I rose to attention, and he confirmed that I was alone when he entered. He sat on my rack and motioned for me to join him. Every part of me wanted him gone, but I was too stunned to refuse. Clearly still intoxicated, he said he needed to talk about something personal.

Mr. Strait began with his painful past: a Marine Corps Colonel for a father—an abusive alcoholic who forced him and his mother living in constant fear, relieved only during deployments. As a boy, he sometimes prayed those deployments would last forever. He went on to explain how wrestling had become his escape, a sport he excelled in so quickly that by eighth grade his father had hired a renowned coach to train him.

A year into working with the new coach, Mr. Strait entered an out-of-town wrestling match his freshman year in high school. He and his coach shared a hotel room with two beds. Unexpectedly, at one point during the night, after Mr. Strait fell asleep, the coach changed beds and molested him. That was the first of several road trips and nights alone with his coach, and the sexual abuse continued.

Finally, when Mr. Strait was a junior in high school, he mustered up the courage to confide in his mother one morning when his father was on deployment. He told his mother about the coach's inappropriate behavior over the years and although she was shocked, her response was more shocking.

She promised to find a way to cut all ties with the coach and instructed Mr. Strait to never tell his father, fearing for their safety. She pleaded, and he made a solemn promise to his mother, a promise he honored until that moment in my room. It was surprising when he revealed that I was the first person he had confided in since the conversation with his mother.

He explained that his tough outer shell was what his father demanded and shaped, starting with naming him after the god of war, Ares. Every decision about his future had been forced upon him, leaving no room for his own desires. As for the molestation, he spent those years confused because a part of him found pleasure in the acts.

Mr. Strait's revelations compelled me to share that I too was molested as a boy by a neighbor, and it confused me as well. For a moment, I empathized despite the cruelty and abuse he had inflicted.

Frustration and pain radiated from him, causing his voice to crack as he continued. "My old man mentally and physically abused me. My wrestling coach had his way with me for years. And now look what I have done to you. I don't understand why this messed up cycle continues." No words came to mind, leaving us sitting in silence for a moment.

Shortly afterward, he walked toward the hatch, then paused. Mr. Strait said that he had realized I was gay when he caught me gawking at him in the shower the year before. He saw more than mere curiosity in my eyes. "Listen, gay boy. Others might buy the story about your girlfriend, but I see through it." Then he left my room.

Curled deep in my sleeping bag, a chilling uncertainty hit me suddenly—there was no telling what either Mr. Strait or Brittany might do next. He was far more unpredictable than I'd ever imagined, and she had already been corrupted by the rush of power.

Out of nowhere, another one of Mami's dichos slipped into my thoughts: "En boca cerrada no entran moscas"—flies don't enter a closed mouth. It was her way of saying that silence can be a form of protection. In that moment, wrapped in fear and confusion, it felt like the only safe choice I had.

A whirlwind of emotions consumed me as I lay there, struggling to fall asleep. Shame pressed down on me—not for anything I had done, but simply for being gay. The humiliation from Mr. Strait and Brittany scraped at my sense of safety, leaving me raw and exposed. A deep dread gripped me at the thought that everything I'd worked for—my dreams of becoming an officer, my scholarship, my future—could slip away. And yet, beneath all that panic, one thing remained certain: my secrets would stay locked inside me, no matter the cost.

7 WHEN THE MONSTER WASN'T IN A COSTUME

My childhood Halloween memories were dear to me. At school, teachers dressed up and handed out candy, adding to the festive atmosphere. After classes, my brother, friends, and I roamed our neighborhood in homemade costumes, relishing the thrill of trick-or-treating. The streets buzzed with children clutching buckets or paper bags filled with treats. I especially appreciated neighbors who, if they ran out of candy, offered spare change or dollar bills.

Celebrating and honoring the Mexican holiday, Dia de los Muertos, on November 1 was also a tradition in our home. Every year, Mami constructed a colorful altar filled with flowers and fruit surrounding photographs of our deceased ancestors. My parents told stories to celebrate and honor their memories, and this tradition instilled a connection in me to some of them, especially my abuelita, my maternal grandmother, because I believed that she was my guardian angel.

When I closed my eyes and concentrated, I could hear her soothing voice singing the Spanish nursery rhyme every time I got hurt and cried, "Sana, sana, colita de rana. Si no sanas hoy, sanarás mañana."—Heal, heal, little tail of the frog. If you don't heal today, you'll heal tomorrow. Being hugged and rocked while hearing the nursery rhyme always did the trick.

Years of dressing up in costumes, traversing the neighborhood for candy, and celebrating Dia de los Muertos were special and innocent memories. However,

Halloween 1995 was quite the opposite.

A more severe freshman boil was looming over us like a dark cloud from the beginning of the semester. By the middle of October, the storm was quickly approaching because things were going downhill for the P-Company class of 99. We were under a relentless magnifying glass and admittedly slipping up on the little things—nothing was getting past our upperclassmen.

One pair of shoes didn't have a spit shine—ding. A freshman was overdue for a haircut—ding. A freshman got caught cutting the mile—ding. No freshmen were in the dorm to help a senior with his uniform—ding. With every ding came another freshman boil threat coupled with hazing either after morning chow or study hours.

After evening chow in mid-October, instead of being excused for study hours, Master Sergeant unleashed a furious tirade, decrying our freshman class as worthless. Weeks of accumulated minor offenses had pushed him to his breaking point. Once his rant ended, Master Sergeant sternly cautioned us that our lack of improvement would undoubtedly lead to a more severe freshman boil.

Later in the week, Master Sergeant delivered our next freshman assignment. Halloween was upon us, and our company tradition included a character named, Mr. Crow— a scarecrow-like figure holding a pitchfork in one hand and an unopened bottle of Jack Daniels in the other. I assumed the name Mr. Crow was derived from scarecrow, but it was disappointingly tied to Jim Crow. We dressed him in dingy overalls, a long-sleeved plaid shirt, and boots. His head was a large jack-o'-lantern. Once again, Justin's creativity was put to good use.

We set him up in a chair in the middle of the fourth deck passageway. Since Mr. Crow was vulnerable and unable to protect himself, my classmates and I were responsible for his safety. To that end, we created a schedule to stand watch around the clock until Halloween, excluding the hours of lights out.

Why did Mr. Crow require protection? Mr. Crow needed protection because of a longstanding tradition with the company on the second deck. Every year, the second deck freshman class tried to destroy him and steal his whiskey. As no previous class had succeeded, we couldn't be the first to break this tradition.

The end of October was also regiment inspection season. Our company inspection was scheduled for Thursday morning before Halloween, and we weren't present during the inspection. When we returned to the dorm after classes, our rooms looked like the aftermath of a tornado. Unfortunately, we failed miserably. Richard and I were in disbelief when we saw the extent of what they had done to our room. Our mattresses were in the middle of the room, and Richard's rack was separated from mine and laying sideways on top of the mattresses. Most of our belongings were also scattered across the room. Fortunately, our uniforms were left intact.

Richard and I were at a loss for words for a moment, but we didn't have time to waste. We immediately set our books on the vanity and began to reassemble the room. Every surface was cleaned to bring order back to our space. Nearby, the sounds of our classmates cleaning filled the air. After some time, I paused and signaled to get Richard's attention because the floor was eerily quiet.

My contemplative whisper broke the silence, "Listen. Why isn't there any yelling? Where are the sophomores and other upperclassmen?"

Richard smirked and shrugged his shoulders, "Bunkmate, they're probably off somewhere planning our untimely demise."

I chuckled and nodded, "I think you're right, bunkmate. There's no point in cleaning if we're doomed. It was nice knowing you."

We chuckled and returned to the task at hand. Our room

was spotless before we left for evening chow. When we fell out into the passageway, only Master Sergeant was present. There was no sign of the sophomores or any other upperclassmen. After dinner, we received orders for our rooms to be inspection ready by the morning and got dismissed for study hours. Something was up because there was still no sign of the sophomores.

Nature called in the middle of the night, and I had to use the head. Relieving myself in the sink was the last thing I wanted to do. It sounded like the coast was clear, so I hopped into my shower shoes and quietly backed out into the dimly lit passageway. In the periphery, I noticed movement and heard sounds coming from one end of the passageway. Mr. Strait was helping another sophomore walk to his room. They were in full utilities and left a trail of what appeared to be mud on the deck. I rushed back into my room before they saw me.

It appeared that the sophomores faced punishment because we failed the inspection. Then fear pierced my thoughts. "If they've been getting punished for hours, then what the hell do they have in store for us?"

Suddenly, the hatch opened. I locked it up at attention before I could holler my greeting, and the person told me to shut the fuck up. I recognized his voice and silhouette with the small amount of light from the passageway behind him—it was Mr. Strait. He walked toward me, and his potent stench of sewage almost made me gag.

His face was covered in camouflage paint and mud, but I could see his eyes. Mr. Strait was apparently fatigued because he struggled to speak. He took a drink from his canteen before he said anything. The sophomores must have been punished for hours because of our miserable inspection results. When he finally spoke, his voice was raspy and strained, but he made his point crystal clear. "You didn't see a damn thing tonight, ya hear me, freshman Lucho? Go on and nod so I know that we are on the same page."

A quick, frantic nod made it clear the message had been received.

He continued, "You and your sorry-ass classmates are gonna pay for the hell we just went through—the disgrace y'all brought onto our company. Now, haul your ass into the rack. Not a peep about this, freshman Lucho. Not to your bunkmate. Not to a soul."

I jumped into my rack and pulled my sleeping bag over my head. After Mr. Strait closed the hatch, Richard startled me when he whispered, "You awake, bunkmate? We are doomed, aren't we?"

I lowered my sleeping bag because just as I expected, Richard's face was looking down at me from the side of his rack. I told him, "I can't imagine what's in store for us, but it won't be good. Let's get some rest and don't repeat whatever you heard."

To make matters worse, the company on the second deck of our dorm ambushed our classmate standing watch over Mr. Crow the evening before Halloween. Every hatch swung open immediately after our classmate standing watch shouted that we were under attack. The fourth-deck passageway was over capacity when additional cadets from both companies ran up the stairs to join the rumble.

Richard and I ran out into the passageway and immediately hit a wall of men swinging, shoving, and even choking. I didn't anticipate the level of violence. Then I saw axe handles being swung, helmets being struck, and blood splattering on the bulkheads and deck. In the middle of the chaos, I heard a cadet from the other company repeatedly shout, "You're not supposed to use weapons." Mr. Strait was near me and responded, "We make the damn rules around here, and you're standing on our fucking deck!"

Despite our efforts, Mr. Crow got destroyed, and his bottle of whiskey was never seen again. We were the first class that allowed this to happen.

On Halloween after dinner, Master Sergeant scolded us for not protecting Mr. Crow and failing the regiment inspection. He ordered us to change into our physical training gear, and the sophomores stormed out of their rooms in full utilities and campaign covers shouting that our freshman boil was about to commence.

The boil started with an intense run around campus. We stopped several times along the route to do standard calisthenics—push-ups, leg lifts, monkey fuckers, star jumps, and mountain climbers.

We returned to the mile after an hour or so and stood in formation in front of McKibbin Hall. I was drenched in sweat. Before he dismissed us, Master Sergeant told us, "I don't know what the sophomores have planned for you, but I'm certain that you deserve it all. My advice is that you stay together to survive this evening's boil."

He ordered us to fall out in the ready room and told us to strip down to our underwear.

"You're fucking kidding me," was the first thought that crossed my mind. A realization hit - I was wearing a jockstrap under my shorts. The mental image of me running around with my ass cheeks exposed was unsettling. I feared that the freshman boil included axe handles, and the thought of being beaten with wood on my bare ass was terrifying.

Heavy metal music intensified as we raced up the stairwell. A sophomore was standing at the top of the stairwell on the third deck and ordered us to low crawl across the deck to the stairwell on the other end of the dorm. There we were greeted by another sophomore who ordered us to duck walk up the stairwell to the fourth deck and low crawl to the ready room.

To my surprise, Master Sergeant stood in the center of the ready room, arms crossed and eyes scanning us. Justin and I ran around him and stood with our backs to the window. The rest of our classmates rushed in and formed a circle around Master Sergeant. He watched as we stripped down to our underwear and left the room after he said that our stench was horrendous.

We tossed our clothes and shoes under the bottom bunk. Fortunately, a few of my other classmates were also in a jock strap. One of my classmates regretted not wearing underwear. The fear was palpable, and Master Sergeant wasn't exaggerating—our body odor was intense. It was unsettling not knowing what our maniacal sophomores had in store for us.

Time was limited, and we suspected that they were going to bust the door open at any moment. We linked arms and waited.

Though everything felt chaotic, one small silver lining remained—Justin and I were next to each other. When I looked over and caught his smile and wink, it offered an intimate reassurance that everything would be okay.

I returned the smile and felt the warmth of his forehead when he pressed it against mine. Amidst the chaos, Justin's steady voice cut through, firm yet reassuring. "Focus, Mauricio. You've trained for this. We've trained for this. We've got this."

I stared into his eyes and mouthed, "Hell yeah we've got this."

Justin's voice rang out, sharp and commanding. "Listen up, class of 99. Think back to FHW and our first pep rally. They'll try to break us, isolate us, but we must stand united. No matter what happens, do not let them take any one of us."

Seconds later, four sophomores stormed through the door and charged at us. The force was so intense that Justin and I cracked the bottom pane of the window with our backs. Only a few of us noticed the damage. Suddenly, the sophomores backed out into the passageway to get a running start. They charged at us again and the glass pane shattered. I lost my balance and would've fallen out of the fourth-floor window onto the cement pathway below if Justin hadn't grabbed my arm and yanked me back into the room.

Justin was spot on because true to form, the sophomores aggressively plucked us apart one at a time. Each time, they closed the hatch behind them to leave us in suspense.

Since I was the first one in the ready room, I was the last one out. I prayed that I wouldn't have to face Mr. Strait. Alas, my prayers went unanswered. Mr. Strait ordered me out of the room.

He closed the hatch behind me and ordered me to low crawl toward the center of the passageway. The moment I dropped to the deck, I realized it was slick with some kind of oily liquid. My elbows and knees slipped with every push—I couldn't get traction and move forward.

The upperclassmen laid thin strips of towels along one side of the deck to prevent them from losing their balance. Mr. Strait walked alongside me until he kneeled to shout into my ear and taunt me, "Come on now, freshman Lucho. I don't have all damn night. What's the hold up? You need a push, gay boy? Looks to me like you're stuck."

His breath reeked of alcohol. I shouted, "Sir, no, sir."

He grabbed my neck from behind and told me, "Quit trying to advance—it's not getting you anywhere. From where I'm standing, it looks to me like you need a hand." No one was around to see what he did next. He rubbed his palm along the floor and began to spank my bare ass with the lubricant on his hand. The force increased with each spank, and I began to slide forward. Then I improvised and pushed away from the bulkhead with my right foot to glide away from him.

He caught up to me when I landed in another oily patch. The spanking continued, but this time he didn't remove his hand. The spanking turned into groping. He squeezed and rubbed my ass cheeks before he pressed his fingers against my anus. All of a sudden, he penetrated me with his fingers. I jolted forward to get him out of me, but he quickly caught up and rammed his finger deeper inside of me. The lubricant and penetration burned. Then he dragged me several feet along the floor by my rectum. There was no one around, and I couldn't believe what was happening.

We reached our destination, and Mr. Strait opened the hatch. He pressed his boot into my backside and shoved, sending me gliding into the room. Towels on the deck stopped my slide.

Although it was dark, I could make out the silhouettes of several upperclassmen scattered around the room—laughing, waiting, and watching. One of them ordered me to get on my feet and lock it up at attention. The towels helped me keep my footing as I snapped to attention.

Before I could steady my breath, a blindfold slid over my eyes. The world went black. Someone gripped my arm and marched me forward. As I passed, another upperclassman slapped my ass—hard—igniting a wave of laughter.

In his unmistakable voice, Mr. Strait interjected, "Be careful with this one. I hear he likes to be spanked." His vile statement triggered more laughter.

They shoved me into a chair. The interrogation started instantly, their voices circling me like vultures. "Are you really a faggot, freshman Lucho? Rumors say you're a cocksucker."

I answered, "Sir, no, sir."

The same upperclassman leaned in so close I could feel his breath on my cheek. "I've got a scenario for you. If freshman Fischer had his cock bitten by a snake… would you suck the poison out to save him?"

I hesitated—a flicker of panic—before answering, "Sir, no, sir."

Mr. Strait's voice cut through the room like a blade. "He'd suck freshman Fischer's cock even without a snakebite." More laughter. All at my expense.

A moment later, his presence closed in behind me. I felt his breath against my ear—hot, deliberate. "You're on contract, freshman Lucho," he said. "You do anything we tell you to do. Do you understand?"

My stomach dropped. "Sir, yes, sir."

"Open your mouth," he ordered. "And lean forward."

The room fell silent. Then came the sound of a buckle and zipper being undone, followed by trousers sliding. I was certain—absolutely certain—what they were about to force me to do. I wanted to resist, to run, to scream, but blind obedience had been hammered into me. I opened my mouth and leaned forward.

A hand gripped the back of my head and pushed me forward. I braced for the unthinkable—the feel of someone's flesh against my lips.

At the very last moment, something cold and solid touched my mouth instead. "Take a bite," Mr. Strait said.

A bowl.

They laughed again—loud, triumphant, delighted by my terror. The humiliation itself was the goal.

The contents of the bowl were unclear at first. After a couple bites, I suspected that it was dog food because of the texture. While I had never eaten dog food, it wasn't awful. I flashed back to eating hot bowls of menudo when I was a kid and swallowed the substance quickly like I did with tripe to avoid its slimy texture as much as possible.

Mr. Strait grabbed my ears and yelled, "Open your mouth and show us that you swallowed it?"

Master Sergeant ordered me to open my mouth and confirmed, "He is clear. Take freshman Lucho to the next room?"

Mr. Strait pulled off my blindfold. He told me to stand up and pushed me toward the hatch. He spanked my butt and hollered, "Drop to the deck and low crawl out of here and down the passageway toward your room."

Once again, the slippery passageway made it impossible

to advance. The repeated pounding of my forearms and insides of my legs caused intense pain. Mr. Strait stood over me the entire time and hollered so I could hear him over the music being blasted.

He barked, "You're not going to give up on me, are you, freshman Lucho?

I shouted, "Sir, no, sir."

"That's right. You cannot quit, freshman Lucho. You belong to me and are not going anywhere."

I shouted, "Sir, yes, sir."

He ordered me to stop low crawling. I was exhausted and froze. My entire body was covered in whatever lubricant they used, and my ass crack was fully exposed.

Mr. Strait initially pressed a combat boot on my lower back. Then he went lower and shoved the ball of his sole between my ass cheeks and applied the same amount of pressure. Once again, I deeply regretted wearing a jockstrap that evening.

No one was around to see what was happening, and he took advantage of the darkness and chaos. Then I felt his hand between my ass cheeks, again, and he rammed a couple fingers inside of me.

Mr. Strait pulled me by my rectum toward the next hatch and released me to open the door. I struggled to advance, so he pulled me into the room, and I came to a screeching halt in front of the vanity. He closed and bolted the door behind us. I assumed I was sliding into the next interrogation room, but I immediately noticed that the deck was dry and there was no towel. There also were no other upperclassmen in the room. He had me all to himself.

Confusion, fear, anger, and helplessness simultaneously overwhelmed me. Every ounce of me felt shattered as I lay motionless on my belly in the dark room. The music wasn't as loud with the hatch closed. Unexpectedly, Mr. Strait grabbed my ankles and spread my legs apart. I looked back and saw him unfastening his belt and utility trousers.

Before I knew it, Mr. Strait mounted and began to hump me until he got fully erect. He repeatedly told me that he owned me and that I was his gay boy. I thought to myself, "Even if I yell for help, no one is going to hear me."

Humping me wasn't enough to quench his needs. My hope that he would get himself off by rubbing himself against me dissipated when I felt the all too familiar shooting pain from being penetrated with little compassion. Pulling away was no use because he tightened his grip around my neck and forced himself deeper inside of me. As his ramming intensified, he moaned in my ear, "Who owns you, gay boy?"

I had no option but to concede, "Sir, you own me, sir. I belong to you, sir."

It felt like I was being ripped apart as he aggressively raped me. There was no time to spare because the others had to be expecting us.

The pain was excruciating, but I told myself that it would be over soon. It was odd what I recalled during the event. Strangely, I thought about a politician from Texas, a billionaire, who ran for governor. I couldn't recall his name in the moment, but I remembered the off-the-cuff statement that ultimately led to him stepping out of the gubernatorial race. In front of workers and reporters, he compared inclement weather to a woman being raped. His famous last words were, "If you cannot do anything about it, you might as well sit back and enjoy it." His woman opponent took that statement to the bank and became the next governor.

In his final moments before climaxing, Mr. Strait tightened his grip around my neck, and I struggled to breathe as he released. After the thrusting stopped, we struggled to catch our breath while he remained deep inside of me. Before dismounting me, he wanted to hear it again. "Tell me one more time. Who owns you, gay boy?"

I responded, "You own me, sir."

My intestines were filled with air, and his fluids and the lubricant that was used on the deck burned the tears in my rectum. Every part of my body was in pain. When his heavy breathing ceased, Mr. Strait released my neck and pulled out of me. He had the nerve to say, "If you gave me something, you're going to pay for it—severely." Then, as if I were nothing more than trash, he ordered me to stay on the deck while he got dressed. We left the room, and he dragged me by a hand down the passageway to join my classmates.

When we reached the room with my classmates, the overhead light stung my eyes and lit what looked like a murder scene. My classmates were on display, and a few upperclassmen, including Master Sergeant, watched angrily as I joined the pile. Everyone was covered in the lubricant. They appeared to be lifeless, and Mr. Strait told me to jump on the pile and play dead. He intentionally told me to lay on my back because he didn't want to draw attention to the hand marks on my ass cheeks or any evidence of the rape.

I sought refuge at the edge of the pile, wedging myself between two classmates. Swiftly, I flipped over, concealing my vulnerable backside, and tightly shut my eyes, blocking out the nightmarish reality. The distinctive click of a Polaroid camera pierced the silence, capturing the disturbing scene, followed by the lingering stench of our sweat-soaked bodies.

Amidst the aftermath, only Mac questioned my and Mr. Strait's prolonged absence. Without hesitation, Mr. Strait promptly shifted the blame onto me, deflecting any scrutiny.

The torturous boil had finally come to an end, yet we were left entangled, lying atop one another for an excruciating thirty minutes until the return of Master Sergeant.

His voice resonated with authority as he delivered a somber warning, a reminder of the dire consequences awaiting those who continued to disgrace our company or engage in further misconduct. The message was clear— shape up or face the inevitable repercussions. "Get to your rooms, clean yourselves up, and hit the rack. Physical training is first thing in the morning, and I expect you to be ready," he commanded in a cold, no-nonsense tone.

My fond memories of Halloween as a boy were shattered the night Mr. Strait raped me. That was the first time I encountered true evil. The real monsters weren't in masks or stories—they were the people who hid their darkness in plain sight.

I begged God to erase that night, to wipe away the scars it carved into my soul.

Instead of commemorating my abuelita that Dia de los Muertos, I found solace in recalling her voice as I wrote a letter to Mami. I yearned to be held and hear the comforting nursery rhyme: "Sana, sana, colita de rana. Si no sanas hoy, sanarás mañana."

8 LOVE IS COMPLICATED

The weeks after Halloween blurred together in a haze of pain and silence. For several days, I faced fresh blood from the rectal tears, a constant reminder I couldn't escape. I also couldn't tell anyone what happened. Even seeking medical help felt like an impossible risk. What would Top Brass do if they found out?

I would lie awake at night, consumed by terrifying thoughts of HIV and other diseases that might be slowly taking hold in my body. My mind spiraled for hours, trapped in an endless loop of scenarios. When I finally found a small clinic that offered anonymous testing, I could barely breathe while waiting for the results. The steady tick of the clock only tightened my chest.

When the doctor called me into a room, tears formed in my eyes before he even spoke. The results came back negative across the board, but the relief felt hollow—I was still carrying the secret of the attack alone, still unable to tell a single soul what had happened to me.

In the days leading up to Thanksgiving, I eagerly anticipated the football game in Fort Worth and the prospect of spending the holiday with Justin and his family. Yet, I was also disappointed to miss the holiday in Houston. Amidst these emotions, I struggled with the desire to tell Justin that my feelings for him were beyond friendship, but I knew that revealing this truth about myself had the potential to jeopardize our relationship and my future in the military.

Early in the week of Thanksgiving, my classmates and I agreed on a plan to carpool to Fort Worth for the game and march-in. Justin surprised me when he told me that his mom had invited me to be a guest at their home and join his family for Thanksgiving. I couldn't wait to meet everyone and thank her in person for the kind gesture.

We departed campus in Justin's minivan just after 1500 hours on Wednesday and spoke very little because Justin wanted to focus on the road. I enjoyed looking at the open fields and cow pastures along the way. The tranquil journey gave me time to process my thoughts and build up the confidence to tell him when the moment was right.

As we pulled into his home's driveway just after 1800 hours, a movement in the window caught my eye seconds before Justin's brother darted out of the front door. Soon after, his mother and sister emerged, and before we knew it, their loving family was beaming with excitement. For a moment, everything felt right.

Mrs. Fischer was a petite woman with short, blonde hair and topaz blue eyes. She had a calming presence and spoke with a warm, Southern drawl. She introduced me to Justin's siblings, Jeff and Jenn, as they rushed to hug their big brother. Mrs. Fischer welcomed me with open arms, and Jeff generously offered to help unload our uniforms and bags.

We arrived famished, and Mrs. Fischer had a hot dinner waiting. It was refreshing to eat a delicious, home-cooked meal for a change. I wasn't exaggerating when I told his mom, "If tonight's dinner is any indication of how incredible your Thanksgiving meal will be, Justin and I might not even fit in our uniforms come Saturday morning." She blushed and rushed to give me a second helping.

I offered to clean up and do the dishes, but Jeff and Jenn assured me that they would take care of everything. Mrs. Fischer then told me that I would be sleeping in Jeff's bedroom because he frequently slept on the couch in the family room after a night of playing games. Despite my offer to sleep on the floor in Justin's room, they insisted I take Jeff's bed.

Justin led me upstairs, giving me a quick tour of the second floor. He pointed out the restroom and Jeff's room, where I found my bag already placed on the bed and my uniform hanging on the closet doorknob. He told me to change into my pajamas and to meet him across the hall in his bedroom.

When I entered his room, my attention was immediately drawn to Justin's extensive set of books. I wasn't surprised when he told me that he read them all, but I was astonished when he pointed out the ones that he reread multiple times. Another bookcase held numerous video game cartridges. I paused for a moment when I saw the photo of his father on the desk. "Your father was a handsome man. And you are his spitting image."

Justin grinned, giving me an exaggerated flutter of his eyelashes before teasing, "So, does that mean you think I'm handsome?"

It was difficult to maintain a straight face. Finally, I caved in and chuckled before feeding him the validation he wanted. "Quit fishing for compliments you handsome devil."

Justin chuckled and retrieved a few of his yearbooks and a large photo album. "People didn't always consider me a handsome devil. An ugly duckling would've been more fitting growing up."

We sat down on the floor and looked through the yearbooks and album. I enjoyed learning more about his past. He was a studious boy and the years with braces and pimples weren't his most attractive. Among the photos, we stumbled upon a handful that included young Brittany during their summers away at camp, and she was always pretty.

Justin saved the most important pictures for last—photos

of his girlfriend, Kate. She was a beauty as I expected. Unfortunately, she and her family went skiing every Thanksgiving, so it wasn't in the cards for us to meet in person that holiday.

When I began to struggle to keep my eyes open, we agreed that it was time for bed. I thanked Justin for welcoming me to his home and for being my best friend in the Corps. With that, I made my way across the hallway to Jeff's room and passed out the moment my head touched the pillow.

Justin's mother prepared a full diner-style spread for breakfast. There was little talking at the table because everyone was busy enjoying the home-cooked food.

Taking the initiative, I offered to tackle the dishes while Justin volunteered to put away the leftovers. After we wrapped up, he proposed a sightseeing tour of Fort Worth since I had never been. His siblings, eager to join, raised their hands in anticipation. Justin drew out his response just long enough to tease them before finally saying they could come along.

Mrs. Fischer had already done plenty that morning, but we were all appreciative—and a little surprised—when she insisted on paying for us to go to the movies. Jeff eagerly suggested a spy film that had just been released, and everyone agreed.

On our way to downtown Fort Worth, we drove past Justin's high school, which looked like a junior college campus compared to Houston Aviation Academy. Fort Worth's cultural district included botanical gardens, museums, and vast collections of art. Justin explained that many wealthy families and philanthropists had shaped the city, and their generosity was visible everywhere. We eventually parked in a downtown garage and explored the historic district on foot.

An iconic art-deco movie theatre was the final stop on our tour. We arrived just in time to buy some of the last tickets available. The movie was thrilling and suspenseful, and Jeff was overjoyed when I sweet-talked an employee into giving him a movie poster and a pin.

Fragrant aromas filled the house when we returned. Mrs. Fischer had spent the entire day creating a perfect Thanksgiving feast. The meal was out of this world, and everyone admitted to being completely stuffed and ready for a nap afterward.

Once again, I volunteered to load the dishwasher, and this time Jeff and Jenn put away the leftovers. They operated like a team, without a hint of bickering. It was clear that Justin's parents had raised a loving, well-mannered family.

Justin and I walked up to his room after we completed the chores. As he reclined on his bed, he said, "The others think you're engaged because you're such a good actor, but I know you better than that. You've been off since we left campus. Is it because you're missing your family?"

I responded, "You're right, it's just... being away from my family, especially during the holidays, it's been messing with my head. I definitely miss them, but being here with you is special, and I wouldn't want to be anywhere else in this moment."

After a brief pause, he sat up and looked at me. "Mauricio, there's something I want to show you. I've never shared this with anyone before." His words left me momentarily speechless.

Justin walked over to his closet and pulled out a shoe box that was tucked away in the back of the highest shelf. We sat in the middle of his bedroom on the floor, and he removed the lid from the box. He took a deep breath before explaining, "This box," Justin began, "contains letters my dad used to leave on my desk every time he went on the road for work." Hearing Justin's words and seeing the sadness in his eyes left me aching for him.

He opened the first letter and slowly read it to me. His

trembling voice gave way to tears running down his cheeks The urge to wipe them away and hold him was overwhelming, but the last thing I wanted in that fragile moment was to make him uncomfortable. Instead, I listened attentively, my own eyes stinging, and placed a hand on his leg. "It's okay to grieve. It tells me how much you love and miss him."

I thanked him for sharing the precious letters and asked him to continue reading.

Before continuing, Justin told me that many nights he fell asleep crying because he missed his dad so much. Reading the letters was cathartic, and hearing his words connected him with his father in a special way.

The emotion of the moment loosened something in me. When he finished reading the letters, it felt like the only chance I'd ever have to tell the truth.

"Justin... I need to get something off my chest, something deeply personal. When I applied for the Marine Corps scholarship, I lied about being straight. I know I'm not supposed to admit that, but keeping it from you feels like dishonesty. Justin, I'm gay. And to make it even more complicated... you're the first guy I think I'm falling in love with."

Justin paused for a moment, his fingers gently sealing the box of letters. He then sat in silence and stared at the wall. I couldn't help but wonder what was going through his mind.

The seconds felt like hours. The silence was uncomfortable, so I whispered, "I'll head over to Jeff's room and let you rest."

Before I stood up, Justin stopped me. His eyes softened with unwavering support as he assured me, "Mauricio, I don't care, and your secret is safe with me. I need you to know—your friendship has been the most unique experience of my life. You're the first gay person I've ever met, but if I'm being honest, I think I've known all along. I'm not gay, but that doesn't change how much I care about you. I love you as a friend, and your friendship means a great deal to me. From the moment we met, there was something effortless between us—like we just clicked. And my instinct, from the start of FHW, has been to protect you—to have your back the same way you've had mine."

His words made me feel relief at first—sharp and overwhelming—followed by something quieter and more complicated: grief for the hope I'd carried, gratitude for the kindness in front of me, and a sense of safety I hadn't felt in weeks. My chest ached with all of it at once, and for a moment, it was hard to breathe.

He leaned over to hug me, and my body felt lighter—as if a massive weight had been lifted. Then he looked into my eyes and told me that he wanted to remain best friends for life.

After carefully returning the box of letters to his closet, Justin turned around and surprised me. "Forget Jeff's room tonight. Keep me company and spend the night in my room."

I nervously accepted. Not wanting to make things uncomfortable, I quickly offered, "I'll sleep on the floor. It's not a problem at all. Let me go brush my teeth and grab a pillow and blanket from Jeff's room."

It was warmer in the house than the night before, and when I returned to Justin's room, he was stripping the comforter off his bed in his tighty-whities. Even though I'd seen him completely naked plenty of times, I instinctively looked away, nervous he'd catch me staring.

I lay out the blanket on the floor alongside his bed and placed the pillow directly below Justin's pillow above. I watched him settle into bed and pull the sheet over himself while I undressed. He watched until I was in my underwear and then asked me to turn off the light.

After I lay down on the floor and pulled a bed sheet tightly over me, we talked for a few minutes about meeting up with our other classmates the next day to practice for the march-in. We also talked about the pep rally that was going to be held at the Fort Worth Historic Fairgrounds.

Justin considerately asked if the floor was comfortable, and I assured him it was fine. Unexpectedly, he offered, "There's plenty of room in my bed. You can join me up here—but don't get any ideas, mister. We can sleep head to toe if that works for you."

"Are you sure you'll be comfortable, Justin?" I asked, hesitant but appreciative of the offer.

I heard him scooting to one side of the bed before he confirmed, "Yes, I'm sure. Get up here."

Before long, we were both lying on our backs, head to toe, side by side. I could feel the heat of his body and the sweat on my palms. My mind raced, a whirlwind of thoughts colliding at once. To break the awkward silence, I asked him if he had ever had his face scratched. He paused for a moment before confirming that having his face scratched intentionally by someone was something he had never experienced.

I shifted to face him and rolled onto my side. For a moment, I watched his chest rise and fall in the darkness—steady, unguarded—and wondered if he had any idea what he did to me simply by existing.

"Close your eyes," I whispered.

He did, without hesitation. That trust nearly undid me.

I lifted my hand and let my fingertips travel across his forehead, slow enough to feel the warmth of his skin, careful enough to disguise the tremor in my hand. From there, I traced the familiar lines of his face—the curve of his cheek, the angle of his jaw. His breath deepened, a soft involuntary sound escaping him, somewhere between a sigh and something more instinctive.

He'd always loved the way scalp massages felt, especially before I buzzed his hair, and the way he melted under my touch now was achingly familiar.

As my fingers drifted through his hair, I murmured, "A girlfriend taught me this, years ago. We used to do this for each other before we… before anything else. It was grounding. Very intimate."

One of his eyes cracked open. "You had a girlfriend?"

I nodded. "She was my first serious girlfriend, and we were together for years. Stories for another time."

He smiled faintly and closed his eyes again. "Keep going. Please."

The plea landed like a spark in the center of my chest.

I let my hand wander across his torso, down his legs. If anything, I was revisiting his body, and he never pulled away.

"You comfortable?" I asked softly.

"If I'm not, you'll know," he said.

I swallowed hard. "Fair warning—I'm not great with boundaries."

He gave a small laugh. "You don't scare me, Mauricio."

God help me, I wished I did.

When I asked him to turn onto his stomach, he did so without a flicker of doubt. I let my hand follow the tension along his shoulders, the dip of his spine, his glutes and hamstrings, the places where I suspected stress lived inside him. Each time I paused, he stayed perfectly still, breathing slow, surrendering to the moment with a trust that made my chest ache.

My nerves were a live current under my skin—desire braided tight with guilt, fear, and the sharp awareness that I was trespassing on sacred ground. Every inch of him seemed to radiate warmth, and every instinct in me fought between restraint and the selfish, impossible wish for more.

He didn't stop me. He didn't flinch. He didn't ask questions.

That trust thrilled me. And terrified me.

At one point, my hand hovered, suspended between where I was and where I knew I shouldn't go. I froze—not out of fear of him, but fear of myself. Of ruining everything.

When I finally whispered, "We should sleep," Justin didn't argue. He turned onto his side and said, "Thank you. That was… incredible."

The room went quiet. My pulse did not.

We ended up not sleeping head to toe after all, and I slept very comfortably. At one point during the night, I woke up to find Justin's arm around me, and I was holding onto it tightly. Everything seemed normal as we got out of bed and dressed the next morning. Justin mentioned that sleeping with me was the first time he had ever shared his bed as an adult.

As a way to thank the family, I offered to cook a Mexican breakfast. They had never heard of migas con huevos and Mami's green and red salsas sounded tempting enough to say yes. Justin drove me to the grocery store before the rest of the family woke up, and I was fortunate to find all the ingredients—tomatillos, peppers, cilantro, avocados, tomatoes, sour cream, onions, cheese, and flour and corn tortillas. I was surprised to find some of the ingredients because I thought they would be too ethnic, but Justin explained that there was a large Latino community in Fort Worth.

Justin was impressed by my skills in the kitchen, and I shared that I learned by watching my mother. I couldn't help but smile as I reminisced about standing on a chair, rolling flour tortillas as a child. "I learned from one of the best tortilla makers in Mexico," I said, my voice filled with pride. "My mother makes the most sensational Mexican dishes, and I can't wait for you to taste her food. Sharing it with you will make it ever more special."

With a grin, Justin replied, "I'll dream about your mother's food until then."

The alluring smell of the sizzling bacon for the breakfast tacos summoned the rest of the family and everything was prepared and set on the table by the time they joined us in the breakfast room.

It was evident that the family loved the Mexican breakfast, as it was devoured quickly. Mrs. Fischer even asked for the avocado cilantro salsa recipe, and I promised to leave it for her.

After breakfast, we got dressed and drove over to the football stadium to join the rest of the company for march-in practice. During the drive, I replayed the night in my head—half mortified, half wanting to freeze time.

When we arrived, I maintained my distance from Mr. Strait, yet still overheard him telling the other sophomores a family commitment would keep him from the pep rally at the Fairgrounds. I breathed a quiet sigh of relief.

After we got dismissed, my classmates and I agreed to meet at the entrance of the Fairgrounds at 2200 hours so that we could walk around and visit the dance halls. Tens of thousands of students and alumni were expected for the pep rally because of the short distance to Fort Worth, so my single classmates were excited by the favorable odds of finding a good time.

As fate would have it, we stumbled upon Brittany at the first dance hall. I caught her glancing in our direction a few times.

The dance hall's volume was pumped up, the liquor and beer were flowing, and the floor was filled with couples twisting and turning. During one of the DJ breaks, I felt a tap on my shoulder and turned to see Brittany standing there.

She flashed a sly smile and asked, "Well hello, freshman Lucho, may I have the next dance?"

Despite my suspicions, I smiled and managed to say, "It would be my pleasure," though the words felt heavy on my tongue.

Brittany exchanged pleasantries with Justin, inquiring about his family's well-being. He reciprocated, asking after hers.

Then the DJ announced to find a dancing partner because

the next song was about to begin. I held her hand and walked her to the edge of the dance floor. I took the lead, cupped her hand and shoulder, and off we went doing the Texas two-step.

A few steps into our dance, Brittany leaned in close so that I could hear her over the music. "Ari, I mean Mr. Strait, has been actin' really distant lately. He takes his sweet time to return my calls, and he isn't staying over as much. Tell me, freshman Lucho, have you noticed anything suspicious? Seen other girls hangin' around him?"

Instead of answering right away, a deliberate pause allowed me to carefully craft my response. I wanted to seem like I was genuinely considering whether there was anything worth mentioning. After a moment, I looked into her eyes, then leaned in and spoke into her ear, "If you're worried about Mr. Strait and another woman, I can assure you there's nothing to stress over. I see him every day, and he's never with any other women."

She appeared relieved. "Thank you, freshman Lucho." Then with a smirk that made my stomach twist, she added, "I know I can trust you… especially after that night."

My response about not seeing him with other women was no fabrication, but it also wasn't the entire truth. I wasn't going to tell her what he had done to me on Halloween night, or how he continued to summon me to his room afterward. And to complicate matters even further, a small part of me had begun to look forward to our interactions.

Brittany sighed dramatically before continuing, her voice filled with emotion. "He's the love of my life, freshman Lucho. I dream about marrying him. I am completely in love with him—I can't eat, I can't sleep, and sometimes, I can't even think straight because I worry about losing him." She leaned in just a little closer, her voice dropping to a hushed, dark whisper. "The Lord only knows what I'm capable of if he were to cheat on me."

She caught me off guard with what came next. "I love him, you know... just as I suspect you love Justin." Her tone was smooth, calculated. "I see it in the way you look at him—your eyes light up and you never stop smiling when he's around." She let the words settle before adding, "I've never thought Justin was gay, but is there something between you two? You can trust me to keep your secret."

I looked directly into her eyes and firmly stated, "Brittany, we are best friends, plain and simple. Justin is completely in love with Kate, and there isn't a gay bone in his body. And as for me, I'm with Marisol."

My patience was wearing thin, so I intentionally stepped on her toe to refocus our attention on dancing. After apologizing, I lied and told her that I needed to count to keep rhythm with the beat.

When the song ended, she thanked me for the dance and exited the floor alone, after getting the information that she was seeking. Justin naturally wanted to know what we discussed when I regrouped with him and the gang. I warned him that I feared she was obsessed with Mr. Strait and that she was capable of anything. I joked that Mr. Strait needed to be careful or else he was going to end up like John Wayne Bobbitt with his member in a dumpster.

The talk with Brittany served as a wake-up call, reminding me to dial down any overt displays of affection for Justin. It was time to channel the acting skills honed over four years in high school drama club.

Moreover, the talk also shed light on Brittany's potentially volatile nature. As the saying goes, "Hell hath no fury like a woman scorned." If she were to uncover any infidelity on Mr. Strait's part with me, her reaction could be dangerously unpredictable.

On Saturday morning, the march-in was a success and we decimated Fort Worth College. While we were at the game, Marisol was kind enough to drive from Houston to Fort Worth to pick me up at Justin's house.

While we waited for Marisol, I expressed my gratitude to Justin's mother and siblings for their warm hospitality. Their beautiful home had become my sanctuary over the holiday, where I felt like a cherished member of the family.

As the time came for me to bid farewell, Mrs. Fischer reassured me that I was always welcome to return for future visits. Just before Marisol arrived, I couldn't resist sharing a dicho with Mrs. Fischer and Justin, one that pertained to guests: "El muerto y el arrimado a los tres días apestan."—the dead and the houseguest start to stink after three days. It was a light-hearted way to acknowledge that, sometimes, even the most welcomed guests can overstay their welcome or become a burden. They enjoyed the humor of my mother's warning and admitted that it could be true.

Marisol pulled into the driveway, and Justin and I stepped outside to meet her. I watched her face carefully as she climbed out of the car—the way her eyes flicked to Justin, assessing him with that blend of protectiveness and curiosity only she could pull off.

Justin smiled, offering his hand and a gentle "It's so good to finally meet you." His mom stepped outside too, welcoming Marisol inside and asking if she needed water or anything for the drive. Marisol, ever polite but guarded, shook her head.

She complimented his hazel eyes, and he replied that she was just as beautiful as I had described. I sensed that something unspoken passed between them: an understanding rooted in the complicated feelings both carried for me in different ways.

After a few minutes of small talk, I loaded my bags into Marisol's trunk. She handed me the keys, a familiar gesture that brought back the comfort of home. We said our goodbyes—and then we hopped in the car.

Leaving Justin stung, but the thought of being with Marisol and seeing my family eased the ache, balancing sadness with something close to hope.

As soon as we backed out of the driveway, Marisol wasted no time in asking the burning question, "So, did you tell him?" I drew in a deep breath, bracing myself before diving into everything that had happened.

Looking back on my first trip to Fort Worth and Thanksgiving of 1995, it was a truly memorable experience in countless ways. The warmth and generosity shown by Justin's family made me feel not only welcomed but also eased the ache of being away from home during such a special holiday. Listening to his father's letters and supporting Justin through it all brought us even closer, solidifying our bond.

Gratitude filled me for Justin's understanding and acceptance when coming out to him, and relief settled in knowing my confession of love hadn't scared him away. The occasional daydream of a world where we were together was impossible to ignore. But deep down, I understood and respected he wasn't gay or bisexual, and I valued our friendship above all else.

But even in that warmth, my body hadn't forgotten what it had endured only weeks before. Some nights I still lay awake, waiting for the panic to settle, or feeling phantom echoes of pain that weren't fully gone. The fear came in flashes. Yet being in Justin's room, listening to him breathe beside me, something inside me finally quieted. Not everything, not all at once. But enough to remind me that safety could still exist in my life.

Our intimate moment in Justin's bedroom was as unique as the affection and love we shared, an experience that held both innocence and longing, and one that I knew would forever hold a cherished place in my memories. I eagerly anticipated whatever the future had in store for us.

9 BLOOD FOR A BUCKLE

Since the start of FHW, the upperclassmen had drummed into us the importance of earning our Texas Star Buckle. This milestone required completing the ultimate test, the pinnacle of our fall semester in the Corps. Earning the brass buckle, adorned with a raised Texas star and the defiant motto, "Come and Take It," wasn't just a badge of honor—it was a rite of passage.

We were forewarned about the hell night we would endure to claim this emblem of tradition and resilience. The buckle, echoing the fierce independence of the Texas state flag, symbolized the rugged spirit of early Texas militias. To wear it was both a privilege and an honor.

According to our traditions, the evening before torch the tower, which fell on Thursday, November 30, 1995, was the pinnacle hell night. It was the milestone that my classmates and I, along with every other Corps freshman, were anxiously dreading and ready to complete. I anticipated nothing short of hell from the sophomores to earn our Texas Star Buckle.

My classmates and I could only speculate because no specifics were disclosed about what hell night would entail. The sophomores did an excellent job, once again, concealing their plans from our eyes and ears.

By Thursday morning, the suspense was thick from the start—only Master Sergeant showed up for morning formation. Sloth physical training was cancelled, so we joined our classmates for the regular workout. Even in the chow hall, most upperclassmen from the other companies were nowhere to be seen.

The dorm was eerily peaceful the rest of the day. We were ordered to wear utilities to evening chow. Once again, very few upperclassmen were present during dinner formation on the mile. As for P-Company, there were no upperclassmen in sight except for Master Sergeant.

Dinner felt like my last meal, and I consumed a pitcher of water on my own so that a lack of hydration wouldn't be my downfall. After we finished our meals, we assembled in formation in front of the dining hall and marched to the dorm.

Master Sergeant brought our march to a standstill halfway to McKibbin Hall with a sudden order to halt. His voice boomed, announcing the arrival of "hell night" for the P-Company class of '99. The challenge was clear: we needed to complete anything prescribed by the sophomores to earn our Texas Star Buckle, a symbol of tradition, honor, and accomplishment.

As he spoke, something inside me locked into place—I felt ready to face any challenge or obstacle with my classmates. He asked if we were ready, and with a resounding roar, we affirmed our readiness, our voices united in fierce determination.

Master Sergeant wasn't finished. His voice thundered with authority. "I want the entire campus to hear P-Company's class of '99. Have I made myself crystal clear?"

Our response was deafening, "Sir, yes, sir!"

He wasn't satisfied and demanded more from us. "You are the best and mightiest outfit in the Corps! You can do better than that. Give me more intensity! Have I made myself crystal clear?"

We dug deep and unleashed a roar even louder. "Sir, yes, sir!"

Then came the final command. "Get to the fourth deck and find a bulkhead. P-Company class of '99, fall out!"

His words and my classmates ignited a fire in my soul. We stormed McKibbin Hall with determination. Our roars reverberated across campus—a declaration that we were united and ready to face hell night. We formed up four to a bulkhead in the passageway, standing shoulder to shoulder as I fought to steady my breathing after the sprint to the fourth deck.

The sophomores burst from their rooms the moment it was quiet, dressed in utilities with campaign covers. They were fired up, ready to deliver an evening of relentless hazing. "To the ready room!" they barked. Mr. Strait nearly blew out my eardrum when I asked for permission to pass. "Get the fuck out of my face, freshman Lucho!"

Shouting filled the air, and Richard and I were shoved around as we scrambled for the ready room. The sophomores managed to pin us against the bulkhead just outside the ready room's hatch, snarling like hungry dogs over a scrap of raw meat.

Finally, Richard and I seized an opening. We broke free and dove through the hatch into the ready room, gasping for breath. Someone in the passageway slammed the hatch shut behind us, sealing us in.

Master Sergeant stood in the middle of the room with our right guide holding the P-Company guidon, the flag that distinguished our unit. My classmates and I squeezed in tightly at attention around them. Their intense stares and stillness in the ready room felt ominous as we waited for the axe to fall.

The hatch suddenly flew open and slammed into the closet wall with a deafening bang. Mr. Strait shouted, his voice slicing through the air like a whip. "Fall out—one to a bulkhead. Move it, now!"

We exited the ready room and spread out across the deck. The chaotic environment was reminiscent of the last night of FHW when they made us believe WWIII was underway.

Master Sergeant paced the passageway in deliberate silence before coming to an abrupt stop in front of me. His eyes scanned the ranks like a hawk sizing up its prey. "Hell night is a time-honored tradition—one that separates the weak from the strong before torch the tower and the most important game of the season, against our archrival. This is your chance to prove yourselves—not just to me, but to each other. Show me your physical and mental strength, intestinal fortitude, and teamwork. No one gets left behind. Is that understood?"

I felt our response deep down. "Sir, yes, sir!"

Mr. Strait kicked things off with standard hazing in the passageway. What had winded me early in the semester suddenly felt routine. I barely broke a sweat after thirty minutes of calisthenics. My confidence level was high, and my classmates that I got to see also appeared unfazed. Master Sergeant noticed that we were holding up strong and told the sophomores to turn up the pressure and move on to the second phase of the night.

We zipped down the stairwell like a current of electricity. The exit hatch nearly came off its hinges during our mad rush to leave McKibbin Hall. We assembled in platoon formation, and even though the sophomores were in charge of the evening, our other upperclassmen watched in the periphery.

An array of dizzying physical challenges continued in front of the dorm before we duck walked to the columns. Duck walking for two hundred yards was unbearable to say the least. When we reached the columns, I was winded, sweating, and a little lightheaded.

We got a small break to drink water and recharge before the sophomores led us in a sprint to the park down the road. When we reached the park, we resumed standard physical training, as the sophomores delivered spiel after spiel about courage, honor, loyalty, dedication, and tradition. Before we moved onto the next part, we received another break to hydrate.

After we put the canteens away, we ran toward the recreation center at a fast pace. At that point, my combat boots were soaked and heavy, and my cammies were drenched with sweat. Our next stop was uncertain, but I figured that we were going to be taken to the jungle obstacle course a few miles away. It was rumored that one of the sophomores almost died the prior year in the sewers around those parts, and that the others carried his comatose body out to revive him. That must have been why Master Sergeant emphasized not leaving anyone behind.

Instead of the jungle obstacle course, we were led to the construction site of the future presidential library in north campus. Despite the no trespassing signs, we jumped the perimeter fence as ordered and descended into the huge pit where the foundation was being poured for the massive structure. It looked more like a track for dirt bikes, with multiple inclines and huge mounds of dirt, but it was the ideal setting for a physical challenge.

As we made our way through the construction site, the rest of our upperclassmen watched from the fence line. My wet cammies rubbed parts of my forearms, elbows, and inner thighs raw, but the stinging pain was tolerable until the order came to low crawl through three pools of standing water.

In the dark, they appeared to be just that to the sophomores and Master Sergeant. Unfortunately, the upperclassmen got it wrong. Muscle fatigue and chafing were nothing new, but this was different—an excruciating, unfamiliar burn that made every movement feel wrong after low crawling through the first pool. The pain throughout my body exponentially worsened after we completed the second and third pools of water.

Nothing could have prepared us for the fact that the pools of water were filled with lye and other cleaning chemicals. Later, we learned that the construction company building the library had cleaned the residue from inside the cement barrels and dumped the solution into the pools. Chemicals, mud, and pebbles from the cleaning pools had seeped into my cammies. The chafed areas of my body were being scraped raw with every step.

The pain was severe, but the sophomores had no idea what was going on and they continued with hell night. The chemicals from the pools permeated my arm and leg wounds and burned the rest of my body below my neck, including my genitals. Thankfully, my face and more importantly my eyes were spared. A few of my classmates weren't as fortunate, and when we got our next break, I watched with great concern as they doused their faces with canteen water.

Once we ascended from the construction site, I forced myself to stay in formation for nearly a mile despite the unprecedented pain. Eventually, a classmate and I began to fall back, and Mr. Strait ordered us to return to formation. I refused to quit, but all I could manage was a slower pace.

Master Sergeant approached me and the others falling back, and one of my classmates courageously broke the silence and yelled, "My balls are on fire, sir!" I immediately followed and shouted that my legs and arms were burning as well.

I glanced over and caught Master Sergeant locking eyes with Mr. Strait. His voice sounded concerned. "What exactly was in those construction site pools, Strait?"

Mr. Strait admitted that he wasn't certain, and Master Sergeant ran up to several of my classmates to ask if they were burning. The responses were identical. Everyone he asked acknowledged feeling intense burning and pain across his body.

Master Sergeant summoned the sophomores as we continued to run, and although none of us heard what was said, once we arrived at the east entrance to campus, we stopped in front of the steps of the facilities building.

Master Sergeant ordered us to run to a tree several meters away and jump for leaves to prevent us from hearing their discussion. The most injured of us hobbled over with assistance from classmates.

Company Commander joined Master Sergeant and the sophomores to discuss the grim situation and oversight at the construction site. After their discussion, we returned to the dorm at a much slower pace. They continued to yell and harass us, but Mr. Strait surveyed from a distance instead of participating further. I suspected the construction site was his idea.

As for me, my excruciating pain was off the charts. The cement-mixed chemicals permeated my wounds and began to dry and harden. This also caused my uniform to bond with my skin. Every movement of my legs and arms felt like scabs being ripped off my body. With no other options, I continuously pulled the cammies from my open wounds to reduce the friction.

We returned to the dorm, and the sophomores were pitiless as they chastised us for being weak. I stood at attention in agony. The message from Mr. Strait that made my blood boil was merciless. "You're all a disgrace—weak, pathetic, and unworthy. You haven't earned a damn thing."

Master Sergeant gave the order for us to fall out, and I mustered every ounce of strength to shuffle my way into the dormitory. Pain seared through my body with each step. At the bottom of the stairwell, I clung to the railing, taking a moment to steady myself as classmates rushed past in a blur. The weight of exhaustion and humiliation settled on me, threatening to crush what remained of my spirit.

In that vulnerable moment, one of Mami's dichos surfaced, and I closed my eyes, drawing in a deep breath: "Camarón que se duerme, se lo lleva la corriente."—the shrimp that falls asleep gets swept away by the current. She meant it as a warning against complacency, a reminder to stay alert and prepared. Yet as I gripped the railing, the truth became painfully clear: no amount of vigilance could have prepared me for the physical toll and careless injuries I had endured that night.

As my classmates passed by, a few asked if I needed help, but I waved them off—too proud, too afraid of looking weak. I braced myself to take the first agonizing step when suddenly Justin's hands clamped down on my shoulders, stopping me cold.

Without a word, he grabbed my wrist, dropped into a squat, and lifted me onto his shoulder in a fireman's carry like I weighed nothing. Then he powered up the stairs to the second deck, his voice ringing out—firm, unwavering, and filled with loyalty, "I've got you, Mauricio. You carried me once—now it's my turn. Hold on, buddy."

We reached the fourth deck, and there was no time for big thanks. Justin helped me hobble to the nearest bulkhead while the sophomores continued to rant and rave. Mr. Strait acted like nothing was wrong and called us pussies for whining about a little pain. Not long after, Master Sergeant took charge and ordered us to hit the showers.

Richard and I entered our room and when I saw that the coast was clear, I told him I didn't want to see what was under my cammies. I peeled off my blouse and t-shirt, and my elbows and forearms were bleeding. I undid my belt and struggled to drop my trousers because the mud and cement mix was glued to my legs. The pain was unbearable when I ripped the trousers apart from my wounds.

Richard's eyes widened the moment he saw my legs. Then, he blurted out, "Holy shit, bunkmate, I think you need to go to a hospital."

"Let me shower and clean the wounds first," I responded, determined. Without hesitation, Richard grabbed my shower supplies and helped me as I hobbled toward the head.

The image of one of my classmates when I entered the head will forever be imprinted in my memory. He was standing naked in the sophomore shower stall, covered in mud and blood, like a scene from a horror movie. His entire body trembled violently as the water painfully struck his open wounds. Our injuries appeared similar, and the water only seemed to intensify his agony.

I asked if he was okay, and he muttered in a broken voice, "Whatever was in those pools is still burning me, and the cement won't come off." His eyes were wide with fear and pain. I was at a loss for words, horrified by the sight before me. The shower, meant to offer relief, had turned into another layer of torture.

I fearfully stepped into the first stall and took a deep breath before I turned the two knobs. Within seconds, I knew exactly what my classmate in the next stall was feeling. As the water rushed down my body, the intensity of the pain increased. I'd never been burned by acid, but his description was dead on. I didn't have the balls to scrub or touch my legs, so I allowed the water to remove the debris. I stood there trembling from the pain for minutes as my open wounds began to surface. My inner thighs, starting from my knees upward, were completely raw and red. I was missing several square inches of skin.

The only option to clean my wounds thoroughly was to use my washcloth and soap. I felt like that fox I always heard about, who had to bite off his leg to survive. I knew that it was going to hurt, but I had to clean my wounds to prevent the possibility of infection. The soft cotton cloth felt like steel wool. Tears poured down my face. There were also pebbles lodged in my wounds.

Feverish scrubbing ultimately cleaned my open lesions. Another classmate was waiting in line for my shower stall and appeared to be in shock. He was bleeding through the sludge on his legs, crotch, and arms. When I finished, I helped him step into the shower before I returned to my room. The sound of him screaming felt like a dagger in my chest and enraged me. My mind raced with questions. "What the hell were they thinking? Why would they do this? And why did we let them?"

Richard was getting dressed when I returned to our room. We weren't sure if hell night was over, so we had to garner our strength to face the rest of the night. Richard was much better off than me, and as the night progressed, I noticed that most of our tall, long-legged classmates were far less injured. His elbows were slightly rubbed raw, but other than that and some strawberry burns on his inner thighs, he was good to go.

Our hatch was open, and we could hardly talk with the sophomores running up and down the passageway, shouting for us to report to the ready room. I turned to Richard and asked, "What else could they possibly have planned for us?" With a determined look in his eyes and a small shrug, he whispered, "I'm not sure, bunkmate, but let's finish this."

After I removed my towel, Richard's jaw dropped and his eyes widened in horror at the sight of my legs—raw, bloody, and torn up. "Oh my God, bunkmate, what the hell did they do to you?" Without hesitation, he told me to stand still and gathered my physical training gear. Holding me up, he carefully helped me get dressed, trying his hardest to reduce the pain.

As I got dressed, we listened to the sophomores and the rest of the upperclassmen talk about the extent of everyone's injuries. The shouting died down as reality—and fear—began to set in. Then Mr. Strait entered our room, looked over my legs, and told me to follow him.

Ten of us were taken to the county hospital because of our injuries. Justin volunteered to help me down the stairs and rode with me and Mr. Strait to the hospital.

Our classmate who was bleeding through the sludge on his legs, crotch, and arms in the head was immediately admitted to the emergency room, and we waited for an update in the parking lot for an uncomfortably long time. Mr. Strait knew that we were all going to be punished severely for this hazing event, and I could sense his anxiety. After no update and several awkward minutes of sitting in his car listening to Nirvana, he had the nerve to ask if I could tolerate the pain and avoid seeing a doctor.

This selfish motherfucker wanted to avoid the county hospital calling the university or police to report the hazing. Even though he asked, I didn't have an option. I was infuriated, but I agreed to pass on receiving the care and cleaning that I needed.

Knowing that his ass was on the line, Mr. Strait reached a breaking point and stormed into the hospital to get a status report. Justin and I remained in the car and talked about the evening and our concerns. Justin informed me that his cock and balls were chafed and burning. He told me to turn around to see, and he pulled his shorts down to show me his cock. I cringed after seeing that his poor head was completely rubbed raw. Even worse, his nut sack was oozing pus.

His pain was obvious, but he still managed to joke through it. "I hope I can still have kids after this because I've always wanted a big family."

It lightened the mood to talk and laugh a little before Mr. Strait returned. He appeared to be quite upset and told us that our classmate was extremely hurt. Parts of his body exhibited third degree burns, and he was going to remain in the hospital until his wounds were properly cleaned and disinfected. After the update, we began heading back to campus along with my other classmates who got talked out of seeking medical care.

During the drive back to the dorm, Mr. Strait spoke to us in an unfamiliar manner. It felt too informal, and Justin and I didn't know how to react or respond. I anticipated that it was a trap and hoped that Justin was thinking the same thing. We attentively listened to him describe how they had methodically planned our hell night. Come to find out, the construction site was improvised and not part of the original plan, and he was responsible for the deviation.

Fortunately, we found a parking space near our dorm, so I didn't have to walk very far. It was just after midnight, and Mr. Strait told us to join the others in the ready room. Justin offered to carry me up the stairs again, but I asked him to walk behind me instead, to catch me if I fell.

When we reached the ready room, I turned the knob and attempted to open the hatch, but it was being blocked by something on the other side. I pushed a little and a classmate whispered, "Hold on a sec—let me get out of the way." Once the hatch opened, we saw our classmates sprawled out across the ready room. The scene was reminiscent of Halloween. Half of them were asleep, but everyone came to after a few minutes.

Although we were ordered to remain silent, one of our classmates asked about the others. I couldn't help but respond, "Our other classmates are heading back to the dorm, but one of them is in the emergency room and staying as long as necessary to clean and disinfect his wounds." Justin added details about the third-degree burns, and I could see the horror in their faces as they processed the gravity of what had happened.

Justin and I found a spot in one of the closets, so I moved some shoes and slept as far back in the dark space as possible. I tried my hardest to restrict movement and reduce the pain in my legs and arms.

Over the next ten minutes or so, one after another, our severely injured classmates joined us in the ready room. After everyone got settled in the dark, we attempted to get some shut-eye.

A sudden bang against the hatch made us jump. Mr. Strait shouted, "Fall out class of '99!"

Without hesitation, we scrambled to obey, opening the

hatch and darting into the passageway, some of us slower than others. As we assembled in the passageway, the sophomores hollered for us to lock it up. Then came the words from Mr. Strait that made my stomach drop. "Don't think we're done with you pussies. Last night was only round one."

I wanted to believe they were just trying to get in our heads, but deep down, fear gnawed at me. I suspected they were telling the truth.

Master Sergeant told everyone to shut their suck. A heavy silence fell over the passageway just as Company Commander stepped out of his room at the far end. He started toward us, slow and deliberate, his eyes scanning each of us with a focus that felt sharper than usual—concern buried beneath command presence. He walked the entire length of the passageway, taking in the injuries, the exhaustion.

When he reached the end, he stopped and asked, "Are any of you going to quit?"

We unanimously replied, "Sir, no, sir!"

His voice was filled with conviction as he continued. "Many before you have risen to the occasion, and I'm challenging you to dig deeper and push past the pain. Do you have the intestinal fortitude to finish hell night, and do you truly believe you deserve the Texas Star Buckle?"

Without hesitation, we roared in unison, our voices stronger, more determined than before, "Sir, yes, sir!"

Company Commander was convinced. "You have proven that you're stronger than you realized. You have endured and you have fought through pain. But more than anything, you stand together—as one class. That's what makes you unstoppable."

His words inspired me and burned away exhaustion and doubt. As he finished, he gave the final command. "Fall out in front of the dorm. Let's finish this together."

The sophomores remained upstairs while we assembled

in platoon formation in front of the dorm. Master Sergeant took a head count and handed us off to Company Commander.

Company Commander marched us over to the capitol building at the main entrance of campus, a long distance that felt longer because of the sharp pains I felt with each step. We halted at a sacred site on campus, in front of the bronze statue of our founding president. I looked up at his Texas Star Buckle and couldn't stop myself from thinking, "Was everything we have endured worth this?"

Before long we heard someone marching toward us. I glanced over to see who was approaching and saw our seniors marching in a single file. They halted directly under the statue and turned to face us. Then Company Commander ceremoniously positioned each of us directly in front of a senior, one squad at a time.

Company Commander gave the order, and the seniors awarded us our Texas Star Buckle. Despite my injuries, in that brief moment I felt no pain—only fulfillment and triumph. I had earned it.

The ceremony concluded with the morning sun warming our backs. With only a couple of hours of sleep, I could barely stay awake during our march back to the dorm.

We received the command to fall out immediately after halting in front of the dorm. Company Commander told us to take our time up the stairs. He knew that several of us were badly injured and didn't want to hurt us more by making us run up four flights.

Richard stopped me before we entered the dorm and asked if I needed help. I shook my head, pushing through the exhaustion. "I can manage."

He offered a small grin. "I'm proud of you bunkmate."

His words meant more than he probably realized. I was equally proud of him. "Right back at you, bunkmate."

Richard and I reached the room, stripped down to our underwear, and hopped into our racks. As soon as my head hit the pillow, I crashed out. I didn't think about how much my legs hurt or the fact that Antoine and Marisol were in the process of driving to University Station for the most significant game of the year.

Just as I drifted into REM sleep, a tapping on my chest startled me awake. At first, I thought I was dreaming—until reality clicked into place. Standing over me was a Top Brass captain. He must have noticed my confusion, because he repeated himself: he was there to investigate hell night.

The captain ordered us out of our racks. Richard instantly jumped down from his rack, sharp and ready. I tried to follow, but excruciating pain pinned me in place— my sleeping bag had fused to the raw wounds on my legs. Overnight, the oozing pus had dried into a crusty adhesive, anchoring me to the sleeping bag.

I apologized to the captain, struggling to free myself. He kindly told me to take my time, though his eyes were probing. Meanwhile, he began inspecting Richard's body and asking questions about hell night.

Richard's injuries were isolated to his elbows, and the wounds had lightly scabbed during our brief nap. Slowly peeling the sleeping bag apart from my legs was a disgusting and painful process, and the captain appeared stunned when he saw the extent of my injuries. His first question was direct, leaving no room for ambiguity. "Freshman Lucho, did any of your upperclassmen pour acid or any other hazardous chemicals on you during last night's events?" Richard and I looked at each other before I responded, and the captain sternly told me to answer the question.

"Sir, none of our upperclassmen poured acid or any hazardous chemicals on me, sir," I replied.

He pressed on. "Were you burned at any point last night?"

"No, sir," I answered, more firmly that time. "No one burned me."

He crouched to inspect my wounds. After a moment, he rose and leaned in close, voice firm and deliberate. "Then walk me through the events of the evening, freshman. And don't leave out a single detail."

I held nothing back as I recounted every detail of hell night. When I finished, I made sure to reiterate that no chemicals had been poured on me, and I hadn't been burned. The captain ordered me to get dressed and report to Master Sergeant's room with the others. I assumed it was because of the extent of my injuries. As I slowly put on my physical training gear, Richard peeked out of the hatch and spotted more Top Brass pacing the passageway.

When I entered the room, Master Sergeant directed me to squeeze in between two of my classmates on his worn-out couch. The scene took me back to waiting outside the principal's office for a scolding and detention. No one made eye contact. The tension in the room was thick, so I stared down at the deck.

Master Sergeant had reached a boiling point and sounded annoyed as he told us that Top Brass suspected we had been tortured with acid and fire during hell night. He seemed more irritated by the investigation than concerned about our injuries or potential punishments. Watching him mock and degrade real officers in front of us left me disappointed. It wasn't the conduct of a leader or future Marine Corps officer. In that moment, I lost a great deal of respect for him.

It also felt like Master Sergeant was campaigning—seeking validation for his frustration and trying to pull us into his resentment. Instead of taking accountability or showing concern, he was focused on justifying himself.

He asked each of us if we agreed with the interrogation and had anything to say. When it was my turn to respond, I followed suit and nodded my head indicating that I had nothing to say. However, I had plenty to say, but I knew better. I wasn't going to go against the grain because I knew with absolute certainty that everyone in the room would turn on me.

I thought to myself, burning with fury and disbelief, "You deliberately hurt us, and now we might face expulsion for this. My academic and military careers are on the line. One of our classmates is in the emergency room. I can barely walk. You're responsible for our safety and well-being, and you miserably failed. And now you've got the audacity to talk shit about real officers who are doing their jobs, responding to reckless students playing soldier? I believed you were a leader. I respected you. But now… I realize how wrong I was. You should be ashamed of yourself."

Shortly after my thoughts settled, Top Brass hauled Company Commander and Master Sergeant away for questioning. The real culprit, Mr. Strait, stayed back in the dorm, and I silently prayed for the truth to prevail so that he would be punished.

Minutes after I returned to our room, the phone rang. Antoine and Marisol were driving to University Station but had stopped in Brenham for gas and to call me from a pay phone. I warned them about my injuries and apologized— our plans would have to change.

Celebrating our first torch the tower, the most anticipated event of the year for every member in the Corps and attending the game against our archrivals were out of the question for me. Despite the countless hours I had sacrificed for torch the tower, I could barely walk and was too fatigued to participate.

Antoine and Marisol arrived at the dorm and called my room from the phone downstairs. I told them to come up but warned them not to freak out when they saw me. Despite my warnings, their excitement vanished the second they entered the room.

"Holy shit, XO. This is fucked up." Antoine's usual lightness vanished; his voice came out flat. "What did they do to you?"

Marisol's eyes widened as she took in my legs and arms. She covered her mouth, shaking her head, and I watched the horror in her face harden into rage.

"How could they do this to you, Mauri?" she said through clenched teeth. "This cult is insane. I told you it would be."

Richard and I explained the details of hell night and that they just missed a Top Brass investigation. They were in utter disbelief and wanted to get me as far away from the mile as possible. Marisol began to pack a bag for me so that we could head to the nearby hotel where she reserved a room for the weekend. In the meantime, Antoine called a friend in Houston, a former co-worker from SpaceWorld Amusement Park, and asked for advice from her mother who was a nurse.

Marisol asked about Justin, and I described how he carried me up the stairs and went with me to the hospital. Richard and Antoine simultaneously covered their packages and cringed when I described that his poor cock and balls had been rubbed raw. In spite of the injuries, they were glad to hear that Justin was well overall and that his family was coming into town for the weekend.

Since Richard was physically able, I gave him my ticket to the game so that his younger brother could attend in my place and told him to cheer extra hard for me. He gave me a hug and left to meet his girlfriend and family.

Antoine helped me down the stairs and to the car while Marisol carried my bag. The mile transformed into the largest tailgating party I had ever seen. Cadets and visitors packed the space as far as the eye could see in every direction, and there was a rich, smoky aroma of Texas barbeque in the air.

We cut the mile and walked past droves of excited folks on the way to the parking garage. Antoine stopped at the pharmacy for an ointment and pain reliever. The nurse said that I could bandage the wounds, but that the bandages would ultimately dry and stick. To prevent infection, I needed to remove and reapply the bandages daily. I opted for the other option which was to allow the wounds to dry and scab.

Antoine and Marisol brought booze from Austin, so we drowned our sorrows, managed to laugh hysterically, listened to music, and watched the festivities on the television. Our reunion felt like the sleepovers we had at Antoine's house throughout high school. The silver lining of my injuries was that I got to spend the weekend catching up with my oldest friends. A reunion of the three musketeers was what my soul needed.

On Saturday, we watched the big game's opening ceremony, and I was sad that I couldn't be with my classmates during the march-in. They looked sharp on the screen, and I caught a glimpse of Richard and Justin when they passed in front of the university president's box. Throughout the game, I watched the screen closely whenever the cameras panned into the crowd, hoping to spot one of my classmates.

Unfortunately, we lost the game to Capital College. Marisol and Antoine relished in the victory even though they weren't football fans. We spent the rest of the evening finishing off the booze and enjoying our reunion.

On Sunday, check-out was at eleven, and we were hungover and hungry when we left the hotel. We stopped for breakfast tacos before returning to the mile.

Marisol and Antoine were surprised that the mile was immaculate after the weekend's events, especially the torch the tower tailgate. Antoine helped me walk up the stairs while Marisol carried my bag. Throughout breakfast and our journey to my room, I repeatedly declined their offers to kidnap me and take me to Austin for a few days. Honestly, I wanted to go with them.

Their final plea was in my room while they helped me into my rack. They were worried about my injuries and potential punishments. They also feared that my careless and irresponsible leaders would hurt me more. Before they left, we reminded each other that we would be reunited in a few days back in Houston for winter break.

After they left the dorm on Sunday, an unexpected visitor dropped by my room. I looked up from my rack and saw that it was Company Commander. I rose to attention and greeted him as quickly as I physically could. As he approached me, the stench of alcohol intensified. Then he opened his mouth, and his breath was acidic and foul. I had never seen him so intoxicated. When he stopped in front of me, he pulled out a small bottle of whiskey and took a swig.

He slightly swayed as he processed his thoughts. "Freshman Lucho, I watched you and your little friends walk across the mile from my room, and damn, did you look pathetic. I can't undo your injuries, but I need you to toughen the hell up and take your pain like a man. I, your classmates, and the future of P-Company need you to walk like you've got some damn pride. We are under the relentless magnifying glass of Top Brass, and if you and the others keep limping around like broken little pussies, we're all screwed. My ass is on the line, and you need to suck it up. Do you understand me, freshman Lucho?"

Hearing that from the leader I'd admired since his welcome letter left me completely disillusioned. His role was in jeopardy because of reckless behavior that happened under his watch. And he wanted me to act like I wasn't injured to rescue his ass and avoid bad optics. The voice in my head yelled, "I'm sorry that I can't walk like normal, you asshole! Every step rips my scabs open, and walking slower is the only way to keep from bleeding all over the damn place. What kind of selfish, sorry excuse for a leader are you?"

Instead, I responded the way an obedient freshman should respond, "Sir, yes, sir."

He replied, "I'm glad we're on the same page, freshman

Lucho. Carry on." With that, he turned and stumbled out of my room, the odor of cheap booze lingering in his wake. In that moment, whatever admiration I had for him shattered. The pedestal I had placed him on crumbled to dust, leaving behind nothing but disappointment.

Once I was alone, I lowered the blinds and stripped down to my underwear for some sleep. This required slowly lowering and peeling parts of my sweatpants off my wounds. I stretched out on my sleeping bag to air out my wounds and prevent my legs from sticking to anything.

Richard returned before study hours and caught me up on the investigation. Top Brass, campus police, university officials, our upperclassmen, and numerous parents were involved. Several parents with clout threatened lawsuits if our company faced expulsion. Company Commander's father was a major donor to the university and led the pack. A sophomore's father was a member of the Texas government, an alum, and a major donor. Powerful parents and the fact that the university couldn't handle another hazing story in the media gave me hope that we would avoid expulsion.

I chose to delay telling my parents about the horrors of hell night or the extent of my injuries until I got home for winter break. There was no point in worrying them from a distance. Instead, I prayed that my wounds would rapidly heal.

When I should have been studying for finals, I felt ambivalent about almost everything. Hell night—our injuries, the threat of expulsion—had me asking whether it was really worth a goddamn buckle. Was the abuse and bullshit hazing I had endured making me more honorable or a better leader? And more importantly, was hiding my authentic self to be admitted to a group that didn't welcome my kind the right thing to do? Sadly, I knew the answers to these questions and doubts.

The semester had taken turns I could never have

predicted. Winter break was the time I needed to reevaluate what truly mattered to me.

10 HAPPY NEW YEAR IN HOUSTON

Final exams ended for me almost halfway through December, and I was relieved and ecstatic to go home, but physically and mentally fatigued. Grades would be available via telephone after the new year, and I was hoping for the best but expected mediocre results. Scholastic probation would jeopardize my scholarship, so I needed at least a 2.0 grade point average to avoid the dreaded 'scho pro'.

The wounds across my legs and arms had scabbed for the most part, and I continued to move slowly to avoid ripping them open, despite what Company Commander said. Marisol and Antoine completed their final exams and were kind enough to swing by University Station to retrieve me on their way home from Austin.

Richard bolted home the prior day, so I had some time to decompress in our room while I packed and cleaned in solitude. Like a typical student going home for break, I filled a bag with dirty laundry and left everything else behind. While I waited for Antoine and Marisol to arrive, I stared out the window and relaxed to Annie Lennox's Diva CD softly playing in the background. Justin was on my mind.

It felt like all my Christmases were coming at once because Justin surprised me with plans to bring in the new year in Houston. The details of his visit were falling into place, and I hand delivered directions to my parents' house. My goal was to make his first trip to Houston and our home an occasion we would cherish for the rest of our lives.

The excitement of Justin's upcoming trip was suddenly

disrupted by an unexpected visitor. Mr. Strait standing at my hatch surprised me. Of all people, he had come to check on my injuries and say farewell. "Remain seated, freshman Lucho," he said as he stepped inside.

Rumors circulated that he was facing severe consequences for hell night, and for the first time, I sensed something I never expected from him—regret.

"Freshman Lucho, I really want you to get better and enjoy your break. I would also like to pick up where we left off when you are back to 100 percent. You have been missed these past few days."

His words rang hollow. He wasn't there for me; he was there for himself. He didn't care about my emotional numbness. Luckily, the phone rang, sparing me from the need to respond. He took it as his cue to leave, but not before delivering one last unexpected remark.

"I may check in on you over the break, freshman Lucho." And just like that, he was gone, leaving behind more questions than answers.

Antoine called from downstairs and offered to drive onto the mile to pick me up in front of the dorm and reduce my walking distance, but I laughed it off and said that he would probably get me into more trouble. Instead, I told him about the alley behind the dorm and asked him to park there.

Marisol was already waiting downstairs when I arrived. The moment she saw me, she pulled me into a tight hug, holding on like she never wanted to let go. Meanwhile, Antoine grabbed my bags and started loading them up.

Shaking her head, she let out a frustrated sigh. "This place makes me furious! I still can't wrap my head around how reckless these assholes were. They should all be expelled for what they did to you."

While I agreed with her, I shot her a look and subtly gestured for her to cut it off. I whispered, "Please try not to get me killed today. Let's just get the hell out of here."

Every step still sent a jolt of pain through my body, but I forced myself to walk like I was fine—mainly to put Marisol and Antoine at ease. As we reached the car, I took one last glance at the dorm, its towering presence, a reminder of everything I had endured.

After slipping into the back seat, I whispered under my breath, "See you in a few weeks, McKibbin Hall."

Marisol got to choose the road trip music, so we listened to her favorite band, 10,000 Maniacs. Natalie Merchant's angelic voice helped me sleep peacefully during the entire ride to Houston.

Mami and Papi stood at the front door, their faces lighting up the moment we pulled into the driveway. I wore sweatpants so that the scars wouldn't horrify my parents, but the second I stepped out of the car, Mami's expression shifted.

"Mijo, why are you limping?" she asked.

I forced a small smile, brushing it off. "I'll explain later, Mami."

Marisol and Antoine exchanged a glance but didn't push. Without a word, they helped me unload my bags, their presence grounding me for just a little longer. As they got ready to leave, Marisol gave me one last hug.

"Call me if you need anything, XO," Antoine said, squeezing my shoulder.

After settling into my room, I finally gathered the courage to show my parents the scars. The second Mami saw them, she gasped so sharply it was like the air had been knocked out of her lungs. Then came the explosion in Spanish.

"Oh my God! Oh Saint Jude! No, no, no! What did they do to you, my loving son?" Her voice cracked as she screamed—hands flying to her face before she spun around in a fury.

Papi tried to calm her down, but she wasn't having it. "This is not over! We're going to sue that damned university! Those lousy people are going to pay for what they did to you!"

She paced back and forth, her rage growing by the second. My battle wounds weren't just mine anymore. Mami had taken them personally, like she had been the one dragged through hell night.

I lied and said that it looked worse than it felt. Truthfully, it was agonizing, but I managed to calm her down by telling the full story and explaining that the construction site was an honest mistake. The fact that several parents were advocating for us not to get expelled helped. Thank heavens that my words calmed her down, and she immediately switched into nurture mode. Mami said that her chicken mole would help me get better, and I knew that she was correct. There was no remedy better than Mami's healing cooking.

Walking continued to be painful my first week back, so I was a couch potato and watched hours of television instead of doing anything productive. News spread quickly through the freshman phone chain that the looming expulsion got dismissed because of the parents with clout. Mr. Strait, Master Sergeant, and Company Commander received a gentle slap on the wrist and had to pay the medical bills for my classmate who went to the emergency room and his local hospital during break. A hazing incident that extreme at a premier university should have made national news. But no one leaked a word.

By the time Christmas Eve rolled around, I was doing much better from a mobility perspective. I was happy to be home with my family and focused on being fully recovered for Justin's visit to Houston. My itchy scabs had reduced substantially, and I was walking normally again. Mami fully focused on nurturing me back to good health, and her delicious Mexican cooking and love accelerated my recovery. It wasn't just the food. She poured her love into every soup, every pot of chicken mole, every bowl of rice and beans, every tamal, every tortilla.

Mami put my gift-wrapping skills to good use while she finalized Christmas Eve preparations. The dining and living rooms were set for our immediate family, a handful of cousins, and Marisol and Antoine. As always, when the clock struck midnight on Christmas Eve my two nieces tore through reams of gift wrapping while the adults took photos and celebrated their joy.

I was practically fully recovered when the most important event of winter break arrived—Justin's visit to my home for New Year's Eve weekend. I planned a weekend filled with many 'firsts' for my dear friend, and I hoped that he would cherish my final gift for the rest of his life.

Justin drove in from Fort Worth on Friday and arrived just in time for a hearty, Mexican dinner. I asked my brother to be home so that everyone could meet my dearest friend in the Corps. Justin arrived and was immediately swept away to the dining room by Mami for introductions to the family. She liked him right off the bat because he showed up with a pumpkin pie made by his mother. An empty-handed guest was bad etiquette according to Mami.

While they got acquainted, I dropped Justin's bag off in my bedroom. Everyone was crammed in the dining room and seated around the table. Justin and my chairs were at the center of the table so that everyone could talk with us. Mami needed help with the food, so I served four platters of steaming tamales and several side dishes and bowls of creamy avocado salsa. She told us to dig in after she sat down.

I did most of the talking at first, and Justin smiled the entire time as he savored the rich food. We struggled to hear each other over the family's loud talking, which wasn't uncommon. I warned him about how loud the dining room could be, but you had to experience it to really appreciate a loud Mexican family at the dining table.

Justin was tired from the drive and the full belly of

tamales knocked him out. The arrangements were that he would sleep in my bed, and I would crash on the couch. As expected, he offered to switch, but I refused like a good host. I pointed out the restroom on the way to my bedroom.

Before leaving the room, I smiled and gripped his shoulder. "I'm going to help my mom clean up while you shower and get ready for bed. I've planned a fun weekend for us, so make sure you get some good shuteye tonight." Just saying it out loud made me even more excited.

First thing Saturday morning, I drove Justin to my boyhood barrio for breakfast tacos at my favorite Mexican restaurant. The hostess immediately recognized and hugged me. She also asked for my two friends, referring to Marisol and Antoine. After I explained that I had been away for college, I introduced Justin. I told her in Spanish that he was my best friend from college and that he had heard about their incredible cooking for months. The flattery made her blush, and she welcomed Justin.

Fortunately, the chorizo and bacon tacos lived up to my hype. The waitress stared in our direction a few times because we raced and engulfed the first order of tacos. She wasn't surprised when I placed a second order and pleased that we loved the food. When we paid, the cashier looked at the ticket and said that we had impressive appetites. Justin told her that the food was delicious and beyond his expectations. She told Justin to return any time he wants good Mexican food and for me to say hello to my parents.

We pulled away from the restaurant parking lot, and I asked Justin to open the glove compartment. He fumbled through the stack of papers at first, so I explicitly told him to open the white envelope on top. The look of excitement in his eyes when he held up the two tickets for SpaceWorld Amusement Park was priceless. He had never been to the Houston amusement park, and the gift was perfect for a fellow roller coaster enthusiast.

SpaceWorld held deep meaning for me and taking him there felt like sharing something essential from my past. The park was the backdrop for some of my fondest memories from my formative years. I led him to the exact spot where my brother had challenged me to conquer my fear of roller coasters—a moment marked by both tears and triumph. I pointed out the rides I worked on during my first job in high school, reminiscing about the sense of independence it gave me.

We made our way to the back of the park, where the field and amphitheater stood—the venue of my first concert, Erasure. At the time, I didn't yet have the language for what that night meant. Unbeknownst to me then, it was my first gay concert, with a flamboyant singer and a predominantly gay audience. It was the first time I danced freely, feeling a sense of community I hadn't known before.

Justin and I burned through our substantial breakfast calories throughout the morning at SpaceWorld, walking thousands of steps, standing in queues, and yelling at the top of our lungs with our hands raised high above our heads on every roller coaster in the park. We were two thrill seekers in our element, and we purchased matching SpaceWorld keychain souvenir picture viewers with our picture together as a memento.

Before we left the house, Mami warned me that the kitchen would be closed, so I had a unique restaurant in mind for dinner. I asked Justin if he had ever eaten Pho, Vietnamese soup, and as I suspected, he said that he had never heard of it but was willing to try anything at least once. We went to midtown, a large East Asian community filled with shops and authentic Vietnamese restaurants.

The appetizer plate of steaming Vietnamese fried eggrolls, fish sauce, and a heaping pile of lettuce and herbs was new for Justin, so an impromptu lesson on how to eat them properly was necessary. I had been in his exact spot the prior summer with my dear friend Vo—my gay "big sister" and mentor—who immigrated from Vietnam in the '70s with his family. Vo introduced me to the restaurant and taught me the ins and outs of Vietnamese cuisine, along with how to be a young gay man. Without a doubt, he's the reason for my addiction to fish sauce and pho.

Justin was no stranger to Chinese eggrolls, so dipping them in sweet and sour sauce was the extent of his egg-roll etiquette. Wrapping a Vietnamese fried eggroll in lettuce along with cilantro and peppers was new for him, and he was skeptical about the fish sauce after he got a whiff. I insisted, "I promise that your taste buds are going to thank me." After following my lead and a couple of bites, Justin was an instant believer, and the order of eight fried eggrolls vanished in minutes.

The main course was a bowl of pho with three types of meat and extra noodles. I showed him how to load the bowl of steaming soup with fresh vegetables and various sauces. Then we practiced how to coordinate the chopsticks with the soup spoon. Once again, Justin was a natural, and we enjoyed and slurped our bowls of pho until the last morsel.

Ms. Thuy, the restaurant's namesake and daughter of the original owners, was at the cash register when we paid our check, and she loved it when I told her how much we enjoyed her food. Our bellies were full when we made our journey home, so Justin quickly faded into a pho coma while I carefully drove to not disturb or startle him.

When we arrived at the house, Justin showered first and was in bed and under the blankets when I knocked and opened the door to say good night. I figured he was asleep, but he asked me to come in and close the door. Without giving it a second thought, I walked into the room and took a seat at the edge of my bed. Justin sat up, looked into my eyes, and asked if I would scratch his body the way I did in Fort Worth.

"I don't mind at all. I'm happy to scratch you but let me lock the door first." I lifted the sheet to crawl into the bed and saw that he was naked. Seeing him naked shocked me, and I suspect that he got a kick out of my rise because he chuckled, "I hope you don't mind. I figured I would save you the trouble."

I told him to roll over so that I could scratch his back. Fortunately, he passed out a few minutes into the scratching, and I didn't face the temptation to ask him to roll over. I gently rolled out of my bed, silently tiptoed out of the room, and watched television on the couch until I dozed off.

Sunday was New Year's Eve and the day of my final gift to Justin. He wasn't expecting anything else from me, but I saved the most meaningful gift for last.

Mami's shuffling around the kitchen woke me up at the crack of dawn, so I joined her to help prepare breakfast. We listened to cumbias and danced around the kitchen like old times. The aroma from heating the tamales on the comal filled the house. I prepared scrambled eggs and boiled the vegetables for fresh salsa. Mami also rolled out a couple dozen flour tortillas. Once the table was set, Mami called for everyone to join us for breakfast.

Justin agreed that the tamales were even better the second day after being reheated on the comal. Since Justin devoured and repeatedly complimented her cooking, Mami said that he was always welcome in our home.

After we showered and got dressed, I drove Justin up Telephone Road and pulled into an obscure parking lot near Houston Regional Airport. There was one other vehicle in the parking lot, and Justin had a playful grin on his face when I stopped the vehicle. "Alright, Mauricio, spill it! Where are we?"

I turned off the truck and told him to open the glove compartment to see the first part of this gift. He mumbled that I had already spoiled him enough, and I promised that this was the last one. I was on edge as he unwrapped the small, flat present.

Justin tore off the wrapping paper and appeared confused as he examined the gift. "It's a book of some sort. Hmm... please don't be offended, but... what is it?"

I laughed and told him, "It's a logbook."

Poor Justin's confusion deepened. "A logbook... like a logbook for a pilot? What am I going to do with a logbook?" His tone was a mix of curiosity and amusement.

I was beaming and dying to tell him, but I held out for a few seconds. Finally, I conceded and shouted, "Hurry up and get out of the truck, and I'll explain!"

I could barely contain my excitement as we stepped into the hangar, the familiar scent of aviation fuel and the sight of sleek aircraft made my blood pressure rise. I turned to Justin with a huge smile.

"Justin, if you're going to be the sensational aviator that I already know you're destined to be, you've got to start somewhere," I said, my voice brimming with anticipation. He looked at the logbook and his expression shifted from curiosity to realization.

"You're holding your first pilot's logbook—to record flying hours you rack up. I imagine that by the time you retire, you'll have several logbooks and tens of thousands of hours logged. But today, you're going to record your very first flying hour with me and my former flight instructor."

Justin appeared shocked as he took it all in, and it made the surprise all the more worth it. He belted out, "You've got to be kidding me, Mauricio." His voice echoed throughout the hangar. "Are you serious? I mean—this is insane!" He ran a hand through his short hair, his energy radiating off him.

"This is certainly the coolest thing anyone has ever done for me. Mauricio, I cannot believe you. I'm actually going to fly today!"

I pointed at the Cessna 172 parked in the hangar. "You see that plane? You're going to fly it today. And when you're an old, crusty, four-star general in a few decades, I want you to remember that I gave you your first flight lesson. So, buckle up, buttercup. Today's the day you take to the skies!"

Justin pulled me in for a tight hug. His voice was filled with gratitude as he repeated, "Thank you! Thank you! Thank you!" He pulled back just enough to look me in the eyes. "This is the most thoughtful gift I've ever received. I can't believe you did this, Mauricio."

He shook his head, laughing softly, still in shock. "Man... you really outdid yourself."

The flight instructor walked over and introduced himself to Justin. Then he jokingly said to me, "Tell me your name again," before he hugged me. He was my flight instructor in high school. Fortunately, he was available and generous enough to work on New Year's Eve as a favor for a former student and future Marine Corps officer. Those were his exact words.

Inspecting the exterior of the plane was the first lesson. I hopped in the back seat and Justin joined the instructor in the front. The instructor gave Justin a brief overview of the instruments, starting with how to steer the airplane. Steering with your feet took some time for me to get used to, but Justin was a natural.

We taxied to runway 17 for Justin's first takeoff and flew south after we got cleared by air traffic control. Being a smaller runway on the West side of the airport, we weren't in danger of running into an enormous passenger jet. The instructor asked if we had a destination in mind, and I requested Galveston so that we could fly along the coast because it was such a unique experience to watch the waves crashing into the beach from a low altitude. Justin was radiating excitement when he looked back at me and admitted that he had never been to Galveston.

It was a clear day with perfect visibility and little to no wind, the ideal conditions for planes that weigh very little. We couldn't have asked for better weather.

Justin's turns were smooth, and the instructor showed us that an open door could be used like a rudder while in flight. When we reached the beautiful gulf coast, we cruised at a low altitude and followed the shoreline to the Galveston airport so that Justin could attempt his first landing.

His grip on the yoke, the plane's "steering wheel", was firm, and Justin looked very focused and a little terrified. I reassured him, "Listen to the instructor and you'll do just fine. You've got this. And don't forget to breathe." Luckily, there were no crosswinds, and he nailed his first landing.

As soon as Justin shut down the engine and parked the Cessna near the hangar, the instructor gave him an approving nod. The moment I stepped down from the plane, I was met with an enormous bear hug.

Justin's grip tightened as he continued shaking his head in disbelief. "I'm never going to forget this moment, Mauricio. I still can't believe you did this for me. This has been incredible!"

I wanted to freeze that moment with his arms around me. I leaned in and whispered, "And I'm never going to forget the genuine joy in your eyes. Seeing you this happy is the best gift I could've ever received. It means the world to me. Justin, you mean the world to me."

The flight instructor interrupted, "Alright gentlemen— I've got to get back to Houston for a hot date. Hit the head and have some free coffee. We depart in ten minutes."

After the head and coffee break, we hopped back into the plane and continued Justin's flight training. We followed interstate 45 back to Houston Regional Airport and around halfway, I asked the instructor if he could teach Justin how to recover from a stall.

The instructor responded without hesitation. "A stall occurs when there isn't enough airflow over the wings, causing a loss of lift. When the plane senses an impending stall, an alarm will start buzzing, growing louder if no corrective action is taken. If you don't adjust in time, the plane will stall—its nose will instantly drop, and you'll feel your stomach in your throat. That's why practicing stall recovery is crucial." He paused briefly before asking, "Any questions?"

Justin looked like a deer in headlights, and I patted him on the shoulder and told him not to be frightened. "The instructor is going to teach you how to recover from the stall and will step in if anything goes wrong."

I tightened my seat belt just in case, but Justin aced the stalls as I expected. After three exhilarating stalls, we continued our journey back to Houston.

Justin proved to be a natural and successfully landed at Houston Regional Airport, and he was ecstatic about having completed his first flight lesson. When we returned to the hangar, the flight instructor added the first entry in Justin's logbook, and I proudly watched. After the flight instructor said his goodbyes, Justin gave me another bear hug, lifted me up, and spun me around a couple times. I had never seen him so overjoyed and was grateful that I could create that experience for him.

As we journeyed home, I couldn't contain my excitement for our plans to bring in the new year. We arranged to join Marisol and Antoine at Elysium to celebrate the big night. Elysium was Houston's premier gay video bar and dance club nestled in the vibrant and historic Montrose neighborhood, lovingly referred to as the gayborhood.

To my surprise, the mention of Elysium being a gay establishment sparked a look of genuine worry on Justin's face. He chose his words carefully, his concern evident. "Mauricio, does going to a gay bar concern you at all with Don't Ask, Don't Tell?" I knew that he was looking out for us, making sure I was thinking things through. We both knew one photo in the wrong hands could end our careers. There were no guarantees, but I told him that I had been going to Elysium since senior year in high school without any issues. I knocked on my forehead and then tapped on the chair for good luck. It was my way of warding off bad energy, hoping that it would help.

His expression shifted from concern to playful curiosity. "I've never been to a gay club, Mauricio. Will I be safe? Will you protect me if anyone tries to hit on me?" he asked with a mischievous grin.

I laughed and reassured him, "Of course, I'll protect you. But honestly, with those dance moves of yours, I think you'll be just fine!"

With a newfound sense of adventure and safety, Justin was excited to go to Elysium to welcome the new year with open arms. The night would be filled with laughter, celebration, and cherished memories.

Fortunately, we arrived early and beat the line that ended up wrapping around the club. Each cavernous room in the club was full of people dancing to the DJ's hypnotic house music. Since we were underage, we couldn't purchase alcohol in the club. Our workaround was a bottle of Absolut vodka in Antoine's car. We made trips throughout the evening for shots since our wrists were stamped, granting us access to quickly reenter the club.

The four of us danced the night away, and I had to block a handful of guys who attempted to move in and dance with Justin. Young guys could be very aggressive when they were on the hunt.

Before we knew it, the countdown to midnight ended, and the club erupted with cheers as balloons fell from the ceiling. The air buzzed with excitement as everyone sang Auld Lang Syne, welcoming the new year. The four of us embraced in a tight group hug. I leaned into Justin, my voice barely audible over the loud music, and shouted, "I'm so happy that you're here with me. Happy New Year. I love you!"

Justin looked into my eyes and smiled. He released

Antoine and Marisol, fully embraced me, and shouted in my ear, "There isn't another place I would rather be—happy new year Mauricio. I love you too and thank you for an unbelievable weekend."

Marisol jokingly shouted, "Break it up you two love birds, and spread the love." She pulled me away to hug me, and Antoine hugged Justin. Then we switched one more time.

The dance floor stayed packed as the DJ played well into the early hours. By the time we stumbled out at 0200 hours, my pulse was still hammering, my ears were ringing, and my feet throbbed from dancing all night. Then Antoine tossed out a wild idea: "Let's drive down to Galveston Island."

"Seriously? Right now?" Marisol shouted.

Justin grinned, "Why not? Let's do it! That'll make two stops in Galveston for me this trip."

We dashed to Antoine's car, the chilly night air biting at our skin. Within moments, we were racing down interstate 45 to Galveston Island, the thrill of spontaneity driving us forward.

Finding parking along the seawall could be a challenge, but the parking gods were on our side. A vacant spot was available near the iconic Flagship Hotel.

A famous Galveston attraction was the hotel's pier that overlooked the vast expanse of the Gulf of Mexico. The four of us briskly walked through the lobby to avoid being stopped by a staff member.

The cool breeze carried the scent of saltwater as we reached the end of the pier and gazed out at the gulf and looked up at the moon. We stood there in silence for a few minutes, savoring the peace and tranquility of the moment, lost in our own thoughts. The gentle sounds from the waves added to the serene atmosphere.

Justin was curious why the hotel was important to me. I explained that it wasn't simply the hotel, but everything about the island. I had childhood memories of my family playing in the warm water and catching hermit crabs. I pointed to where I used to fish with Papi and Apolo. Near the fishing spot, Mami used to hold my hand and guide me along the granite pier.

My high school memories on the island were almost always with Marisol and Antoine. Many evenings during junior and senior year, the three of us would drive down to Galveston, lay across the hood of Antoine's car, and stare up at the stars—breathing in the salty air, relaxing to the sound of the waves, and dreaming out loud about our futures. Ironically, our parents thought we were up to no good because we missed curfew so often, but they couldn't have been more wrong. Those nights weren't about clubs or parties—they were about imagining the lives we wanted.

When we were alone, I revealed to Justin a heavy decision that had been haunting me for weeks. The night we earned our Texas Star Buckle had crystallized it for me— I wanted out of the Corps and Texas F&E. They weren't for me.

Justin's expression softened, a mix of sadness and deep understanding.

"I get it," he said. "You've got to do what's right for you, Mauricio. You've been carrying so much all year—helping everyone, pushing yourself until you had nothing left."

He paused, choosing his next words with care.

"You don't need the Corps or a uniform to prove who you are—or that you're a good person."

He stepped closer.

"You deserve the freedom to be yourself. You deserve happiness. That's what I'm wishing on that star for you."

He pointed up at the sky.

His words hit something raw in me; my throat tightened. I stayed silent for a minute, fighting back the tears. In that moment, I felt seen, appreciated, loved, relieved, and yet so torn. "I'll finish the spring semester," I promised, my voice barely above a whisper. The news brought a genuine smile to his face, and that special sparkle in his eyes returned. "It'll be fantastic to complete freshman year with you," he said, sounding happy. He pulled me into a tight hug, holding on as if he would never let go. "No matter what, we will always have each other's backs, our freshman year, and years of memories to come."

In that embrace, I found comfort in Justin's unwavering support, a bond that transcended any institution or decision.

We were famished when we left the hotel, and I suggested the oldest Mexican restaurant on the island. Lucky for us, they never closed. It was near Galveston's historic Strand District and inexpensive, so Marisol and Antoine and I stopped by every time we visited.

After the very long night, Antoine dropped us off at home, and I made sure he was okay to drive before he left. We were all still feeling the effects of the vodka, but the greasy food and time spent eating had helped us sober up a bit. Marisol promised that they would get to her place safely. "Don't worry about it," she said with a reassuring smile. "I'll keep an eye on him—we'll be fine."

I nodded, feeling relieved that Antoine wouldn't be driving home alone. "Thanks, Marisol. Y'all be careful."

I followed Justin into my bedroom to retrieve pajamas. From the closet, I watched Justin strip naked and hop into the bed and under the sheet. The floor lamp was dimly lit, and he was staring at me when I looked at him. "Tonight was so much fun, Mauricio. I've never danced like that, so open and free. My ears are ringing, and I'm not tired. Will you scratch me?"

I walked over to lock the door and whispered, "Mami won't understand if she finds us in bed together. Are you sure you are comfortable with this, Justin?"

"I trust you, Mauricio. And I know you respect my boundaries," Justin answered. I changed into my pajama bottoms, and he lifted the sheet so that I could join him.

In the stillness of the silent room, my fingernails gently traced slow, delicate paths along his face and scalp. He was awake even though his eyes stayed shut—the stillness meant he was alert.

I ran my hand down his torso, feeling the rise and fall of his chest with each breath. When my hand finally rested on his heart, I could feel it racing beneath his skin.

He turned over, and I caressed and scratched the back of his body for several minutes. Justin began to replay the entire weekend, and I could feel his gratitude and love filling the room. Not before long, his body twitched a few times, indicating that he was falling asleep. The signal was all too familiar. Then he turned on his side with his back to me and requested, "Would you please hold me until I fall asleep?"

Despite knowing what was right, I felt a surge of anticipation and nervousness. Heightened senses made me look back again to make sure that the door was locked. My voice cracked a bit when I replied, "Of course I'll hold you, Justin."

I scratched the side of his scalp and began to doze off myself. His body twitched a few more times and he began to lightly snore. That was my cue to exit the room or else I would fall asleep next to him.

As I reluctantly released my grip on him, I leaned over and pressed a soft kiss on the back of Justin's head, feeling his stubbly hair tickle my lips. "I love you so much, Justin," I whispered, hoping he could hear me even in his sleep.

Being careful not to disturb him, I slowly rolled out of my bed. The soft glow of the lamp cast gentle shadows along his muscular body, highlighting every feature. I tucked the sheet under him, ensuring he was covered and comfortable, before quietly walking toward the door.

Just as I reached for the doorknob, Justin's voice—still groggy—broke the silence. "I love you too, Mauricio," he whispered. He drifted back to sleep, his breathing soft and steady once more.

For a moment, I stood there, frozen. Hearing that he loved me felt like a gift. Finally, I unlocked the door and tiptoed out of the room, carrying more emotion than I knew what to do with.

We woke up to another one of Mami's hearty meals. She prepared huevos rancheros, black-eyed peas for good luck, refried beans, cactus, rice, and homemade flour tortillas. Justin talked throughout breakfast about everything we did over the weekend and how much he loved his first visit to Houston. I told him that it was the least I could do to thank him and his beautiful family for their warm hospitality over Thanksgiving.

We packed up his things and my parents said their goodbyes. Mami warmly told Justin to visit again soon. As I walked Justin out to his car, he pulled me into another one of his tight bear hugs. "I meant what I said when you walked out of the bedroom last night," he whispered.

I looked at him, confused. "I thought you were talking in your sleep."

He shook his head, his eyes sincere. "There's no one like you, Mauricio. And that makes my love for you unique. It's not sexual, but I know that we've got a special bond. Does that work for you?"

I paused, searching for the right words. "Our bond is special, Justin, and I'll always cherish you." We held each other a little longer.

He then expressed his gratitude for the weekend, stating that the flight lesson was the most memorable part of the trip and something he would remember for the rest of his life.

Before parting ways, Justin retrieved a gift from his bag—four engraved carabiners and a rappelling rope. On one side of the carabiners, my initials were delicately etched, while the other side proudly displayed the emblem "U.S.M.C."

The gifts were precious mementos, reminders of the time we had spent together and our special friendship. We spent several weekends throughout the fall semester racing to see who could assemble a Swiss seat the fastest, and he was proud of me when I finally beat him.

"I love them, Justin. They are awesome, and I will put them to good use—and think of you every time I do."

Justin leaned in for another hug and said, "Now, every time you assemble a Swiss seat, climb, or rappel, remember that I'll be right there with you, ensuring your safety."

The thought of him being there for me was comforting. "I'll never forget. I promise. Thank you."

Watching him drive away left me alone to be fully present in feelings of gratitude, sadness, joy, and love. I tightly held the gifts, savoring the happiest new year I had ever celebrated. Justin had shown me that love came in many forms and that a unique bond could exist between two men, regardless of their sexual orientations.

As I walked toward the house, Mami opened the door to let me know that I had received a phone call. "Who is it, Mami?" I asked. She told me that it was someone from P-Company. "I think he said his name is Ari." A chill ran down my spine. Ari. Why was Mr. Strait calling me?

11 HALF IN, HALF GONE

My parents generously let me borrow the gas-guzzling Ram Charger for the return trip to University Station. Though the AC had long since died, I was grateful the heat still worked—without it, the cabin would've been an icebox in what was proving to be a brutally cold winter. Even thinking about the frigid morning runs and walks to class made me shiver.

When departure day finally arrived, Mami surprised me by keeping her composure—no tears this time. Instead, we shared a hearty Mexican breakfast, a proper sendoff that felt like her way of strengthening me for what lay ahead. Papi wrapped me in a warm hug and chose to stay behind as Mami walked me out to the truck. There, she recited her familiar prayers, asking her patron saint to watch over me and blessing me with hopes for a better semester.

Keeping the radio off filled the drive with a silence I needed to steady my racing thoughts. I was living between two worlds—one calling me forward, the other pulling me apart.

Part of me was genuinely excited to be reunited with my classmates—especially Justin and my bunkmate. Yet beneath that excitement lurked a persistent dread. I felt suspended between two identities: one pulling me toward staying in the Corps, the other already halfway gone.

The university and the Corps—they weren't what I had imagined or hoped for. Thinking about facing Mr. Strait again made my stomach turn. Fear was the first thing that rose in me, sharp and automatic—but underneath it, buried so deep I barely admitted it to myself, was the confusing pull I felt whenever he was near. That mixture—terror layered with something else—was its own kind of trap. Then there was the uncertainty surrounding P-Company's future and concerns over my grades.

My legs and arms bore memory-filled scars from hell night, etched reminders of recklessness, pain, and endurance.

Richard was already settled in our room when I arrived, and his face immediately lit up the moment I entered. "Welcome back, bunkmate! I'm sorry we didn't get to talk much during the break. Are you all healed? And how'd your grades turn out?" He sounded concerned, knowing I had left campus badly injured and filled with anxiety over my academic standing.

I hesitated before answering. "I'm all better now. As for my grades—worst-case scenario, bunkmate," I admitted. "Scholastic probation."

Richard's expression shifted, the pride in his own academic success momentarily clouded by concern. "Damn, Mauricio. I prayed that you'd avoid scho-pro. How'd your parents take it?"

Mami and Papi's disappointment hung over me. They urged me to prioritize grades over the Corps. Yet no one was harder on me than myself. With my Marine Corps scholarship and place at Texas F&E hanging in the balance, failure simply couldn't be an option.

So I made hard choices. Cutting back on partying with my classmates became essential, and staying awake in class took priority—even if it meant standing in the back of lecture halls and auditoriums. Most painfully, I gave up my cherished journaling time, replacing those quiet moments of reflection with hours of focused study.

Richard, on the other hand, filled me with pride when he told me he made the Corps honor roll. I was delighted for my bunkmate because he put in the hours to earn the recognition. Then he shared an even bigger surprise. I had helped influence a major life decision of his. Just before winter break, he started the application process for a Naval ROTC scholarship and was fast-tracked thanks to his stellar high school grades. Days before returning to campus, he learned that the scholarship was his. It was the bright update I didn't know I needed.

I was lying on my rack talking about the holiday break with Richard when Justin appeared in the doorway wearing his trademark grin. "Hey classmates, it's great to see you. I just arrived. Scoot over, Mauricio," he said, nudging me until he had enough space to flop down beside me.

The three of us caught up on the latest rumors, most revolving around hell night and its aftermath. Word was P-Company had been on the verge of being disbanded. Several influential parents had challenged the fallout with Top Brass and university leadership, and, in the end, we avoided expulsion and disbandment by a thread. We were on probation but intact. Some of our upperclassmen, including Mr. Strait, had to pay the medical bills for our most injured classmate.

Later that evening, Master Sergeant ordered us to assemble in the passageway before lights out. We already knew what was coming but hearing it from him made it official.

"Listen up," he barked. "P-Company is under a microscope. Top Brass has made it clear—one complaint of hazing, and this company is finished. We will all be out on our asses—that means expelled. And you can kiss any chance at graduating or a commission goodbye."

The weight of his words settled over me like fog, heavy and suffocating. Two types of probation after just one semester—academic and company—were never part of my plan. I had dreamed of proving myself, of excelling, of making my family proud. Instead, I felt like I was walking a tightrope, one misstep away from losing everything.

Then, in typical Master Sergeant fashion, his tone shifted. "But hell night had an… unexpected outcome." He let the words hang for a moment, his lips curling into a smile. "P-Company's always had a reputation for being the best and toughest in the Corps. But now? Now you're legends."

"Cadets from other companies have been coming up to me, asking if y'all were tortured with acid." He chuckled, amused by the absurdity. "And you know what I told them?" He paused. "That we're not allowed to talk about hell night. Orders from the top."

As preposterous as it was, this boost to our reputation filled Master Sergeant and the other upperclassmen with pride.

Just as we were dismissed, Mr. Strait's voice cut through the noise. "Freshman Lucho, my room. Now."

My stomach twisted. I followed him, stepping into his room and standing at attention.

He shut and locked the hatch. "Lower your sweatpants and underwear," he ordered.

I hesitated, every instinct screaming to refuse, but my body obeyed anyway, despite the knot tightening in my stomach. My skin crawled as he examined my legs, his fingers tracing the scars with an unsettling intimacy. When he told me to turn around, my muscles involuntarily tensed. His hands moved over the back of my legs with slow, deliberate pressure that felt wrong.

When I turned back to face him, something had shifted.

I wasn't prepared for the longing and almost tender sincerity in his eyes. Then, suddenly, he cupped my face and pulled me firmly toward him. Before I could react, his mouth was on mine, his tongue forcing its way past my lips. The kiss was deep. And to my shock, a bright, involuntary rush of pleasure shot through me—confusing, unwanted, and disorienting.

He took one of my hands and guided it to rub the bulge in his sweatpants. Mr. Strait's voice was lower than usual, almost hesitant. "I'm glad you're better," he said, his usual roughness softened. He held my gaze for a moment before adding, "I've missed you and our encounters."

I was shaken. Was he my predator or my lover? He lowered the front of his sweatpants and told me it would be quick. After finishing, I left his room in a daze, my thoughts tangled.

Just as I returned to my room, Mac stopped by to check in. "Sloth Platoon runs start tomorrow, and because of the cold weather, wear your physical training gear under your sweats. We'll run to the recreation center and use the indoor track." He was determined to see us succeed in the PFT Challenge two months away. I wasn't thrilled about extra physical training before dawn, but time with Mac and the others was the silver lining.

That night, I struggled to sleep. Long after lights out, I stared up at the bottom of Richard's bed. The room was quiet—Richard already asleep, his soft breathing steady, but my mind was anything but still.

Everything felt heavier. The semester hadn't even begun, but I was already carrying too much: regret about joining the Corps, my feelings for Justin, academic probation, company probation, my parents' disappointment, and above all, the confusion over what was happening—and what might happen next—with Mr. Strait.

I couldn't make sense of it. My body had obeyed even as my instincts screamed. I wanted to believe I had control, that I had a choice—but deep down, that kiss, that moment, blurred every line I thought I understood.

Had I just survived something? Or surrendered to it?

The thought unsettled me.

In the stillness, I could almost hear Mami's voice—soft and protective. Her blessing made me feel shielded, if only briefly. I wanted to hold on to that feeling and let it guard me from the worst of what was to come in spring semester.

I pulled the sleeping bag tighter around me and closed my eyes, uncertain about the semester ahead—but certain of one thing: I was no longer the same person who had arrived at the start of freshman hell week.

12 LITTLE BY LITTLE

Since the beginning of freshman year, I faced a daunting challenge: my inability to run long distances at a fast pace. Physical fitness proved to be not just important—but critical to being a respected cadet and Marine Corps officer. My military career would hinge on meeting stringent fitness standards and regularly undergoing physical fitness tests.

Besides improving my grades and clawing myself out of scho pro during the spring semester, I was determined to help P-Company claim victory in the 1996 PFT Challenge—the three-mile run based on the Marine Corps physical fitness test.

As the Challenge approached, I reflected on the months of training. Countless morning runs felt like an uphill battle, but I refused to give up. What made the journey tolerable, though, was the support from Mac, Justin, and Richard. They gave up their own time to invest in me—Mac pushing me through sloth platoon runs and Justin and Richard dedicating many of their weekends to help me. They ran beside me and encouraged me every step of the way.

As days stretched into weeks and weeks into months, the changes became undeniable. My endurance grew, my strength increased, and my body moved with a confidence that hadn't been there before. The combination of a healthier diet and consistent training made a noticeable physical impact, so much so that I exchanged my trousers for a smaller waist size earlier in the semester.

Company runs no longer left me winded, and there was

more energy to carry me through each day. Workouts became something to lean into, not just survive, and each push brought a quiet sense of pride. Progress wasn't just physical—it was a reminder of how far I had come.

The eagerly anticipated moment finally arrived, marking a major milestone of the year. For P-Company, the 1996 PFT Challenge stood as something far beyond mere competition. It was the annual opportunity to defend our hard-won crown and prove to the rest of the Corps that we were the undisputed champions.

P-Company had been triumphant for ten consecutive years, so we were the unit to beat. We could choose any day or time slot to run, and Company Commander opted for us to run on the last day of the challenge, in the final time slot. By doing so, we would know the fastest time and what we needed to win.

Companies began to compete in the third week of March, and tensions and trash-talking increased across the Corps throughout the week. We anxiously watched the leaderboard being updated day after day as other units completed the run.

Every morning that week, I paused for a moment to reflect on another one of Mami's dichos: "Poco a poco se anda lejos"—little by little, one goes far. Over the past six months, I'd watched that truth unfold in my own body. Incremental runs had stretched into miles. Miles had become habits. And those habits had carried me farther than I ever expected. Small, steady steps—exactly as Mami promised—had made all the difference.

Throughout the week, the leaderboard was heating up—more companies, faster times—fueling my competitive spirit. By the morning of our run, the time to beat was eighteen minutes and fifty seconds, which was fifty seconds shy of the maximum scoring Marine Corps three-mile run time. It was hard not to be concerned. My last PFT in February nearly made me puke, and that was just under twenty minutes. It was my best run since joining the Corps.

The night before our run, I clasped my hands together and whispered a quiet prayer. I asked the Lord to grant me the stamina to fly like the wind and for our entire company to cross the finish line under the leading time—even if only by one second. Then, I asked my Abuelita to watch over us and keep us safe.

In that quiet moment of prayer, a sense of peace settled over me. I remembered that I wasn't alone on this journey—I never had been. My classmates were with me, the Lord was with me, and so was Abuelita. I could almost hear her voice, reminding me that everything would be okay.

Richard and I woke up thirty minutes early on the morning of the challenge, my stomach twisting with nerves. I had been training for this, but now it was real. Dressed in our physical training gear and ready, we stretched in our room.

As I brushed my teeth, Richard walked up behind me, and I caught his big grin in the mirror's reflection. "You've got this, bunkmate," he said, clamping his hands onto my shoulders with a firm squeeze and a spark in his eye. "I know how hard you've been grinding for this—day in, day out—and it's all paying off. You're stronger, faster, sharper. Today's your day to own it. The challenge doesn't stand a chance against you, man. Go out there and show 'em what you're made of."

Richard's confidence in me was comforting, but it didn't stop the nerves from buzzing in my stomach. I chuckled when he joked that I would miss waking up every morning to run with the sloth platoon.

Master Sergeant shouted the order, and my classmates and I fell out into the passageway. The tension in the air was palpable as he slowly paced in front of us. And then he spoke.

"Listen up, Pirates! This is it—the moment you've bled, sweat, and fought for. Every sore muscle, every blister, every damn second you thought about quitting—it's all led to right now. You've trained like warriors, and today, you don't just run. You prove. You dig down deep and show your intestinal fortitude. You show this Corps, this campus, and yourselves exactly what P-Company is made of. Now envision the victory and earn that legacy!"

He walked over and halted directly in front of my bulkhead, his focus fixed on me—like the next message had my name written all over it.

"When your legs burn and your lungs scream for air, push harder. When your mind tells you to quit, silence that weakness, because you are P-Company pirates—and pirates never quit! Remain focused, stay in formation, and leave everything you've got out there on that course. Now, let's get out there and show these bastards what P-Company is made of!"

The passageway erupted into cheers after his speech. Even the upperclassmen, usually composed and stoic, couldn't hold back. A charge flooded my veins. Every breath, every beat echoed one truth—I was ready. And judging by the thunder around me, so was everyone else.

Mac weaved through the passageway and stopped in front of me, his sharp eyes locking onto mine. He leaned in close, his voice low but steady, meant only for me.

"I know you're ready to shut up every damn naysayer out there," he said. "You never quit, not once—not when you were dead on your feet, not when it looked like you were gonna pass out. That's why I believe in you, Mauricio. That's why I never gave up on you."

Mac's words sparked something in me. A lump rose in my throat, and I had to brace myself to stay grounded. My emotions were running high—not because I was weak, but because he saw me. He saw the struggle behind every mile, every insult I bit my tongue through, every moment I wanted to quit but didn't. Mac knew the pain I had pushed past, and in that moment, I was grateful because he truly believed in me.

He then pressed his forehead against mine just like he had on those tough mornings when I needed a push. "You've got this—now go prove it. Show them what Mauricio Lucho is made of." I took deep breaths to maintain my composure and nodded. His faith boosted my confidence, and I was ready. Ready to prove, not just to them, but to myself, exactly what I was made of.

We received the order to fall out into formation in front of the dorm and roared down the stairwell. This time, one of my classmates slammed the metal door with enough force that it snapped off its hinges. We marched down to the start line. Before the gun fired, Company Commander shouted, "18:45—that means six minutes and fifteen seconds per mile. Let's show them what Pirates are made of!"

As I stepped onto the mile, I was struck by how packed it was. It felt like every company in the Corps had shown up, shoulder to shoulder along the route. Even non-Corps students had gathered, drawn by the buzz around the annual challenge.

Amongst the sea of faces filled with anticipation and excitement was a large group of P-Company family members and friends who had driven in from out of town to cheer us on.

I squinted, my eyes darting across the sea of faces, searching desperately for Marisol and Antoine. The sheer number of people made it almost impossible, but then I heard them.

"Mauricio! XO! Mauricio Lucho!" Their voices cut through the noise, unmistakable and full of excitement.

Relief and joy washed over me when I finally spotted them in the crowd. No matter what, they always showed up for me.

We reached the entrance to the mile where the timekeeper stood at the starting line, his hand gripping a black pistol. He raised it up high and signaled for us to get ready. I took a deep breath, drawing in the energy of the crowd. Then, the timekeeper fired the pistol, and we were off.

A mile into the run, I controlled my breathing and coasted. The pace was fast, but I could have gone faster. Something ignited inside me, propelling me toward the best run of my life.

The run hit a new gear at the two-mile mark. Company Commander gunned it and suddenly we were flying. A couple of my classmates and several upperclassmen began to struggle and break formation. Before I knew it, each step felt heavier, my legs struggling to match the unforgiving pace. My clothes clung to my body, soaked, and my lungs worked double time just to keep rhythm.

Watching my classmates around me struggle, I remembered all the times they had pushed and encouraged me during my own battles with running. During so many runs, they were there for me. Now it was my turn.

"Come on class of 99, you've got this!" I yelled. "We're almost there—just a little more!"

Mr. Strait seized the moment to turn up the pressure. There was no encouragement in his words, no motivation—just cold, sharp-edged contempt.

"Is this the best you can do, you pussies?" he yelled, his voice slicing through the morning air like a blade. "You call yourselves pirates? You're a fucking disgrace! Pick up the pace before I run you into the ground!"

As usual, his words weren't just meant to push—they were meant to degrade.

Mac and other upperclassmen intervened, drowning him out with words of encouragement. Their powerful show of unity steadied us.

The cheers from the onlookers grew louder as we

approached the end. Company Commander shouted for us to pick up the pace and finish strong. At that point, I was drenched in sweat. Finally, we crossed the finish line! We did it! We pushed ourselves to the limit and finished the run.

The time stopped when the last squad crossed the finish line, and then Company Commander called quick time to start cooling us down. Everyone had shown true grit and determination, refusing to give up.

One of the juniors in the sloth platoon walked to the nearest trash can to vomit. I took deep, steady breaths as sweat poured down my body. When we halted, the timekeeper walked over to Company Commander to report the result, and he held a clipboard in front of his face to prevent us from reading his lips.

The timekeeper walked away from Company Commander, and the air around us shifted. The once-roaring crowd fell silent. My chest tightened, my breath caught somewhere between exhaustion and dread.

Company Commander stood there, steadying his breathing, his expression unreadable. His jaw was set, his hands on his hips, and for a moment, I swore I saw a flicker of frustration—or was it disappointment? All I could do was wait, stomach churning, for the words that would decide whether all my sacrifices—every drop of sweat, every ounce of pain—had been enough.

Each second dragged like an eternity. Then, at last, Company Commander made his way toward us to deliver the verdict. "I hate to break it to you, pirates, but your time this year was slower than last year."

My heart sank, and I took a deep breath, bracing for the disappointment. But then—just for a split second—his act cracked, and a smile spread across his face.

"That being said," he continued, his voice growing stronger, "even with a slower time, we defeated every single company. And that means our legacy continues—we are the PFT Challenge champions of 1996!"

The moment the words left his mouth, a roar of cheers erupted around me. "This victory isn't just about speed," he went on, his voice rising above the celebration. "It's about grit. It's about pushing past the pain when your body is screaming at you to stop. It's about discipline, determination, and the unbreakable bond that makes P-Company the best of the best." He looked us over, pride gleaming in his eyes. "You didn't just win a title today. You upheld a legacy. You proved, once again, that P-Company is the best."

The cheers grew deafening, and at that moment, a mix of excitement, gratitude, and relief filled my soul. We did it! I looked around at my fellow classmates, and although we were drenched in sweat and red in the face, everyone appeared overjoyed!

Company Commander continued speaking about our hard work and determination. He also reminded us that this victory wasn't just about winning a competition but about building character and camaraderie within our company.

For a moment, I let the noise fade into the background. I closed my eyes and whispered a quiet thank you to the Lord—for carrying me when I needed him, for surrounding me with people who refused to let me give up. I thought of Mac, Justin, and Richard; their belief in me had been my anchor. Then, looking up at the sky, I blew a soft kiss heavenward for Abuelita. I hoped she could see me.

Company Commander called out the order, and we rushed to form a tight circle around him. With our arms draped over one another, on his command, our company chant exploded like a cannon blast across the mile, echoing so loud I wouldn't be surprised if students on the other side of campus paused to listen. The energy was electric—pure adrenaline and pride. The second we finished, we broke into hugs, high-fives, chest bumps—everything.

Richard, the best bunkmate ever, ran over to me, his

face lit up with joy. Without hesitation, he scooped me up in a bear hug. "You did it, bunkmate! I knew you could do it!" he exclaimed, eyes bright and filled with joy. "You absolutely annihilated the challenge!"

He set me down, but his hands remained firmly on my shoulders, eyes shining with pride. "You've shown everyone what true determination looks like, and I'm so proud of you," he said, his voice filled with genuine warmth.

It was a special moment of pure camaraderie, a testament to the power of friendship and support. Looking into his eyes, I told him, "You're a true champion and the best bunkmate ever! I couldn't have done this without you." Despite being red and dripping sweat, his face was glowing with a huge smile that stretched ear to ear.

Justin was nearby, and I looked over to see him surrounded by his loving family, cheering and congratulating him on the achievement. Amidst the excitement, I sensed that he was searching for me. When our eyes finally met, time seemed to freeze, creating a space of stillness amidst the chaos. His beaming smile grew even brighter, reflecting our special bond.

Without a second thought, he cut through the crowd, weaving between bodies and never breaking our gaze. As he approached, I could see the exhilaration in his eyes. When he finally reached me, his arms wrapped around me in a tight embrace.

"Congratulations, Mauricio," Justin shouted, his voice thick with emotion. "You did it. I knew you would."

I nodded, unable to speak for a moment as the weight of everything hit me.

He pulled back just enough to look me in the eyes, his hands still gripping my shoulders like he didn't want to let go. His voice lowered, full of emotion.

"You didn't just finish, Mauricio—you led. You lifted people up when they were falling behind. You inspired me."

I managed a small laugh, brushing away the tears

forming in my eyes.

"And hey," he added with a grin, "remind me never to bet against you."

"Thank you, Justin," I choked out, my voice just as full of feeling. "I couldn't have done this without you. Mami's dicho was right again."

His grin widened. "The 'little by little' one?"

I nodded. "Yeah, that's the one."

Step by step, day by day, I had pushed forward— sometimes barely crawling, sometimes flying. And in the end, I had gone further than I ever imagined possible.

Before he returned to his family, Justin's eyes sparkled with excitement. "Get ready for a day of celebrating," he said, clapping his hands together. "This is just the beginning."

After Justin returned to his family, I scanned the crowd, my eyes darting desperately from face to face. I couldn't find Marisol or Antoine. Then, I felt a gentle tap on my back.

I turned around, and there they were—Marisol and Antoine, their faces radiant, their eyes filled with relief and joy. "Look at you, superstar," Marisol teased, wiping away a tear with a grin.

Before I could say a word, they pulled me into a tight, joyous hug, wrapping me up as if they had been waiting all day for the moment. "You really did it, XO," Antoine shouted.

My physical training gear was soaked in sweat, but they didn't care. They held on, gripping me like they never wanted to let go. And in that hug, I felt how much they understood what I had gone through to get here. Their happiness, their relief, their unwavering belief in me—it was all there and deeply felt. Feeling their pride as strongly as my own made the victory that much sweeter.

Not long after, Mac spotted us huddled together, deep in conversation. As he approached us, the mischievous look in his eyes gave him away before he even opened his mouth.

"Give it a break, you three," he called out, striding toward us with that easy confidence of his. Then, with a smirk, he turned his attention to Marisol and Antoine.

"Welcome back, traitors," he said, directing the jab at Marisol and Antoine, in jest, of course. Even though we all went to the same high school, attending our archrival university was something Mac would never let them live down.

I barely had time to laugh before he turned to me. "Freshman Lucho, step over here with me for a minute." He was formal since others were around.

I followed him a few steps away, and in an instant, his usual playful demeanor faded. His expression softened, and when he spoke, there was no teasing—just sincerity. There was something different in his eyes—like he had been waiting for the right moment to say this.

"Mauricio," he said, his voice low and steady, "I heard you out there, pushing your classmates forward. That's leadership. That's heart." He paused, letting the words settle.

Then he rested a hand on my shoulder, his grip firm but reassuring.

"I need you to hear this—I'm proud of you."

Like earlier in the passageway, his words hit me hard, like a wave I didn't see coming. All the early mornings, the moments of doubt, the aches I pushed through—they flashed through my mind. And Mac, who had seen me at my lowest, was standing there seeing me at my best.

He didn't need to say much more. In those few words, he gave me something I hadn't realized I was still chasing— validation from someone I deeply respected.

A lump formed in my throat, and I swallowed hard against the rush of emotion. I took a deep breath to compose myself before I said, "None of this would've been possible without you."

Without hesitation, he pulled me into a hug.

But, just as quickly as the serious moment had come, it was gone. Mac leaned back, wrinkled his nose dramatically, and grinned. "You stink!" he shouted. "Now wipe those tears off your face, and let's go talk to the traitors."

I laughed, shaking my head as I followed him back. Some things never changed.

I wiped my tears as a renewed sense of pride—and validation, especially as a member of the sloth platoon—washed over me.

The challenge was officially over, but the celebration had only just begun. We were ready to celebrate the rest of the day, and we made our way back to the dorms to shower and get dressed for the festivities on the mile.

Within a few hours, the mile was transformed into a fair of sorts, complete with barbecue pits, booming music, and a sea of chairs and folding tables. The smell of grilled burgers and hot dogs filled the air, luring in hungry cadets from all corners of the mile. Despite the strict rules against alcohol consumption, kegs flowed freely on each floor of the dorms, and several cadets, including me and Justin, risked the consequences by drinking beer in public.

The festivities on the mile grew wilder as the hours passed. Everyone was in high spirits, laughing and joking around as if they didn't have a care in the world. Marisol, Antoine, and I lost track of time as we hung out with Richard, Mac, and Justin, caught up in the infectious energy of the day.

Unfortunately, Marisol and Antoine had to leave before sunset to make their way to Houston, cutting short their visit with us. They said their goodbyes to Mac, Richard, and others before Justin and I accompanied them to the car.

As we made our way toward the parking garage, Antoine pulled me aside to share an observation while Justin and Marisol walked ahead. "XO, I've been watching Justin all day, and he doesn't look at anyone else the way he looks at you. I know you've said he isn't attracted to you, but it's pretty clear to me that he has some special feelings for you."

I knew exactly what Antoine was talking about—he wasn't the first to notice. But none of that mattered to me. From the very beginning, I had dismissed the idea as wishful thinking, choosing instead to focus on what truly mattered—our friendship.

Back in the fall semester, I had already convinced myself that what Justin and I shared was something rare and meaningful, a bond built on loyalty and trust. His friendship was something I valued above all else, something I would never risk losing.

"I appreciate you telling me, Antoine," I said, forcing my voice to stay steady, even as a storm of emotions swirled inside me. "But that ship has sailed. Justin isn't gay, and he's in love with Kate."

Saying it out loud stung, but it was the truth—the only truth that mattered.

Antoine studied me for a moment, his expression full of understanding. Then, without a word, he pulled me into one of his warm, reassuring hugs.

"I get it, XO," he replied. "I know that you two have a very unique and special friendship."

Justin and I took a long walk away from the mile after we watched Antoine and Marisol drive off. The sky was clear, the moon was bright, and that part of campus was empty and peaceful.

I loved the unplanned moment—just the two of us, walking side by side, letting the evening carry our conversation. We laughed, trading stories about freshman year, reminiscing about the struggles, the pain, and the victories, big and small.

As we strolled across campus, I found myself soaking in every second. I glanced over at him, and in that instant, it hit me. The destination was sweet, but the journey we had taken together was even sweeter. The friendship we had built, the memories we had made—those were the things that truly mattered.

By the time we made our way back to the festivities, a deep sense of gratitude settled in my chest. No matter what the future held, the victory and the memories were ours to hold onto forever.

13 TRUTH COMES TO LIGHT

Throughout my youth, Mami and Papi instilled one simple tenet: thou shalt not bear false witness. In our home, a lie—once uncovered—brought swift consequences. Mami would often recite a familiar dicho: "La verdad, tarde o temprano, sale a la luz." As I grew older, the truth of her words revealed itself repeatedly. No matter how deeply you bury something, no matter how carefully you weave your story, the truth sooner or later will come to light— quietly at first, then unmistakable, like a beam of light cutting through the dark.

When it came to me and Mr. Strait, the truth had been buried under layers of deception for far too long. He wasn't just controlling—he was calculated, always several steps ahead—convinced he could pull the strings without anyone noticing. But manipulation breeds overconfidence, and sooner or later, even the most cunning puppet master misses a string. That is when the whole performance begins to unravel.

Since the start of the spring semester, he had everything under control. He was the one pulling the strings, and I willingly played along. But during the first weekend of April, he slipped—and the lies came crashing down.

The first Friday of April was a university reading day for final exam preparation. Campus customarily emptied out, but I decided to stick around because I desperately needed to work on a paper. Justin and Richard planned to go home along with the majority of our other classmates.

On Thursday evening, my classmates and I were standing at attention on the bulkheads in the passageway, eagerly anticipating our early weekend liberty. Master Sergeant took roll call, and one by one, we reported our weekend whereabouts.

Mr. Strait was nearby as I waited for my turn to report. When I reported that I would be staying in the dorm the entire weekend, I caught Mr. Strait pivot toward me. My update had evidently caught his attention.

After my update, I overheard Mr. Strait talking to one of the other sophomores. He mentioned that Brittany was driving to Fort Worth early Friday morning, and that he planned to stay on campus to work on a project. The deliberate volume in his voice signaled his real motive—letting me know he'd be alone.

Richard left the dormitory shortly after we were dismissed, leaving me alone in our room. I was exhausted and went to bed early, hoping to recharge and tackle my paper first thing in the morning. But as I lay there in the darkness, I couldn't shake the feeling that Mr. Strait was planning something.

It was refreshing to sleep in on Friday morning. A couple cold Pop Tarts helped jumpstart my mind, and I diligently worked through the morning. Before I knew it, my stomach rumbled, and I decided on some real sustenance for lunch—pizza! A large pizza seemed practical—half for lunch and the other half for dinner.

The afternoon flew by, and I set a goal to work until 1700 hours. Just as I logged off my bunkmate's personal computer, the phone rang. I wasn't expecting a phone call, so I stared at it until the ringing stopped. A few seconds later, it rang again, and I told myself I'd better answer—it might be an upperclassman.

"Good afternoon, freshman Lucho speaking, sir or ma'am."

"It's Mr. Strait, freshman Lucho. I'm sure you're

preparing for exams, but are you at a point where you can give me your full attention—now?"

"Yes, sir. I was just logging off the computer," I replied.

He told me that Brittany was out of town and that he wanted my company. Before I hung up, I asked if he had any special requests.

There was a brief pause before he spoke, his voice dropping to a commanding whisper. "Wear your physical training gear—and a jockstrap. The hatch will be cracked open. No one sees you go in, understood? Once you're inside, bolt the hatch. Quietly."

I confirmed, "Ay, ay, sir. I will be there shortly, sir."

After I changed into my physical training gear, I ran down the passageway and looked both ways to ensure the coast was clear before entering his room. As instructed, I bolted the hatch and stood at attention in front of the vanity, facing the window. He was listening to music, but not loudly.

Mr. Strait stood up from his recliner and disrobed, revealing himself, nude and semi-erect. Then he walked over and passionately kissed me on the lips. Before long he stepped behind me and told me to raise my arms so that he could remove my shirt.

In an instant, he turned me to face the vanity mirror. "Lean forward and put your hands on the counter." I was already familiar with the position.

Mr. Strait surprised me when he reached around and fondled me over my shorts—this was a first. Then he inserted his thumbs under my shorts waistband and slid them around to either side of my hips. Without warning, he squatted down behind me and pulled my shorts down with him.

"Step out of your shorts and spread your feet apart," he ordered.

Admittedly, the sensation of his tongue against my back and gentle bites sent shivers through me—they were sharp and undeniably titillating. My breaths grew heavier, and I could tell that my trembling turned him on.

Before long, he gave me the next set of instructions. "Rest your chest on the sink, reach around with both hands, and spread your cheeks."

I obeyed him, tried to relax, and he continued. He moaned softly as he rimmed me.

Then he stood up and said, "I'll try not to be as rough this time, I promise." Unlike some encounters, he was patient while he penetrated me.

The room was warm, and we worked up a sweat. Suddenly, he locked me into a full nelson, slipping his arms under my armpits and locking his hands behind my neck. Knowing I was helpless triggered a sexual rage in him; the pounding intensified. I began to worry that the sounds could be heard over the music.

My voice vibrated from the pounding when I attempted to say that he needed to slow down because we were being too loud.

He listened and slowed down. This gave us a moment to catch our breath.

Just as Mr. Strait started back up, I thought I heard a faint clicking sound coming from his hatch, but whether he did or not, he continued without hesitation. I strained to listen, and a second later, there was no doubt—another distinct click reverberated through the air.

I snapped my head to the left as the hatch creaked open and gasped. Standing there—of all people—was Brittany, gripping a key in her trembling hand. For a second, I couldn't believe it was really her. She looked nothing like the beauty who always turned heads. Her hair was a mess, her eyes hollow with exhaustion, the dark circles beneath them making it clear she hadn't slept in days.

Brittany's gaze met mine, a mixture of shock, desperation, and fury. She had walked in on her worst nightmare, bringing with her a twist none of us had seen coming.

It took a few seconds for Mr. Strait to realize she was standing in the doorway. When he finally spotted her, he threw me forward and backed away from me. He was gasping for air and told her to get inside and bolt the door. She walked in and was rendered speechless by what she had discovered—God knows I would've been.

At first, my body froze, unsure of what to do next. Instinct pushed me to create some distance between me and both of them, so I retrieved my clothes and made my way to the window. As I dressed, I couldn't help but wonder what I was going to say to Brittany.

Brittany's voice shattered my thoughts as she screamed, "How could you do this to me? You told me that you loved me." Mr. Strait lunged toward his stereo system, frantically turning up the volume as he signaled to Brittany to lower her voice.

He tilted his head and asked, "What are you doing here, Brittany? You're supposed to be in Fort Worth. And tell me—how exactly did you manage to get a copy of my key?"

His words, slow and deliberate, hung in the air like a trap, shifting attention off himself and onto her. I finished dressing and turned to face them—knowing he was already rewriting the narrative in real time.

Apparently, Brittany knew that Mr. Strait thought he could outsmart anyone. But she had outsmarted him when he wasn't paying attention, making a duplicate of his backup key without him realizing he ever lost track of it.

She knew the backup key was in his desk and that he never checked whether it stayed there.

Her voice cut through the loud music. "You think you're so clever, Ari Strait," she spat, her voice trembling with a mix of anger and anguish. "You never even noticed when I took your precious backup key."

Mr. Strait's face paled as Brittany continued. "You think you can just cheat and get away with it? I knew something was off with you since the start of the semester. You grew distant, secretive. And then, when I saw your blinds closed on random afternoons, I knew. I lied about my trip to Fort Worth because I had to find out the truth."

Her eyes blazed with fury as she hurled the key at him, her voice rising to a scream. "Take it! I never want to see it or this room again. I never want to see either of you two again. How could you betray me like this, cheating with another man?"

Mr. Strait stood there frozen as the key fell to the floor. The room held its breath, the weight of Brittany's revelation hanging heavily in the air. The shock of the accusation—cheating not with another woman, but with another man—left Mr. Strait speechless.

Brittany's eyes filled with tears, but she didn't falter. "I thought I knew you," she choked out. "But I guess I never really did."

Mr. Strait was clearly crafting a manipulative response in his head, desperately hoping to defuse the explosive situation. He took a deep breath, trying to calm his nerves, and approached Brittany, still unclothed and sweaty.

But as soon as he got close, she raised her hand to stop him in his tracks.

"Don't come near me, Ari Strait, and get dressed for heaven's sake," Brittany spat out. "How long has this been going on?"

Mr. Strait appeared to struggle—truly struggle—for the first time since I'd known him as he conjured his response. Predictably, he lied and told her that it had just started.

I was fed up with the lies, so I found the courage to speak the truth. Before he could continue, I interrupted him and looked into her eyes, "Brittany, let me explain."

Mr. Strait didn't let me get a word out. He snapped, razor-sharp, "Shut your damn suck, freshman Lucho." His eyes locked onto mine—cold, unblinking—a silent threat not to defy him.

"What are you afraid he'll tell me?" Brittany intercepted. She paused and stared into my eyes. "Tell me the truth," she demanded, her eyes searching mine for answers.

I drew in a slow breath, forcing myself to steady the shaking inside my chest before speaking.

"Fuck you, Mr. Strait," I said, my voice trembling with pent-up anger and exhaustion. "I'm tired of being your bitch. Today, the truth's going to come to light because it always does. And I don't give a damn who you tell that I'm gay, because if you do, I'll tell everyone that you are as well."

They both stood there in stunned silence. Mr. Strait's face contorted with a mix of fury and fear, his carefully constructed facade beginning to crumble.

I proceeded to reveal the truth. "Brittany, his betrayal and abuse have been happening for months. After our three-way last semester—which you helped initiate—he started calling me to his room. Then he raped me on Halloween night, leaving me torn apart both mentally and physically. The weekly calls have continued ever since. I'm sorry you're hearing this now."

As soon as the words left my mouth, Brittany's expression turned from disbelief to devastation. Tears streamed down her face as she stared at me. For a brief moment, I thought she might faint, but instead, she turned her fury on me. Brittany lunged toward me, her hands shaking with anger, and struck me with slaps across my face and chest.

The force of the blows stunned me, and I stumbled backward, clutching my face in shock. But Brittany wasn't finished. She continued to rain blows down on me, swinging wildly as anger overtook her.

I recoiled, shocked by her sudden outburst, but before I could react, she grabbed my shoulders and stared into my eyes with a fiery intensity.

"I told you in Fort Worth how much I loved Ari—he's my

everything—and I can't bear the thought of losing him. You knew what you were doing, freshman Lucho, and you lied to my face. You lied to my face."

I denied her accusation. "I didn't lie to you on that dance floor, Brittany. I told you that I never saw him with another woman, and that was the truth. I couldn't tell you what was going on between us because his retaliation would be severe, and you know this! He would report me for being gay and end my military career." She looked down and paused as she processed what I said.

Mr. Strait saw an opening to manipulate the narrative. With a calm and calculated tone, he shifted the blame onto Brittany, playing on her emotions and vulnerabilities.

He twisted the truth, telling her that her choices had pushed him into all of this. He insinuated that it was her idea to invite me into their bed that fateful night after the pep rally, and that he had been left unsatisfied because she'd insisted on withholding sex until marriage.

Mr. Strait played the victim, painting himself as a man whose needs weren't being met by his girlfriend. He went on to suggest that Brittany should be grateful that he hadn't cheated on her with another woman, assuring her that she was the only one he loved.

Once again, deceptive words masked his true intentions. He knew exactly how to twist the knife, leaving Brittany confused and uncertain. "You're my girl, Brittany, and I love you. Please forgive me," he pleaded, his voice a masterful blend of sincerity and desperation.

Seeing her falter stunned me; his manipulation was working. She was caught in his web, her eyes flickering with a mixture of anger and uncertainty.

As Mr. Strait's manipulative tactics tightened around her, I felt baffled. How could she still be slipping toward him after everything she'd just heard?

It was as if she was under some sort of spell, unable to see the truth right in front of her.

"Brittany, don't listen to this snake," I urged, trying to cut through his lies. "He is lying. You know the truth." But my words seemed to bounce off an invisible barrier.

"I love you, Brittany," Mr. Strait repeated, his voice dripping with false sincerity. "We can get through this together. Just give me a chance."

Her expression softened, and a cold dread settled in my gut. Then Brittany directed a pointed question at Mr. Strait, one that cut to the heart of the matter.

"What if he gave you AIDS?" she asked, disgust sharpening every word. "His kind have been dying all over the news because of the AIDS epidemic. It's God's doing—because his kind are an abomination."

Her words hit me like a sledgehammer, and my body went cold. It was a hateful and hurtful thing to say, but I wasn't surprised given her cruelty.

Despite the anger rising inside me, I refused to let her words break me. With firm resolve, I turned to her and said, "Brittany, it's not surprising to hear how you really feel about me and the gay community at large, but this isn't about disease or divine punishment. This is about his lies and manipulation. Oh, and by the way, you don't have to worry about Mr. Strait because I don't have AIDS. And in case you missed it, he is one of my kind whether you want to accept it or not."

Mr. Strait, his facade of control slipping, told me to shut my mouth. But Brittany stood her ground, crossing her arms in defiance.

"How do you know that you don't have AIDS?" she demanded. "Answer me!"

I disclosed to them that I got tested in Houston during winter break—the results came back negative. "And I have only been with Mr. Strait since my last test. If I do have HIV or AIDS, then the only way I could have it is if he gave it to me."

Mr. Strait snapped, "Enough—both of you. I don't have

HIV or AIDS, and for the record, freshman Lucho is the only guy I've ever been with. So let's stop dragging this AIDS nonsense into the conversation and move the hell on."

The tension in the room became unbearable, and I needed to leave. I needed to wash off Mr. Strait's sweat and odor, all of it clinging to me like a film.

"I'm done here," I said. "You're both twisted and belong together. Brittany, I'm sorry I didn't tell you the whole truth in Fort Worth. But you need to understand that he has been using my sexual orientation as leverage against me, and I've been afraid of what he might do to me since I met him. But the fear and your hold on me end today."

I briskly walked between them toward the hatch and as I reached for the knob, Brittany had to have the last word. "Ari and I are cut from the same cloth, freshman Lucho," she said, her words dripping with venom. "You don't know what I'm capable of doing either."

Her words hung in the air like a dark cloud, leaving me with a sense of dread and unease. Whether it was a threat or a warning, it sank deep. And what would happen next?

After a long, scalding hot shower, I returned to my room and locked the hatch, feeling like a prisoner in my own dorm. As I ate my cold pizza and listened to Annie Lennox's Diva CD on my boombox, I couldn't shake the feeling that I was on borrowed time.

In bed that night, my mind was filled with conflicting emotions and questions, each one carrying its own weight of uncertainty and fear. Would Mr. Strait retaliate? Would Brittany's threat materialize into something more menacing? What would Justin and Richard think of me? What would become of my friendships with the rest of my classmates and Mac if they discovered my sexuality? How would my family react?

The weight of it all felt suffocating. I grappled with a sense of alienation, an overwhelming feeling of being an outsider in a world that didn't want me as I truly was. The

Corps and my military dreams, once sources of pride and aspiration, had become a nightmare.

14 THE TAINTED CELEBRATION

With the spring banquet on the horizon, a current of excitement swept across the mile, contagious and impossible to ignore. This marked one of the final milestones in our freshman journey. The Corps was buzzing with energy, eager to claim bragging rights for the year ahead. The stakes were high, with awards and recognition on the line, and the race was on to see which company would come out on top. P-Company was determined to take the crown.

Despite the festive atmosphere, I couldn't shake the feeling that something sinister was brewing in the days leading up to the banquet. Celebration loses its sweetness when intuition whispers that danger is already at the door.

My gut told me that something was off. Mr. Strait, the once voracious and abusive figure who had summoned me to his room on multiple occasions, had been curiously silent since Brittany's discovery. And the rumors of a rift between him and Brittany, his twisted debutante, had yet to be confirmed.

Instead of getting tangled in a negative thought spiral, I poured all my energy into Justin. He had worked tirelessly to earn the highest honor in our company's freshman class and was notified in advance so that he could invite his family.

Master Sergeant granted liberty at noon on Friday, earlier than normal. Several of my classmates had reserved hotel rooms for the weekend, including my bunkmate.

Richard reserved a room for him and Becky so that Marisol and I could stay in the dorm.

Justin and Kate also planned to stay in the dorm. I repeatedly reminded myself to be excited—and part of me truly was—to finally meet her in person. But underneath that, there was a little envy I couldn't deny. Kate was undoubtedly the love of his life. And while I tried to be happy for them, a part of me still hurt.

Marisol drove in from Austin and met me at the dorm with curlers in her hair, her dress, and an overnight bag in tow. As Marisol and I caught up and got ready, I tried to focus on her stories about exams and life in Austin, but my mind drifted back to Justin's constant chatter about Kate.

I decided to shine my shoes one more time while Marisol curled her long, brown hair. Soon after, Justin knocked before opening the hatch and poking his head into the room. "Mauricio… Marisol… are you two decent?" he whispered.

"Get in here, crazy!" I chuckled. The moment had arrived, and my feelings instantly changed when I saw her. I couldn't help but smile as he introduced us to Kate. She was exquisite, with a regal appearance and calming presence that made me feel instantly at ease.

Justin began the introductions with a gracious tone. "Kate, allow me to introduce the wonderful Marisol—Mauricio's girlfriend, whom I've spoken so much about. She attends Capital College, our archrival, but let's not hold that against her."

I set my shoe and rag down on the deck and rose to my feet. Kate greeted Marisol with a warm hug.

Then she turned to me, eyes bright, and said with a playful smile, "Mauricio, I started to doubt you were real. I've been anticipating this moment for almost two semesters."

Her words instantly disarmed me. All I could do was smile. There she was—the girl Justin loved—and she made me feel like we were old friends.

She approached me with graceful warmth, arms open and eyes glowing with kindness. As we embraced, her voice landed softly in my ear.

"Mauricio, it's truly a pleasure to finally meet Justin's dearest classmate in person."

When she pulled back, she looked into my eyes with a serene smile.

"After everything I've heard from Justin, I feel like I already know you. I've imagined this moment more times than I can count, and I'm genuinely so happy it's finally here."

What else could I say? "The feeling is mutual, Kate. It's wonderful to finally meet you in person. You're exactly as Justin has always described." She was a gorgeous brunette with crystal blue eyes, tall and slender with long, straight hair past her shoulders. Her angelic face had delicate features.

A quick glance at Justin revealed that signature smile, the kind that said everything without a single word. In that silent exchange, I could practically hear him say, "Told you so." And he was right.

I asked Kate about the drive with Justin's family, and her soft laugh carried a playful wit. "The drive from Fort Worth was a bit long," she said, "but I managed to sneak in a nap while Mrs. Fischer drove." Then she leaned in slightly, her eyes gleaming. "They're so excited to see you, Mauricio. Honestly, I think they might be more thrilled to see you than to watch Justin receive his award."

She paused just long enough for the teasing to land, then turned to Justin with a smirk. "I'm kidding, honey. Mostly."

After everyone laughed, Marisol cracked the whip and reminded us to get ready for the banquet. "Time check, folks. I'm almost done with my makeup, and then I need help with the dress. Mauricio and crew, you need to start getting dressed as well."

Justin snapped to attention and gave an exaggerated salute. "Aye, aye, ma'am," he replied. "Clearly your time with Mauricio in JROTC didn't wear off. We'll hustle—it won't take us long to get dressed, promise."

Before they hurried off to change, I let them know that Marisol and I would swing by Justin's room to pick them up. I wanted the four of us to walk to the banquet together and arrive side by side.

Marisol commented on how quickly I had gotten ready, but I could tell from her tone that she saw right through me—she said I looked distracted. As I helped her zip up her dress, she didn't dance around the subject. She directly asked me, "How are you really feeling after finally meeting Kate?"

I took a deep breath, trying to find the right words. "If I'm being honest, there's a part of me that feels devastated. It's the simplest way to describe it. But I've known that Justin isn't like me—he's not gay. Still, that doesn't change the fact that he loves me, just in his own way, and that love has meant more than I can put into words." I looked at Marisol, my voice softer now. "And I'm equally grateful for you—for your love, your friendship, and your presence right now. I'll be okay. Truly. Thank you for being here with me."

I asked Marisol, "Do you think Kate understands that Justin loves me?"

Marisol grinned confidently. "My love, she knows. A woman always knows. He lights up when he sees you, and he always has. I could see it in her eyes. I guarantee that she is feeling a little heartbroken too. But you bring him joy and have made this hell of a year tolerable for him. You two have been a blessing to each other."

I smiled at Marisol. "You look absolutely breathtaking. Once again, you're going to steal the show."

We hugged and then made our way down the passageway to meet Justin and Kate.

During our descent to the ground floor, Justin suggested that we switch partners on the way to the banquet so he could talk to Marisol, and I could spend more time with Kate. I chuckled and agreed, mentioning that Kate's sexy, strappy high heels would make her tower over me.

As we exited the dorm, Marisol took Justin's arm and Kate took mine. They quickly broke ahead of us, and I suspected that Justin intentionally sped away with Marisol to give me and Kate some privacy. "Slow down, you two," I shouted after them.

Kate gave my hand a gentle squeeze, her tone both reassuring and lighthearted. "Don't worry about them, Mauricio. Let's take our time. These heels are new, and I swear they're already conspiring against me." She glanced down at her shoes, then met my eyes again, her expression softening into something more serious. "But really—I'm glad it's just us for a moment."

"Mauricio, I've pictured this moment for months—truly. Where do I even begin?" She smiled, her eyes shining with sincerity. "Among all of Justin's classmates, you're the one he speaks of most. You're the most special to him. He's told me, more than once, that if it hadn't been for you, he would've walked away from his scholarship and the Corps. I hope you know how much you mean to him. He loves you in a special and unique way."

I came to an abrupt stop. Kate stopped beside me, her expression curious but calm. I then turned to her. "He told you that he loves me, and you're... you're comfortable with that?"

"Absolutely, Mauricio," Kate replied without a moment's hesitation. "He's told me on several occasions, and I'm genuinely grateful he's had you by his side this year. He gives you full credit for helping him tolerate freshman year and for being the one who steadied him when everything felt like too much. The bond you two share—it's something he deeply cherishes. And, honestly, so do I."

Her sincerity meant more to me than she could have known. I never imagined that she would describe Justin's true feelings for me.

I hesitated for a second, searching for the right words. Then I finally said, "Kate, I really do love Justin—more than I've ever loved any man. And no matter what, I'll always want what's best for him. That's you. I'm honestly happy that you have each other."

"I know you do," Kate said softly. "I know your love for him runs deeper than friendship—it's something rare and beautiful. And the truth is, he's incredibly lucky. Not many people get to be loved so fully by two people who are truly devoted to him." Her expression was gentle as she leaned in to embrace me.

Our embrace was abruptly interrupted when Justin called out for us to hurry up. I glanced ahead and saw that several of our classmates and their dates had already gathered in front of the dining hall, waiting for us to join them for a grand entrance.

Kate and I joined the group, and we entered the hall. Justin and I escorted the ladies to their seats before he requested that I accompany him to say hello to his family, who were seated in the VIP section at the front of the hall. Without hesitation, I gladly accepted, excited to see Mrs. Fischer, Jeff, and Jenn.

Jeff ran over to hug Justin before we reached the table. While they hugged, I pulled out Mrs. Fischer's chair, and she greeted me with a firm embrace.

Mrs. Fischer's eyes shimmered with pride when I congratulated her—the kind of pride that can only come from watching your son be recognized as the top freshman in our company, and maybe even the entire Corps. I looked into her bright blue eyes and said, "It's so nice to see you, again. And congratulations, Mrs. Fischer. You've raised a future Marine Corps general."

Before we could say more, Justin leaned in, his voice full

of playful urgency. "Okay, enough, you two. Let me hug my mom and give her a kiss—we need to get back to our table."

An unsettling wave of discomfort rushed through me as we made our way back to the table. Then I saw the source—Mr. Strait's piercing gaze locked onto us from the neighboring table. The discomfort elevated further when my eyes shifted and landed on Brittany, seated beside him. There she was, composed and seemingly untouched by everything that had happened between us in his room—as if none of it had ever occurred. The sight of them together was shocking.

How could she have possibly forgiven him so easily? The reality was disturbing. She likely shifted all the blame onto me, refusing to own up to her actions in our entanglement. And the thought lingered—would she seek revenge against me in the future? The uncertainty gnawed at me.

After we took our seats next to each other, Brittany startled me when she appeared behind us, wrapping her arms around both Justin and me in a fictitious display of friendship. Justin, unaware of the extent of my relationship with Brittany and Mr. Strait, responded politely, wishing them both an enjoyable evening.

I waited for Brittany to return to her chair before I looked over at Mr. Strait's reaction. His displeasure was evident, and it wasn't hard to make out what he muttered to her, "What the fuck was that?"

The banquet started, and I was impressed by the number of servers present. The atmosphere was formal and elegant, and the Corps chaplain led us in prayer before the first course was served. As we ate, the clink of cutlery, shouts, and laughter filled the hall.

For the main course, we had our pick between a slice of roast beef or a roasted chicken breast, both served alongside mashed potatoes and steamed vegetables. I will admit, I had braced myself for the usual bland, rubbery banquet food, but we agreed that it was far better than we expected.

Conversations flowed easily around our table. When dessert arrived—platters of cake slices and cookies—everyone seemed to savor each bite. Everyone, that is, except for Justin because of his dietary restrictions.

After we completed the final course, the commandant of the Corps rose to the stage to extend his welcome and deliver his address. The next speaker began handing out awards, and we erupted with cheers when we learned that P-Company had won the award for outstanding company of the year.

As Company Commander received the trophy, my mind drifted to his drunken message after hell night. My disappointment in him overshadowed what should have been a glorious moment.

The announcement of the outstanding freshmen by company brought a wave of excitement, peaking when Justin's name was called for P-Company. As he made his way to the stage, Kate beamed with pride, and Marisol nudged me, whispering, "Try not to be so obvious. You're glowing more than she is."

Finally, when they announced the top freshman in the class of 1999, the moment felt electric. The second Justin's name echoed through the dining hall, we jumped to our feet and exploded in cheers! My chest swelled with emotion—I couldn't have been prouder of him.

We continued to applaud and cheer while Justin returned to our table. Without hesitation, he threw his arms around me in a tight hug. I told him that I was proud of him, and he replied, "I couldn't have survived freshman year without you." After he hugged Kate, our classmates and several upperclassmen congratulated him.

As we wrapped up, word spread from the upperclassmen to gather in front of the dining hall—Company Commander had a message for us.

As instructed, we assembled around Company

Commander. He held up the award for the best company of the year and proudly declared, "You earned this! We showed everyone that P-Company is the best. And freshman Fischer, you made us all proud today."

Company Commander was visibly emotional as he took a deep breath and continued to speak. His voice cracked, but he composed himself and asked us a question before we headed back to the dorm to continue the festivities, "Who is the number one company in the Corps?"

We shouted our cheer at the top of our lungs, and it echoed across the entire mile. Onlookers waited for us to finish before continuing to shout their congratulations.

Back at the dorm, kegs were set up in the heads and everyone was ready to celebrate. My classmates and I reminisced over the past two semesters, and our guests enjoyed hearing the stories. Justin and I were inseparable, once again, with Kate and Marisol by our sides.

Hours passed, and when the time came, folks began to retreat to their rooms and hotels. The festivities couldn't go past midnight or else the campus police would show up. I gave Mrs. Fischer a huge hug before she left with the kids. Marisol and I headed to my room as the passageway lights were turned off.

Marisol was exhausted and told me that she was going to change into my boxer shorts and t-shirt, brush her teeth, and jump into the rack. I stood in front of my hatch to give her some privacy and took the moment to soak in the silence of the empty passageway.

My heart skipped a beat the moment Justin stepped out of his room. Without hesitation, he walked straight toward me and pressed his forehead against mine. His voice was low, meant for me alone, as he whispered, "If our ladies weren't here, I'd crash with you tonight." His words sent a flutter through my chest, and despite everything, I couldn't help but feel a rush of excitement.

I laughed and told him to return to Kate, but a part of

me longed to be with him. He looked at me with a hint of sadness in his eyes and said, "I'm not joking, freshman Lucho," before he turned to walk away. I watched him fade into the dimly lit passageway.

As I brushed my teeth and looked in the vanity mirror, I replayed the talk with Kate and Justin's words after receiving his awards. They were the kind of moments I would carry for the rest of my life.

Marisol was asleep when I climbed into the rack next to her. After I drifted off to sleep, I was jolted awake by blood-curdling screams echoing from the passageway. Marisol shook me hard, her eyes wide with terror. "Mauricio, oh my God, what's happening out there? That's Kate! I know it is!" Her voice was filled with panic.

I leaped out of bed and threw on a shirt. We raced to the door, flung it open, and peered out into the dimly lit passageway. Kate was standing there, screaming hysterically.

"Mauricio, Mauricio, anyone, please help Justin!" she cried.

Marisol and I ran down the passageway while puzzled faces peered out from open doors. When we reached her, Kate sobbed, her voice breaking between gasps. "I woke up and found Justin seizing on the floor!" Kate explained, her voice shaking with panic. "Then I called 911—but he won't stop! He won't stop seizing! Please, Mauricio, do something—please go inside and help him! I don't know what else to do!"

I ran into Justin's room and saw that he was lying on the ground, covered in foamy vomit and blood. He was still seizing. I looked around for any clues and noticed that an opened care package filled with cookies and desserts was on his desk. Nothing else seemed out of the ordinary.

Marisol joined me in the room and gasped, "Oh my god, oh my god, oh my god."

I told her to grab towels and help me turn Justin on his

side to clear his airway.

Seconds later, Master Sergeant entered the room and asked, "How long has it been?"

Kate replied that she had dozed off while Justin was eating cookies from the care package that I had delivered to his room during the banquet. When she woke up, he was on the floor seizing and bleeding from a gash in his forehead.

"I didn't send a care package," I shouted when suddenly ambulance lights lit up the mile. Master Sergeant ordered, "Clear the damn passageway. The paramedics are coming up."

The paramedics rushed into the room. With urgency, they lifted Justin onto a stretcher, and Kate and I instinctively flanked his sides, desperate to stay with him.

"Marisol, please—find Richard and tell him to meet us at the county hospital!" I implored. My mind raced, but I forced myself to focus. "And someone—anyone—find Justin's mom. She has to know what's happened!" Justin's family needed to be informed without delay.

Master Sergeant, amidst the chaos, inquired, "Does anyone know where his family is staying?" Kate quickly responded, "The University Inn on Texas!"

Master Sergeant replied that he would contact the family and then head to the hospital. I also heard him say that we needed to locate and inform Company Commander.

As we stepped out of McKibbin Hall, I tried to reassure Kate. "Justin's one of the strongest people I've ever known. He'll pull through. I believe that. Try not to worry."

The paramedics led us to the alley that dead-ended at the back of our dorm. Upon arriving at the ambulance, we were informed that there was only room for one person to ride with Justin. Without hesitation, Kate offered to ride up front, leaving me to ride with Justin.

On our way to the hospital, I held onto Justin's leg, which

had stopped trembling. The paramedics worked diligently to resuscitate him, but despite their efforts, he didn't regain consciousness during the ride.

At the hospital, Kate and I were ushered into the room and told to stay back as the medical team surrounded Justin. They moved swiftly, intubating him and connecting him to the telemetry monitor. We stood side by side, frozen in place. Then, just as my hope began to fade, a single beep cut through the commotion. My knees nearly gave out, and I clutched Kate's hand. "Thank God," I cried, tears welling in my eyes, "He's still with us."

Members of our company gathered at the hospital, quietly waiting outside the room. When the family arrived, the staff invited them into the room and pulled Mrs. Fischer aside to speak with her.

A nurse approached me and Kate and gently asked, "Is there anything I can do for you right now?" Desperation filled my voice as I pleaded, "Please, just do everything you can to bring Justin back. Give him your absolute best care."

Moved by my plea, the nurse placed a hand on my shoulder. She promised to pray for Justin and assured us the entire medical team would do everything in their power to help him. Then, she offered us snacks and water and suggested we rest in the waiting area to be more comfortable.

But I couldn't bring myself to leave Justin's side—I had to stay, just in case he woke up. Kate stayed with me, without question.

We quietly stepped to Justin's bedside, each of us taking one of his hands. I didn't recite a formal prayer—I just spoke to God from the depth of my heart. "Dear Lord, please have mercy. Spare Justin, give him the chance to live the life he's meant for. He's the best of us, and he has so much left to give this world. If a price must be paid, let it be mine."

When I glanced at Kate, she reached across Justin's body and gently took my hand in hers. Her voice was barely audible as she whispered, "He'd say the same for you."

Seconds later, my eyes shifted to Mrs. Fischer and the medical team. The doctor spoke softly, but whatever he said struck like a sledgehammer—I saw it in her face. The light drained from her eyes, and her expression froze, sending a chill straight through me. Then, as if the weight of it all became too much to bear, Mrs. Fischer broke down. Her sobs were raw, uncontrollable, as she buried her face in trembling hands. The sight shattered what little hope I had left.

She cried out, her voice breaking with anguish. "No—no, this can't be! Lord Jesus, please, don't let this be real. Wake me up from this nightmare—I'm begging you!"

Jeff and Jenn rushed to her side, wrapping their arms around her as she uncontrollably sobbed and begged God to not take her son. Her desperate plea left me frozen.

Kate heard everything and began to sob. By the looks of things, they had all lost hope. But I refused to give up on my best friend.

I leaned in close and pleaded, "Please, Justin... open your eyes. Everyone's here, mortified and pulling for you. We need you. I need you to open your eyes."

The weight of memory hit me—what he'd once told me about his dad—and my voice cracked as I begged again. "Please don't answer God's call, Justin. It's not your time, my friend. Please... just open your eyes."

Mrs. Fischer walked over to me and Kate, her steps unsteady. She reached for my hand, her fingers trembling, her eyes filled with unspeakable sorrow. Her voice broke as she spoke the words I had dreaded.

"Mauricio... Kate... it's every mother's worst nightmare. The doctors—they just told me Justin isn't going to make it. My baby... my beautiful boy... he had a severe reaction to something he ate. He's always been so careful because he's deathly allergic to peanuts. But this time... this time, he went too long without oxygen. They've done all they can.

He's… he's brain-dead now. These machines—they're the only thing keeping him here. The damage… it's irreversible."

The news struck me like electricity, and the room seemed to spin around me. Before I could even catch my breath, Kate's anguished cry shattered the air.

"No! No—this can't be happening!" she sobbed. "We're supposed to get married! We had our lives planned—he wants a big family… we were going to build that together! Please, no, not Justin… not like this!"

Then Mrs. Fischer cried out, "First my loving husband and now my darling son. Lord, why have you forsaken me?" In a burst of emotion, she threw herself on top of Justin. "I have to hear my son's heart beating." Jeff and Jenn wept. Kate walked over to the foot of the bed and watched with tears rolling down her face.

After a few minutes, Mrs. Fischer rose, her voice barely holding together. "They're going to turn off the life support. Please ask everyone to come in," she said, and a wave of grief rippled through the room. One of the nurses opened the door and invited everyone into the room.

One by one, our classmates and upperclassmen stepped forward to say goodbye, but no one could bring themselves to leave. By the time the last man spoke, we were all packed tightly into that cold, sterile space. The room felt heavy with sorrow, as if the walls themselves were straining under the weight of so many broken hearts. Even the hospital staff stood still, heads bowed, sharing in the agony.

The nurse turned off the machines, and the beeping instantly began to slow. Mrs. Fischer held the cross on her necklace and began reciting the Our Father. Everyone joined her in prayer, and I could barely speak through my tears. I held Justin's hand—it was still warm—but I knew his life was slipping away in those final moments.

Shortly after we finished the prayer, the steady beep of the monitors fell silent—his heart had stopped. It felt as if time froze. I stood there, numb, watching myself place a trembling hand over his chest. His body was still, his spirit gone. I swear I felt his soul slip away.

I hugged Mrs. Fischer and told her, "You gave Justin a wonderful life, and he loved and appreciated you beyond words. I'm so sorry for your loss and please know that I'll love him and cherish my memories of him for the rest of my life."

With tears streaming down my face, I stumbled towards the corner of the room, feeling completely empty and alone. Marisol and Kate rushed to my side, offering their support as we watched everyone else pay their respects to Justin's grieving family.

After our classmates, upperclassmen, and the medical team left the room, I turned to Mrs. Fischer, his siblings, and the girls, and softly asked, "May I please have a moment with him to say goodbye?"

Mrs. Fischer nodded, her eyes red and swollen from sobbing. She led everyone out of the room, leaving me alone with Justin's lifeless body.

I sat on the edge of the bed and took his hand in mine. I couldn't believe what had happened—that my best friend was gone forever. I would never see his piercing hazel eyes or beautiful smile again.

"My dear friend," I whispered. "You were supposed to be a general—and you would have been an exceptional one. You had my back when others didn't. You showed me unconditional friendship and love."

I would carry him with me for the rest of my life.

As I looked up, tears streaming down my face, I angrily shouted, "Lord, how could you allow this to happen? Why couldn't you have mercy on Justin—on Mrs. Fischer and the kids?"

Suddenly, there was a knock at the door, and Marisol walked in to join me. She wrapped her arms around me and rested her cheek on my back. She cried with me. I asked her,

"This isn't a nightmare, is it?" And she confirmed, "No, my love. I'm so sorry that this isn't a nightmare."

Then she placed a hand on my arm, her voice soft but steady. "Mauricio, we need to go. You've been up all night, and you have to get some rest." She glanced toward the hallway where Company Commander had been speaking, then added, "I overheard him saying they're planning a final roll call for Justin on the mile. Sounds like the whole Corps will be there. They want everyone back at the dorm by 1700 hours on Sunday."

Tears welled up in my eyes as I pleaded, "I'm not ready to leave him, Marisol. I don't want to leave him here alone and in the cold." Marisol reassured me to take my time and that she would be waiting for me in the car.

I leaned over Justin's still body and ran my fingers through his hair, making little circles as I caressed his scalp because I knew that it relaxed him.

My final kiss touched his forehead, and the only words left in me slipped out: "Rest in peace, brother. Rest in peace, my love. Please visit me in my dreams."

When I walked out of the hospital, I froze. The last two people I ever expected to see were standing there—Brittany and Mr. Strait, locked in a heated argument. As I stared, my eyes were drawn to Brittany. She looked like she was unraveling right there on the sidewalk—her hair and makeup were disheveled, and her face was pale and strained, as if she hadn't slept. Seeing her like that filled me with a deep, uneasy dread.

The loss of a childhood friend and neighbor was undoubtedly taking a toll on her, but there was something else. I boldly shouted out, "What are you doing here, Brittany?" But as the words left my mouth, I realized that I already knew the answer. She stood there, linked to the tragedy of Justin's death in some way.

Brittany sounded distraught when she babbled, "I need to speak with you, Mauricio." Then tears began to stream down her cheeks. Once again, I sensed that she had something awful to reveal.

Slowly, the words spilled out, heavy with guilt. "I'm so sorry, Mauricio... I never meant for any of this. I swear, I never imagined it would end like this. Justin... he was only supposed to get a little sick. I didn't think—I couldn't have imagined—it would go this far."

Brittany's words hit me like a ton of bricks. She had revealed what I'd already suspected—that she had something to do with Justin's death. My mind reeled. What did she mean by "a little sick"?

Then it hit me—the care package on Justin's desk, the one Kate thought was from me had to be from Brittany. That evil, spiteful witch had intentionally poisoned him with peanut-laced treats, all to hurt me.

Rage detonated inside me, fast and crippling. The words burst out before I could stop them. "What the fuck are you saying, Brittany? What do you mean he was only supposed to get a little sick? Are you telling me you did this? You're the reason he's gone? What the fuck did you do?"

Brittany fidgeted with her hands and looked away from me, as if searching for an escape. The sight only fueled my rage. I demanded to know the truth. "Look at me, Brittany. Did you send that care package to Justin knowing that its contents would hurt him? Was this your twisted way of getting back at me because of Mr. Strait? Tell me the damn truth."

As rage continued to consume me, I remembered the first time Mami explained the hidden power inside one of her dichos, warning me to use it only when truly warranted: "Como te ves, me vi; como me ves, te verás."—how you appear, I appeared; how you see me, you will see yourself. It was more than a saying. It was a reckoning, passed down through generations, meant to remind anyone who caused harm that justice always finds its way back. Growing up, I'd heard Mami whisper it when someone had crossed a line, and I believed—deep down—that it carried weight.

In the heat of my fury, the words tore out of me before I could stop them. The moment they left my mouth, something surged through me—not magic, but something older, fiercer, ancestral—making the hair on my arms stand on end. Brittany and Mr. Strait didn't understand the words, but their reactions told me they felt their force. I saw it in the way their bodies went still, as if the air itself had shifted and the weight of what I'd said had gripped their throats.

My rage boiled over, and I lunged toward her. But Mr. Strait stepped between us, his voice stern and commanding. "Freshman Lucho, return to the dorm immediately," he ordered, "and keep your mouth shut about what she said. That includes your little beard waiting in the parking lot. Be in your room when I call you at 1800 hours, and don't make me come looking for you."

I had no choice but to comply. But before I left, I looked into her eyes one last time. The pain, the fury, the heartbreak—it all poured out in a few words. "You will know my pain soon. I promise." Then I turned and walked away.

The car door slammed shut behind me. Confused and concerned, Marisol looked at me and asked, "What's going on, Mauri? What did they tell you? Are you okay?"

I took deep breaths to calm myself down. "I don't even know where to begin," I responded. "But I need time to process everything that just happened. I'll explain when we get to the dorm room."

Brittany's revelation replayed in my mind while Marisol drove us back to the dorm. What should have been a celebratory and momentous weekend had transformed into the most tragic of my life. And with a growing sense of unease, I knew it wasn't over.

15 BOOTS AND UTES AT DAWN

Mr. Strait didn't call at 1800 like he said he would. Instead, he burst through my hatch unannounced, startling me so hard I nearly jumped out of my skin. Marisol was out picking up dinner—meaning he had been watching. Waiting. Listening for the exact moment I would be alone. He knew. He always knew.

At first, he just stood there, his face unreadable. Stoic. Cold. His eyes darted past me, scanning the room for threats, or maybe just avoiding mine. Or maybe... he was looking straight through me. Something in me stiffened; the air shifted.

The moment he said we were leaving the mile for a private conversation sent a chill up my spine. To "blow off steam," he claimed we would run to the obstacle course to talk. But deep down, something felt off—this run wasn't just about cooling down or clearing our heads.

His tone left no room for argument as he ordered, "You're going to meet me behind McKibbin Hall at 0430 sharp. Full boots and utes. And listen carefully—you don't tell a soul that we're meeting or where we're going. Not your girlfriend. Not your bunkmate. No one. Do you understand me?" I nodded to show that I understood despite feeling uncomfortable.

He walked to my hatch, looked both ways down the passageway to ensure the coast was clear, and turned around to tell me one more time, "0430 hours, boots and utes, not a word to anyone. Be there. And don't be late.

Understood?"

I nodded, once again, too afraid to do anything else.

The moment he disappeared, I sat on the edge of my rack, my mind racing.

What was waiting for me out there in the early morning darkness? Why the secrecy? A knot of dread tightened in my gut—something was seriously wrong.

The meeting at the obstacle course felt out of nowhere, hastily invented. I suspected that it was connected to what Brittany had done. But why? What was Mr. Strait's real endgame? And just how far was he willing to go to cover up Brittany's wrongdoing?

It wasn't long before Marisol returned. There were a couple soft taps on the hatch, and she slipped inside and quietly closed the hatch behind her. She came in with her usual warm smile, but the second her eyes met mine, that smile faded. Her expression shifted instantly. Without saying a word, I pressed a finger gently to my lips, urging her to stay silent, and motioned for her to sit beside me on the edge of the bed.

I leaned in close, my voice dropping to barely a whisper as I switched to Spanish—it felt safer that way. "I have to explain what happened to Justin, but I have to start from the very beginning... and tell you things I've never told anyone."

Marisol's entire body froze, and her eyes locked onto mine.

Bit by bit, I began revealing every disturbing encounter with Mr. Strait: the time in the shower with two upperclassman nearby, the night of the threesome with Brittany, the night of the rape that I had buried deep, and countless times that he summoned me to his room to have his way with me. Marisol didn't interrupt once. Her body was still, but her eyes were widening, flicking back and forth as if trying to keep up, to make sense of it all.

Marisol was visibly shaken—she was right to be alarmed

by the revelations. The moment I paused, her questions came fast, frantic, spilling from her lips like water bursting through a dam, and I had no answers.

"Why didn't you tell me, Mauricio?"

"What kind of monster is Mr. Strait?"

"Why didn't anyone say anything? Richard? Justin? Mac? Someone had to have seen something!"

Each question was a cut, slicing into the guilt I had buried for months. Why had I suffered in silence, brushing off the treatment and pain as just part of the challenge of making it through the Corps as a gay man?

When Marisol calmed down, I revealed Brittany's twisted plan. A plan not just to hurt me, but to weaponize Justin's trust and vulnerability as part of her revenge.

I explained how Brittany had sent a care package with desserts to Justin's room under my name to poison him. Marisol didn't know how severe Justin's allergy to peanuts actually was, but Brittany knew all too well.

Slowly piecing together the possible plot, I continued, "Marisol, I suspect that young Brittany overheard her dad talking about what happened to Justin during that awful summer at camp. I can just picture her, eavesdropping while he told the whole story to her mom after getting home—soaking up every detail about Justin's near-death experience and his allergy. I also suspect that she filed away what she heard that day and when the time came, she knew exactly how to use it against him... and against me."

Marisol's voice trembled with anger. "That's insane. How could that debutant bitch do that to someone she's known since childhood? Why, Mauricio? Why would she even think of doing something so cruel?" She didn't hesitate, her tone turning fierce. "You need to call the police—now."

Instead of answering her about the police, I pressed on—laying it all out. I explained Brittany's twisted plan to catch Mr. Strait cheating... only she expected to find him with another woman. I let out a slow sigh. "She got the shock of her life when she unlocked the hatch and found him with me."

"No… no, Mauricio—are you serious?" she whispered, almost breathless. "She caught him fucking you and did all of this… for that? To get revenge against you when Mr. Strait played an equal part in your messed up affair. That's sick."

She leaned in closer, her hands gripping mine as if to steady herself. "That son of a bitch came to see you after I left for dinner, didn't he? That's why you appeared to be in shock when I returned. Tell me what happened and don't leave anything out."

I told her Mr. Strait had something planned for early morning—a run to the obstacle course under the excuse of blowing off steam and having a private conversation. The way he framed it sounded routine, almost harmless. But the secrecy, the timing, the tone in his voice… none of it sat right with me.

Marisol didn't hold back. "Mauricio, you cannot go with him alone. We have no idea what he—or he and Brittany together—might be capable of doing to you. What if this isn't just about talking? What if they're planning something worse? They could try to hurt you and make it look like an accident."

"You're correct, Marisol. This run to the obstacle course does not feel right. Something's off—I feel it in my gut." I paused, then added, "I need your help. We've got to come up with a plan—something smart, something that'll keep me safe. Whatever Mr. Strait is up to, I can't walk into it without being prepared."

"After dinner," I said quietly, "I need you to leave the dorm with your bag and dress—make it look like you're heading back to Austin."

"Get a room at our hotel," I continued, "the one we stayed at with Antoine when we went to watch the big game. Then tomorrow morning at 0430, go to the obstacle course."

She opened her mouth to protest, but I raised a hand to stop her.

"Don't park near the entrance. Find a spot far enough away so that your car won't be noticed. Stay hidden and watch everything. I need a witness, Marisol. In case something goes wrong. There's an emergency phone in a weatherproof box near the rappelling wall. Call for help if something goes wrong."

There was deep concern written across Marisol's face. She pleaded with me not to go, but I felt like I had to face Mr. Strait and hear him out. "I have to do this, Marisol," I said firmly. "And I'll do everything possible to take care of myself. I promise. Now let's eat before the food gets cold."

While we tried to eat dinner, my mind drifted into a spiral of worst-case scenarios. I couldn't shake the thought that Mr. Strait might try something—that he could use the run or the obstacle course as a chance to hurt me and make it look like an accident. The jungle course nearby was another perfect setup—steep drops, muddy ponds, blind spots everywhere. It wouldn't take much for something to "go wrong" out there.

After tossing out the plates and food containers in the trash, I stood still for a moment to steady myself beneath the weight of it all. When I turned, Marisol was watching me, full of worry. I took a breath and forced a small smile. "Hey," I said gently, stepping toward her. "It's time for you to head out. Let me help you get your things together."

I didn't need to say it aloud—she could hear what I was really trying to say, "I'll be okay. You don't need to worry."

While Marisol finished gathering her things, I retrieved an index card from my desk and scribbled down the combination to my padlock. "My journal is in the footlocker," I told her, handing her the card. "If anything happens to me… you'll know where to find it."

I paused for a second, then added, "Everything's in there, Marisol. Every twisted detail about what's happened with Brittany and Mr. Strait since the fall. What he did to me. What I'd buried for months. It's all in that journal."

I still needed to write about tonight—Strait's meeting, and what Brittany had confessed outside the hospital about Justin.

Marisol's hand trembled as she took the card from me. Her eyes glossed over almost instantly, and I saw the tears beginning to pool. We hugged each other tightly—no words, just the kind of embrace that says everything. I felt her arms wrap around me tighter, like if she held on long enough, she could somehow stop time. And for a second, I wanted that too.

I whispered in her ear, "Everything's going to be fine. I promise." I was scared, but I didn't want to add to her anxiety by sharing my fear.

"You can't promise that," Marisol said. "But promise me this—promise you'll fight and return. To me. To Antoine. To your family. Promise me you won't break your mother's heart."

She stepped closer, clutching my hands tightly. "If anything feels wrong, you run. You fight. You scream for help. Do whatever it takes, Mauricio—just come back to us."

All I could do was nod. I pulled her into one final hug. Then she turned, grabbed her things, and walked out.

I stood there in the middle of my room, alone, praying that it wouldn't be the last time I saw my childhood friend.

Until around midnight, I tossed and turned in the rack, caught in a storm of anticipation.

Desperate to quiet my mind, I focused on slowing my breathing, counting each inhale and exhale like a prayer. At last, sleep came—gentle and unexpected.

That was when I saw him. Justin appeared in my dream, radiant and full of life, like he had never left. He came with purpose, as if he had something important to say.

We were transported back to Houston, reliving the very moment when Justin had surprised me with the four engraved carabiners and rappelling rope. The delicate etching of my initials on one side, proudly accompanied by the emblem of "U.S.M.C." on the other. And there he stood, Justin, his gaze penetrating the depths of my soul.

"Mauricio," his voice echoed with a ghostly clarity, "You'll never be alone because I'm here for you, and will always be by your side, no matter what. Don't forget what I repeatedly told you, every time you climb or rappel, I'll be right there with you, ensuring your safety."

Overwhelmed with emotion, tears streamed down my face within the dream. I managed to whisper through my tears, "I won't forget that you're there to keep me safe, Justin. I won't forget. Wait… I'm not ready to go."

When I woke up, my cheeks were wet, and my pillow was damp—proof that the dream had stirred something deep inside me. My thoughts were still hazy, but one thing was crystal clear: Justin had found a way to reach me—to send a message from beyond.

It wasn't just a dream.

It was a warning.

And it hit with the force of certainty.

A vivid image of the obstacle course—its tower and rappelling wall—sharpened in my mind. My gut twisted with suspicion: Mr. Strait wasn't planning just a conversation.

Something darker was brewing.

I needed a plan. Not just any plan—one that put me two steps ahead. One that kept me alive.

I jolted upright and out of my rack to shut off my alarm just minutes before it could shatter the silence of 0330 hours. Time was precious, and I needed every minute—to get dressed, to steady my nerves, and to finish what could be my final journal entry.

Just as I turned on the desk lamp, another one of Mami's dichos came to me like a voice from home, wrapping around me like both a warning and a blessing: "Mucho mejor prepararse para lo peor, incluso cuando esperamos lo mejor."—we must prepare for the worst, even as we hope for the best. Its truth thudded through me, steady and undeniable. With danger closing in, I heard her voice as clearly as if she were beside me, and I braced myself—mentally, physically, emotionally—for whatever waited on the other side of my hatch.

I walked to the closet and reached for my utilities. The uniforms felt different that morning, heavier somehow, like they knew what was coming. The ritualistic act of getting dressed grounded me in the moment.

Justin's voice, or the memory of it, whispered through the silence, guiding me. I followed what I believed was his clue. I carefully tucked away a few small items into my utilities—nothing obvious, nothing Mr. Strait would easily detect if he tried to pat me down. These were my safeguards. They wouldn't stop a bullet, but they just might tilt the balance if Justin was right.

After I laced my boots, I retrieved my journal and sat down at my desk. I pressed it tightly against my chest—clutching it like I was hugging Mami. A part of me couldn't shake the fear that I was writing my last entry.

But when I opened the cover, the words came naturally, details flowed onto the paper. When I finished, I let myself reflect—not just on what brought me here, but on the people who carried me:

My parents, who loved me fiercely.

My brother, who taught me strength.

Marisol, always by my side.

Antoine, my day-one.

Justin... who changed my life.

Richard, Mac—all of them.

Their love and kindness stayed with me. They were the

reason I had to make it through.

When I first arrived at Texas F&E, hope burned bright. I arrived with dreams of growth, of making my family proud, of one day serving with honor. But nothing could have prepared me for the freshman year that followed—a year that rivaled hell, created a tangled web, unraveled secrets, blurred the lines between right and wrong, and changed the course of my life forever.

The red digits on the alarm clock flashed: 04:28.

It was time.

I slipped my journal into the footlocker and clicked the lock shut—a quiet but heavy sound that felt too final. Everything I had lived and endured during freshman year was inside those pages.

I walked to my hatch and whispered one last prayer.

"Lord, Abuelita, Justin... guide me. Watch over me."

Then I opened the hatch and stepped into the darkness— not knowing whether I'd return, but knowing I had to walk forward anyway.

16 THE INCIDENT REPORT

City of University Station Police Department
Incident Report for Case #1996-04-14
Incident Type: Attempted Murder/Homicide
Incident Day: Sunday
Date: 1996-04-14
Time: Approximately 0500 hours
Reporting Officer: [Name Redacted]
Details:

On Sunday, April 14, 1996, at approximately 0500 hours, officers with the University Station Police Department (USPD) were dispatched to the obstacle course at Texas Farming & Engineering University in response to a report of an attempted homicide and an individual found deceased at the scene.

Upon arrival, the first responding officer was met by a female witness, who directed the officer to the area near the base of the obstacle course's rappelling tower. The female witness then directed the officer's attention to the rappelling tower, where a male was observed hanging motionless from a rope, suspended approximately halfway down the structure. The subject appeared unconscious, and the University Station Fire Department (USFD) was requested to dispatch a ladder truck to assist with retrieval.

The witness then pointed out an unresponsive male lying on the ground at the base of the rappelling tower. The subject exhibited no signs of life. Additional emergency medical services were immediately requested through the

USFD.

The witness positively identified the individual suspended from the rope as Mauricio Lucho, a 19-year-old Hispanic male and freshman at Texas F&E. The male on the ground was identified as Ari Strait, a 20-year-old Caucasian male and sophomore at the same university.

According to the witness, Ari Strait allegedly pushed Mauricio Lucho off the top of the rappelling tower during a confrontation. The witness reported that immediately following this act, Mr. Strait appeared to lose his footing and accidentally fell from the tower, crashing head-first into the ground below.

The witness further stated that Mr. Lucho's fall was abruptly halted by a rope or harness system approximately halfway down the rappelling wall. The sudden stop and impact with the wall resulted in an apparent loss of consciousness.

Mr. Lucho was lowered to the ground by USFD personnel and transported by ambulance to the county hospital. His current condition is unknown at the time of this report.

This incident is currently under active investigation by the USPD as an attempted homicide. Preliminary information suggests that the victim and the deceased perpetrator were previously acquainted.

Anyone with information related to this case is urged to contact the USPD at 1-800-222-USPD.

17 FINAL ROLL CALL

Justin and Mr. Strait were raised since childhood to be cadets in the Corps at Texas F&E and military officers. On top of their similar destinies, they had spent countless days at football games with their families, envisioning their futures as students and cadets. Their parallel journeys saw them earn Marine Corps ROTC scholarships, join the Corps, and even join the same company, separated by just one year. In the end, both of their paths were abruptly cut short.

Rooted in deep-seated traditions, Texas F&E paid solemn tribute to fallen cadets through a ceremony known as the Final Roll Call. Against the backdrop of the mile, families and friends mourned the loss of their loved ones.

Sadly, I was unconscious for three days and missed the Final Roll Call held in honor of Justin. Marisol attended in my absence, and she later described the evening to me. Mrs. Fischer had invited her to sit with the family and Kate, giving her a close view of every detail of the ceremony.

Although Mr. Strait also met an untimely end— undoubtedly a tragedy for his loved ones—his name was never spoken aloud. Marisol described that it lingered like a shadow over the mile, heavy with disgrace. His family didn't attend the vigil, perhaps silently acknowledging the shame attached to his name. Being erased felt like a fair punishment for the pain he had caused so many.

Adorned in their formal dress uniforms, over 2,000 cadets gathered in formation on the mile, observing a 30-minute period of silence prior to sunset. Despite the massive number of people, Marisol described the mile as tranquil and somber.

The Final Roll Call was held in honor of Justin, and the P-Company Pirates took their designated position at the center of the mile. They stood in formation behind Justin's grieving family members, Kate, and Marisol, who sat facing the mile's flagpole and the eternal flame of the founder's memorial. From this solemn vantage point, the P-Company Pirates would conduct the final roll call.

Along the perimeter of the mile, thousands of non-ROTC students gathered to pay their respects. Every entrance to the mile, between the dormitories and other buildings, was filled with students standing several rows deep. The onlookers maintained silence, many clutching white candles, as they awaited the commencement of the ceremony after sunset.

Marisol painted an ethereal scene for me. The sun began its slow descent, casting long shadows across the campus as streaks of orange and pink bled into the darkening sky. With each passing moment, the light grew dimmer. Then, as if on cue, the solemn toll of the university tower bells echoed across the campus—each chime a mournful cry into the darkening sky, marking the beginning of the ceremony and honoring a life taken far too soon.

As the tears of family members and cadets fell around her, Marisol sat frozen and wept, consumed by confusion and grief. The prior seventy-two hours had unraveled into a nightmare. Her mind raced, trying to make sense of it all— what had happened, what could have been done differently. She ached for Justin's family, for Kate, for me, and for the classmates now left behind.

Instead of participating in the solemn Final Roll Call, P-Company should have been enjoying the end of the spring semester. The senior cadets ought to have been celebrating and reminiscing about their transformative four-year journey, cherishing the lifelong friendships they had forged.

For the freshman class of '99, it should have been a time of jubilation, marking the completion of the two most grueling semesters of their four-year crucible. Yet, their hearts were heavy with grief.

Mami later told me that during Final Roll Call, my family and Antoine waited anxiously in the county hospital. Mami, consumed by a mixture of grief and hope, fervently directed her prayers to God and her patron saint. She also pleaded for the guidance of her mother, my Abuelita, and other ancestors. Meanwhile, Papi, Apolo, and Antoine grappled with their own emotions while sitting outside in the waiting area for hours.

After the tower bells concluded, Final Roll Call continued with a color guard marching ceremoniously to the flagpole at the center of the mile. Two of the color guard members raised the American flag at half-staff. After they secured the rope and flag, a seven-member honor guard and a single bugler from the Corps band marched toward the center of the mile. Their cadence was slow and ceremonious until they came to a full stop behind the color guard.

This was the signal for the P-Company Commander to conduct the final roll call, and each cadet responded until the call went unanswered. The weeping intensified when Company Commander called for Justin and there was no response.

The honor guard followed roll call with a 21-gun salute. Three rounds of shots were fired, and the bugler immediately followed with a haunting rendition of Taps. Cadets and administrators ceremoniously saluted when the bugler commenced.

When Taps ended, everyone lowered their salutes, and the honor guard and color guard turned and walked off with the same slow cadence in which they arrived. The smell of gunpowder hung in the air while the guards silently marched away into darkness. Marisol said the scene looked haunting.

Justin's family and Kate remained to console each other in front of the flag and eternal flame while the units dispersed and returned to their dormitories in the dark. Company Commander dismissed the unit one row at a time. Marisol watched as our classmates and upperclassmen gave their condolences to Justin's grieving family members and Kate.

Later, when Richard and I had a chance to catch up, he told me what happened that night. He was completely spent when he got back to the room and just wanted to sleep. He shut the hatch behind him and was about to climb into the top rack when he heard a soft knock at the door. At first, he thought he imagined the knocking. But when he opened the door... he was taken aback when he saw Marisol standing there. She looked shattered, like she hadn't slept.

She confirmed that she was exhausted and drained, and her eyes were swollen from prolonged crying. The moment she entered the room, she immediately embraced Richard.

"You, Mauri, and Justin went through so much, and I still can't believe this nightmare is real. How are you? How are you holding up, Richard?" she asked, her voice filled with genuine concern.

"I'm still in disbelief and shocked by everything that has happened," Richard replied. "I don't understand any of it."

Marisol told Richard, "I'm there with you. I'm devastated about Justin and feel guilty for feeling grateful that Mauri survived. I'm heading to the hospital now to see him. But before I go, he gave me this note."

Marisol described how her hands were trembling when she gave Richard the note. She said that he slowly unfolded it, as if he already knew it would change everything. Then he read it out loud, his voice low but steady: "If something happens to me, retrieve my journal from my footlocker. It includes every sordid detail about my encounters with Mr. Strait and Brittany." I also included the combination for the master lock.

They opened the footlocker together, and my journal was right there, exactly where I left it. Marisol looked Richard in the eyes and asked him, "Please keep this between us, at least for now."

She said that he didn't hesitate. "Absolutely," he replied. "I won't speak a word of this."

Before she left, Marisol tightly hugged him and promised that justice would be served. "And if you need anything," she continued, "you have my number. Thank you for being a true friend and best bunkmate. Thank you for not judging him. He always said he lucked out with you. You'll be in my prayers, and I'll call when there's an update."

When she opened the hatch, Richard also made a promise. "Mauricio is a warrior, Marisol. He's going to be okay… I promise."

Marisol later described what she saw when she stepped out of McKibbin Hall. The glow of hundreds of candles. Students gathered for a vigil, their faces lit up in the soft flicker of light. She stood there for a second and wiped away tears that wouldn't stop flowing.

She told me her heart was torn—rage twisting against the need for justice, fear battling with hope. Then she looked back at the dorm one last time, the place that held so many memories—and so much pain. After taking a deep breath, she whispered a prayer that she would never walk through those doors again.

18 RESILIENCE AND REVELATIONS UNVEILED

In my formative years, the teachings I absorbed from both faith and society led me to internalize the idea that something was deeply wrong with me. The trauma from being bullied and excluded, and the weight of shame, lingered in me from my earliest memories.

Deep down, I knew I didn't sprout from bad seeds, nor did I carry any stain of evil or hate. My spirit overflowed with goodness, love, resilience, and an unwavering faith. Throughout freshman year, I faced many odds stacked against me—and through it all, I emerged knowing more about my true self.

While I drifted in unconsciousness at the hospital, I experienced a vivid dream—one I never wanted to leave. Justin stood next to my bed, smiling down at me. I smiled back and asked, "Did I just dream it all? Was it all a nightmare?"

With an apologetic smile, he gave a gentle nod. "No, Mauri… I'm sorry, it's all real," he said softly. "But listen—I need to thank you. For loving me the way you did. For being my best friend."

His warm hazel eyes shimmered, glassy with held-back tears. "I found my dad, Mauri. He's healed… radiant. Better than I ever remembered. And being reunited with him— being whole again—I'm okay now. Really okay."

Justin placed a hand on my chest. "Your Abuelita and I— we're watching over you. Always. And I'll be right here when it's your time, I promise. But that time's not now."

He leaned down and hugged me. "You've got a lot of folks down there who are worried sick about you. People who need you. So you gotta wake up now, Mauri. You gotta go back."

Hearing that he'd found his father and my Abuelita brought a flicker of comfort, though it didn't ease the ache in my chest. I clung to him, desperately pleading, "Please, Justin... I don't want to leave you. Not yet. I'm not ready."

His tone suddenly shifted to firm and commanding, the way only Justin could deliver when he meant business. "Listen up, freshman Lucho—you have to go back. Your family, your friends—people are losing sleep over you. You hear me? They need you." He paused, locking eyes with me. "Have I made myself crystal clear?"

Just as I opened my mouth to protest, his voice softened. "Please... do it for me. Wake up, Mauri. Touch your Mami's hand—she's right there beside you." He gave me one last smile. "Now open your eyes, my friend. I'll see you later."

When I opened my eyes, I had no idea where I was. The room felt hazy—dreamlike—the steady beep of a nearby machine, the sterile scent of antiseptic hanging heavy in the air. Then I saw Mami. She sat beside my bed, clutching her rosary and praying with her eyes closed.

I managed to whisper, "Mami..."

Her eyes snapped open. For a split second, she froze. Then she screamed—a full-body scream, the kind I had only ever heard once before, when Abuelita passed. She began to sob uncontrollably, calling out to God and Saint Jude over and over, giving thanks through a flood of tears. "¡Gracias, Dios mío! ¡Gracias, San Juditas! ¡Mi hijo, mi hijo!"

Moments later, Papi and Apolo burst into the room. Mami wept into my shoulder, clinging as if letting go would undo the miracle. The room spun with noise and emotion. I didn't know what I had been through or why everyone looked at me like I had just returned from the dead.

I asked, "Where am I? What happened at the obstacle

course? Where's Marisol? What day is it?"

Apolo told me we were in the hospital, and I'd been in a coma since my fall. He continued and said the son of a bitch who tried to kill me had fallen and died. That Marisol was fine. She explained to the police everything that took place. Marisol also gave the police a lead about the guy's girlfriend.

Brittany had already been arrested and charged with Justin's death—involuntary manslaughter. When Apolo broke the news to me, I knew in my bones that the curse had come to pass.

"The way you see me... you will see yourself."

I had said those words with every ounce of fury and heartbreak in me—not as a threat, but as a prophecy.

Because of her crime, Brittany stood exactly where I had stood—drowning in the unbearable agony of losing her true love. I suspected grief and regret consumed her. And I hoped that the very pain she had caused me wrapped around her neck like a noose.

Deep down, I also hoped the justice system wouldn't go easy on her. I wanted her to spend years behind bars—not just imprisoned by concrete and steel, but by the memory of what she had done.

I asked Apolo to call Marisol and Antoine to update them on my condition. As he stepped out to make the calls, I took a moment to survey the room. Slowly, details came into focus. I turned to Mami and asked, "What room is this?"

She looked at me, her eyes filled with tears, and said softly, "27."

In an instant, I remembered that room 27 was where Justin had taken his final breath just days before. The pain of his loss reignited with full force.

Mami said I had been unconscious for three days, long enough to miss the ceremony honoring Justin. She grieved for Mrs. Fischer in the way only a mother could after such a devastating loss.

The reality hit hard: she had come so close to losing me. And if my intuition had underestimated Mr. Strait, both Mrs. Fischer and Mami would've been grieving the loss of a son.

Justin and my intuition warned me that Mr. Strait was capable of anything to protect Brittany and conceal what she had done. In his mind, I was the only other person who knew her secret. To anticipate his moves, I tried to think like him and contemplated various scenarios. I asked myself, "What's the simplest scenario to make a death look like an accident on the obstacle course?"

When Justin appeared in my dream and revisited the gifts he had given me, it became clear—the most plausible option for a staged accident was a fall from the top of the rappelling wall. With this possibility looming, I prepared myself.

That dreadful Sunday morning, after I secured my journal in the footlocker, I retrieved four items—two of the engraved carabiners and the rappelling rope that Justin gave me as a Christmas gift, and an additional 15-foot rope. I tied bowline knots on both ends of the additional rope and attached a carabiner to each knot.

I tucked the ropes into my cargo pockets—a calculated risk, a gamble I had no choice but to take. I hoped the early morning darkness would be my ally, concealing the small bulges in my pockets from Mr. Strait's watchful eyes.

At 0430, I heard the clear sound of Mr. Strait's departure from his room. With caution, I waited for him to walk down the stairs to the third floor before venturing out to meet him. When I joined him behind McKibbin Hall, the stench of alcohol overwhelmed me, clearly indicating that he had been drinking throughout the night. An eerie silence settled between us. Without a word, he motioned for us to begin.

The uneasiness in the air was palpable during the run from the mile to the obstacle course. Our cadence followed the slam of our combat boots against the pavement. The roads were dimly lit, the campus silent. Luckily, the darkness gave my eyes time to adjust to the moonlight.

I arrived at the obstacle course slightly winded, but barely a drop of sweat on me. My endurance was a testament to months of rigorous training. Despite this, I purposely bent over, hands on my knees, drawing deep breaths to appear fatigued. It was a strategic move, an act to deceive him into believing I was spent from the run. In contrast, Mr. Strait seemed visibly exhausted for the first time ever. His demeanor showed signs of dehydration, stress, and what seemed like a sleepless night.

Mr. Strait made no mention of Brittany or Justin. Instead, he revealed a challenge: a race to the top of the rappelling tower. True to form, he boasted he would be waiting for me at the top. But his eyes never met mine— fixed instead on the dirt at his feet. That subtle break in character only sharpened my sense that an ulterior motive was at play.

In his usual arrogant manner, he proposed giving me a five-second head start, and I accepted. Except for Justin and Mac, everyone else was oblivious to my true speed and agility on the obstacle course. However, I had a feeling that Mr. Strait would be just as fierce and determined on the course, envisioning him pushing himself to his limits to beat me to the top of the tower, despite being hungover.

"Ready?" he asked. I gave a silent nod.

I took a deep breath, settling into position beside him. His voice cut through the silence, counting down. At "Go," I exploded off the start line, every muscle firing, as if everything—my survival, my future—hung in the balance.

I swiftly maneuvered through the initial obstacles, leaving him behind as I soared through the course like the Greased Lightning roller coaster. Determined not to waste a single moment, I resisted the urge to glance back, knowing any distraction could cost me precious time. I arrived at the rope climb, panting for breath but undeterred. With a burst of energy, I leaped as high as I could, gripping the rope tightly and propelling myself upward, using my arms to ascend before securing my feet.

After reaching the top of the rope climb, I immediately jumped onto the tower's platform, my eyes darting downward to catch a glimpse of Mr. Strait leaping toward the rope. Every second held immense significance. Seizing the opportunity, I retrieved Justin's rope from my cargo pocket and skillfully assembled a Swiss seat while swiftly advancing toward the edge of the wall. Months of training and racing with Justin had honed my skills to the point where I could assemble the seat in the dark, while walking, in mere seconds.

Despite the risk of falling, I deliberately sat on the edge with my legs dangling over the wall, beside one of the platform's hooks. I clipped one carabiner to my Swiss seat and rushed to anchor the rope to the platform with the second carabiner. I had just finished when Mr. Strait stepped onto the platform. I quickly shifted over to block his view of my precautionary measure.

Only then did I notice my gasps for air and the sweat soaking through my utilities—it had been the fastest run of my freshman year. I focused on steadying my breath as he approached.

"Why are you perched on the edge of my tower, freshman Lucho?" he asked, each word forced between heavy breaths and laced with suspicion.

Overwhelmed by a sense of defiance, I answered, "Because I want to savor my victory and this glorious view into the darkness, sir."

He let out a short laugh, clearly stunned. "Where the hell did that run come from, freshman Lucho?" he barked.

My voice quivered—not from fear, but from exhaustion and pure anger—as I yelled, "That run was the result of months of grueling work with Justin Fischer, my classmate who your girlfriend killed. Let's cut to the chase. Why did you bring me here, sir?"

He walked over and stood ominously behind me, his presence suffocating. He ordered me to get on my feet, and although there was a narrow gap between us, he refused to budge, intensifying the difficulty of the balancing task. Fortunately, it was evident that he didn't see I was tethered to the platform. By the time I turned around to face him, the heels of my boots were teetering at the very edge of the platform. Without warning, he gripped my blouse with both hands and pulled me toward him.

"You know damn well you wouldn't have beaten me without that five-second head start," he growled, his voice thick with wounded pride.

Clearly annoyed, I responded, "You set the rules, Mr. Strait, and I obeyed them, just as I've always obeyed you. I've been playing by your rules this entire freshman year, enduring a living hell."

"You think that was hell, freshman Lucho?" he sneered, eyes burning with something darker than hatred. "Hell is where your kind deserve to rot—for eternity."

He had some nerve. I took a deep breath, letting the anger and disgust surge through me, and replied, "My kind? Don't you mean our kind? Well, rest assured, I'll make damn sure you and your murderous she-devil girlfriend have reserved spots in hell, you son of a bitch."

In a fit of rage, he pushed me back with a force that sent me teetering on the edge of the platform, and at that moment, I prayed he wouldn't lose his grip. A lightning bolt of fear cracked through me as I pictured the catastrophic consequences. I could have surrendered to the weight of my body, allowing gravity to pull us both over the edge, but deep down, I couldn't bring myself to kill Mr. Strait. I wanted him to pay for every torment he had inflicted upon me throughout my freshman year.

As he held me perilously over the edge, his grip tightening, he told me he regretted ever crossing paths with me and swore he would do anything for Brittany—his true love. With a sadistic grin, he taunted me, relishing the control he held, and cruelly asked if I wanted him to let me go.

"Ari... don't do something you're going to regret for the rest of your life. I'm quitting the Corps. You'll never have to see me again. For the love of God, stop."

But in his arrogance, he had overestimated his own strength. The grueling rope climb had taken more from him than he realized. His fingers began to slip against the fabric of my blouse, his grip weakening, his balance faltering.

In a sudden, unexpected move, he released his hold on my blouse, causing me to plummet backward over the rappelling wall. As I fell, a brief moment of clarity allowed me to witness him desperately flailing his arms, urgently trying to regain his balance. But fate and gravity had different plans.

Mr. Strait's screams pierced the silence and darkness—proof of the fate he had chosen. They were the last sounds I heard before the rope snapped tight, slamming me against the wall with bone-cracking force. The knots, Swiss seat, and carabiners held. Then everything went black.

With the moonlight, Marisol saw what happened at the top of the platform and both of our crashes—mine into the rappelling wall and Mr. Strait's into the earth. He crashed into one of the perimeter logs and died on impact. She later said I made a thunderous sound when I struck the rappelling wall.

Marisol then ran to the obstacle course's emergency phone and dialed for help. Police, paramedics, and a fire truck arrived within minutes. While Marisol talked with the police, the firefighters used the truck's ladder to lower me down from the wall. They loaded me onto a gurney and transported me to the county hospital with Marisol in the ambulance. From the hospital, she called my parents and Antoine, and they rushed to be by my side.

From my hospital bed, I recounted the relentless mental and physical abuse I endured from Mr. Strait throughout my freshman year to the police, university administrators, and Top Brass. Each story was like tearing open old wounds, dragging me back through the dark chapters of my cadet journey. By any measure, it was excruciating. Yet, with every painful story and detail, I felt a sense of liberation, breaking free from his cruelty.

Everything that had transpired solidified the decision I had started considering during winter break—to quit the Corps and withdraw from the university. Deep down, I didn't want to return and complete the spring semester. But I was determined to finish out my freshman year with Justin, Richard, and my other classmates.

Looking back, my freshman year as a cadet in the Corps was nothing short of extraordinary—a journey marked by profound discoveries and revelations. I experienced true love and forged lasting friendships. But I also came face-to-face with the dangerous seduction of power and the darkness that can lie buried in seemingly ordinary people. The mental and physical hazing I endured went far beyond anything I could have imagined.

And yet, through it all, I had proven to myself that my mind and heart knew no bounds. The journey had revealed my self-worth and the power of my own convictions, separate from any uniform or institution. The dichos repeated by Mami throughout my life had rung true time and time again, guiding me toward good choices. The Corps also confirmed my beliefs in equality, fairness, and justice for people from all backgrounds.

Justin taught me what it meant to love deeply, to admire fully, and to trust in true friendship. I still grieved him—my first love—with profound sorrow. The emptiness he left behind hurt in ways I couldn't describe, but I vowed to hold our memories close, no matter how much time passed.

I would carry Justin's laugh, his radiant smile, and the

twinkle in his hazel eyes with me forever. He made me promise to remember what he told me in Galveston—that I didn't need a title or a uniform to be worthy of respect. That I was already a good and honorable man. That I deserved to be loved—not for who I could become, but for who I already was.

Richard and my bond remained unbreakable, his acceptance of my truth affirming the strength of our friendship forged as bunkmates. When I came out to him at the hospital, he said he knew I was gay all along and wasn't sure about Justin. The part that confused him most was when Justin rushed into our room and hopped on my rack. He didn't care, so he never said anything about the visits. He promised to visit me often in Houston, a testament to the lasting connection we shared.

Most of my classmates turned their backs on me the moment they learned I was leaving the Corps. They swore they would never speak to me again—and they didn't. Not one showed up at the hospital.

The revelation was shattering. We had endured two semesters of hell together, and yet it meant nothing. Their promises of lifelong friendship and brotherhood crumbled—exposed as hollow words, empty loyalty, and false fellowship. Whatever bond we had vanished the moment I stopped playing their game.

When Mac visited me in the hospital, I came out to him. He told me he had always known and that he couldn't have cared less. Back in high school, everyone had their suspicions, but Mac respected me for my work ethic and dedication to being an outstanding cadet and leader.

What weighed on him most was Halloween night. He admitted having a gut feeling that something was off—that Mr. Strait had done something wrong—but he didn't act. We took too long getting to the room where everyone waited, and somewhere in the silence, I looked at Mac and said, "Don't regret anything. Others saw more and didn't help. And thank you—for all that you did for me."

The pillars of my strength—Marisol and Antoine—had never once let go, standing by me with unwavering loyalty through every twist, every fracture, since our high school days. When I told them I was walking away from Texas F&E, leaving behind the Corps of Cadets and my Marine Corps scholarship, they didn't question the decision. They cheered. They saw what I was only beginning to understand: that sometimes the bravest path is the one where you finally choose yourself.

Coming out to my family from that hospital bed was a terrifying moment—but they didn't reject me. I was met with love. Pure, judgment-free, fierce, unwavering love. In their arms, I found more than acceptance. I found freedom. Gratitude surged through me. I was alive. I was loved. I felt seen.

As I stood in the doorway of hospital room 27, one last truth pierced my soul: I had been spared—not by chance, but for purpose. My life wasn't a mistake. I wasn't broken. I wasn't less. God crafted me with intention. Every moment—the love, the pain, the heartbreak, the trials— had carved a path that only I was meant to walk. And no matter how hard the journey ahead, I knew I would never walk it alone.

Justin's voice still echoed in my mind, steady and warm, urging me to rise, to live, to love again. He had said he would be watching—with Abuelita at his side—and I believed him. Their presence surrounded me, not as shadows of the past, but as guardian angels, whispering that my story wasn't over. It was just beginning.

For the first time, I looked out into the world and saw it for what it truly was—full of people who still needed my love. And I would meet that world as I was always meant to—with courage, with confidence, and with love.

I was ready.

ABOUT THE AUTHOR

Mauricio Lucho is a pseudonymous Mexican-American writer.

Writing under a pen name allows him to explore deeply personal themes of identity, power, silence, and belonging with honesty and care. His work draws from lived experience and examines life inside rigid institutions, where loyalty and tradition often collide with truth and self-preservation.

Mauricio writes to shed light on harassment and abuse faced by members of the queer community in the U.S. armed forces during the "Don't Ask, Don't Tell" era—and the ways many of those harms continue, in different forms, to the present day. While elements of his work are fictionalized, its emotional core is rooted in reality.

For years, he struggled to write this book. Like many other goals in his life, completing it ultimately required confronting imposter syndrome—particularly the belief that he was "not a writer"—and the discomfort of revisiting a complicated past decades later.

His determination to finish the story reflects the same resilience that carried him through the experiences that inspired it—and a belief that telling one's story, on one's own terms, is a quiet act of courage.

In real life, Mauricio is a dedicated professional committed to advancing inclusion and fairness around the world.

.

www.ingramcontent.com/pod-product-compliance
Lightning Source LLC
Chambersburg PA
CBHW050314110726
47899CB00007B/2239